EXCLUSIVE

"If I promise to rewrite an entirely honest feature about you, then will you give me an exclusive?"

Desney leaned back on her heels. "How are you going to write honestly about me when you know nothing about my life?"

"I'll attach one of my subwriters to you twenty-four seven," Wade explained.

"I want you to do it," Desney suggested arrogantly.

"What?"

"The only terms I'm willing to accept is for *you* to do the hard work," she jibed. "I want *you* to shadow me twenty-four seven."

"Why are you—"

"It's the only way you'll learn that your subjects are real people, with feelings," Desney interrupted. "Take it or leave it."

"I'll leave it," Wade drawled casually.

She gave an insolent shrug of her shoulders, cast Wade one last thundering glance, and then turned on her heel toward the glass doors.

"Wait!" Wade was out of his mesh chair in an instant. He crossed the room just as quickly. "You want a shadow? You've got one." The words were hardly off his tongue when he grabbed her wrist.

Surprised, Desney brought her arms up in an attempt to break his hold, but that only enabled Wade to tug her into his arms. Their eyes met, and Desney was aware that his features had suddenly softened. He knew he was over-stepping professional conduct to have her interlocked against his hard-muscled frame, and Desney could also sense the brief tremble of his body, making her wonder whether she had affected him in some way. It wasn't so unlike the tremble of her own limbs.

"Twenty-four seven," he purred into her right ear. "Wherever you turn, I'll be right behind you. And by the time I'm done, I'll be telling my readers the color of your lingerie."

INFATUATION

Sonia Icilyn

ARABESQUE
BET
BOOKS

BET Publications, LLC
www.bet.com
www.arabesquebooks.com

ARABESQUE BOOKS are published by

BET Publications, LLC
c/o BET BOOKS
One BET Plaza
1900 W Place NE
Washington, D.C. 20018-1211

All Kensington Titles, Imprints, and Distributed Lines are available at special quantity discounts for bulk purchases for sales promotions, premiums, fund-raising, and educational or institutional use.

Special book excerpts or customized printings can also be created to fit specific needs. For details, write or phone the office of the Kensington special sales manager: Kensington Publishing Corp., 850 Third Avenue, New York, NY 10022, attn: Special Sales Department, Phone: 1-800-221-2647.

First Printing: February, 2001
10 9 8 7 6 5 4 3 2 1

Printed in the United States of America

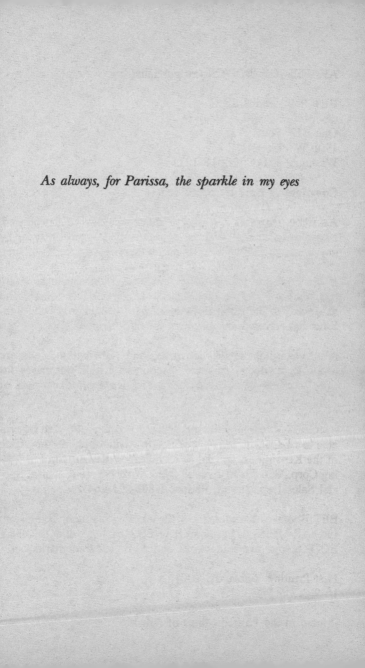

As always, for Parissa, the sparkle in my eyes

One

"Woman," the tall man snapped, his lips tightly clenched in a lame attempt to hold back his irritation. He glared at the intruder who had forced her way into the London office overlooking Euston Road, and grimaced. "I hope you've got a smart-ass lawyer."

"And I hope you've got your lawyer's lawyer," Desney Westbourne replied equally combative, tossing her edition of *Bribe* magazine on his desk. "Where do you get off spoon-feeding the public this pudding of misinformation? I've never been a crack slinger."

"No?" the man returned, his expression one of blatant, almost comical disbelief, "So how did you take Frederick Fitzgerald out so easily? He flew in the air like an eagle," he began, so amused he was forced into sporting the trademark gold-toothed smile. "Only he didn't land like no eagle. You knocked him out stone sober. Now that man must weigh, what . . . two hundred pounds?"

"You're a lunatic," Desney finished. He looked like one, too. An original urban species who talked feisty, dressed wild, and had a creed mentality. With his wiry, muscular body; black panther tattoo; cropped, dyed blond hair; chunky, self-made gold jewelry; and loud street stylings, he appeared more like something on a poster of Britain's most wanted than a professional who could be taken seriously. "Just what kind of writers do you have on staff here?" she gritted out.

"The best," came his Milano-accented reply. "And right now, you're on my time. I want you out of Mr. Beresford's office."

Desney looked around her. The office was flashy. Pale and sleek, full of contemporary power props, silver ornamental pieces, steel furniture, and the highest-quality computer hardware money could rent. In the short term, any magazine with a high profile behind it could get a bank loan to project whatever image it chose. Long term was different, and it was evident this magazine was in for the haul.

"You're not Wade Beresford?" Desney's voice weakened, now realizing why she had not been confronted by anyone on her arrival. The reception desk was not manned, and the staff she saw from across the office had remained seated in their chairs, working diligently.

"No." Her adversary's tone was filled with satisfaction. "I'm Tony Barbieri, his assistant editor."

"I see."

"Then maybe you can see your way out of this office," Tony finalized, indicating with an astute index finger at the double-tinted glass doors that Desney had barged her way through. Making her notably aware that he was not about to brook any further nonsense, he added a deliberate American pleasantry. "Have a nice day."

Desney bit her bottom lip, and hard. *Italians!* she hissed beneath her breath. They always liked to swallow things whole, just like aspirin. While the British preferred theirs dissolved, the Spanish fizzy, and the French as a suppository, Italians liked digesting things in their entire ensemble. And right now, *Bribe*, the Afro-Italian magazine that had taken the European market by storm, had waged war against her burgeoning reputation as a leading black actress, and had decided that the production company she was working for was small enough to be consumed in one quick mouthful.

Such consequences as putting them out of business or sending contracted actors back on welfare held no meaning. As far as Wade Beresford was concerned, Kemet Productions was too tiny to be halved, too minute to be divided. There would be no thought of ruining the company piecemeal. The company and the soap it produced were of the exact portion to be devoured in one fell swoop—just like aspirin.

"Wait a minute." Desney stood her ground directly across the steel desk that separated them, aware that Tony Barbieri was hiding behind it gratefully, as if it were some vast chastity belt, adopting a bad-boy repartee to mask his physical awkwardness at being around her.

Desney knew she sometimes had this affect on men, that her medium build, striking facial features, and illuminating personality could often put men on the defensive. But she had rehearsed what she wanted to say to Wade Beresford, and she would be very firm, very forthright. She wasn't about to be chased away now like some hare into its burrow. "I'd like to arrange an appointment to see Mr. Beresford."

"Woman," Tony Barbieri began again rather uneasily, his tone now bridged in annoyance, "Mr. Beresford has a busy diary. He's—"

"It's Miss Westbourne," Desney interrupted, returning the hardened gesture she had come to recognize in a man's eyes—a sort of patronizing contempt of her gender, which in no way excluded their willingness to use a female in any way that suited them. "I'm sure when—"

Tony wasn't deterred. "At the risk of sounding rude—"

"Is there anything wrong?" a thick Verona accent intruded.

Aware that someone else had entered the room, Desney turned arrogantly and opened her mouth, then stopped herself. The man facing her towered inches above her head. He had long, curly ringlets of black hair styled in something akin to Rastafarian locks. It was smoothed back from his face and hung down his back in a ponytail ending at his shoulders. His skin was a rich honey brown, set off by a pair of green-brown eyes that seemed to penetrate hers in a menacing way. The square jaw line with a cleft at the chin seemed the final finishing touch only God could have placed there to complete this Adonis.

Desney was dazed, consciously noting that he wore a clean white shirt with his tie slightly askew and close-fitting tailored trousers that set him in direct contrast to the man she had already confronted. And by the way he stood there, watchful, his lazy gaze firmly fixed, he might have owned the whole damned place and be checking on the way it was functioning. She swallowed. *Sexy,* she thought suddenly.

Hard as nails, she quickly reassessed, reminding herself that she had not survived in her role as Cinnamon Walker on "It's A Wide World" by telling columnists what she really thought of them. Not when they had the kind of following that *Bribe* had amassed in the short time since its launch into Britain.

Assuming a less hostile approach, she said, "My name is Desney Westbourne. I'm here because I know Cinnamon Walker is news, and as an actress, I expect there to be a little bit of gossip about me here and there. However, I have to take exception when my face is plastered over three pages of your magazine, confusing my personal life with what is seen on the screen. I demand to see Mr. Wade Beresford."

"Well, if it isn't the sex goddess in my office."

Desney's heart sank. Her brows furrowed as she suddenly realized who she was addressing. Such male attraction didn't warrant an ill personality to suit, she thought. "You must be the idiot who's responsible for this . . . pulp bull." She pointed directly at her copy of *Bribe*, hardly believing that this handsome man could be the cause of her problems. "Somehow I thought you'd be taller."

"Sorry to disappoint you," he confirmed, a modest Italian accent detectable as he extended a large brown hand and flashed her a wide monkey grin. "I'm Wade Beresford."

Desney slapped the hand away. His name was familiar enough, but this was the first time she was meeting the man in person. Wade Beresford not only wrote the weekly gossip features for *Bribe*, he happened to own the magazine, too. In a little under two years, he had been successfully sued because of *Bribe*'s unsubstantiated little libels. But Wade had simply written the costly defeats off to promotion and publicity, and the readers—in spite of considerable evidence that the gossip was untrue—kept their allegiance in four languages.

Whenever anything was rumored to have happened in the land of show business—a tale of vice, a tragedy, an overdose, or corruption—it was *Bribe* that legitimized it, made it real to its gullible readers. Wade Beresford was feared by actors, singers, dancers, models, and minor celebrities of the sporting and television fraternities alike. But there were those who garnered his attention, too. It was a case of their needing him and his needing them. His magazine's popularity simply soared.

"I ought to sue you for libel and take you all the way to the Old Bailey," she snapped.

"That's kinda like the Supreme Court, right?" He turned to his colleague and muttered the equivalent in Italian. Desney suddenly found herself in the center of a bilingual joke.

"Don't play ignorant with me," she lashed out, not expecting her voice to sound so low and deep. It made it hard for her to be harsh and disdainful. "You may publish your piece of trash in Italy, but our libel laws reach beyond the Channel here."

"What do you want?" Wade smiled easily. Too easily, Desney thought. It softened all the hardened features in his face and made him appear boyish.

"I want a retraction," she said angrily. "And an apology."

The chuckle rubbed against her ragged nerves. "I can't promise you either," Wade said matter-of-factly, walking boldly toward his desk, where he began to busily shuffle documents in all directions. Dismissing Desney from his thoughts entirely, he sought the artwork he required from among his papers and handed it to Tony Barbieri. "Scan that and edit out the trademark," he ordered. "Get rid of the emblem, too. I don't want any copyright breach."

Tony nodded and eyed Desney rather coolly before he dutifully left the room. Desney watched him leave, her blood simmering that she could actually be ignored this way. She, Desney Westbourne, who had once played Hamlet's Ophelia at the Hackney Empire in London, and had then gone on to Broadway, where she had been nominated for the New York Critics Circle Best Actress Award.

She gazed warily at Wade Beresford, thinking of him as a roguish buccaneer raiding her ship. Even knowing of her presence in the room, he continued to conduct himself rather busily, as though he had hoped she would get the message and silently depart like a lamb in distress. And Desney was distressed, knowing that she was facing the one man responsible for all the lies and conjecture that had been published about her. Did this man not care that she had a reputation?

"I'm curious to know exactly how I've been characterized among your copyright and libel rules," Desney began, realizing that she had suddenly caught Wade's attention. His hand paused momentarily over a bowl on his desk where she could see he kept popcorn.

He afforded her a quick glance and could see all the hell-bent defiance welling up in her cheeks, but it didn't seem to worry him unduly.

"Do you see hard-working people like me in the performing arts as mere objects, like words, that can be manipulated or erased from the pages of your magazine?" she continued. "Because, if so, you've definitely missed your vocation in life."

Desney didn't miss the sudden flash of dark retaliation that fired in Wade's green-brown eyes. She could tell that he could be a dangerous man if he really wanted, and she wondered whether she had been too hasty in crossing swords with him.

His hand dipped arrogantly into the popcorn bowl, and for a moment Desney felt a grip of something like fear in the pit of her stomach as he slowly brought his hand to his full pink lips and slowly crunched on the six toffee-coated pieces. Only after he swallowed did he decide to speak, and the few seconds of patient waiting had frazzled Desney beyond her normal endurance. This was a man utterly in command of himself, and he had the ability to control others by sheer force of will.

"What do you consider to be my vocation?" he asked.

Desney could hardly imagine that this handsome man was really interested in her opinion at all. Whether she gave a true or false answer, it wouldn't stop him from selling magazines filled with the kind of content he chose to publish.

"I think you destroy people's lives," she attacked scathingly. "I believe you see true talent and destroy it at a stroke because it makes you sleep easier at night knowing that you've pulled the rug from beneath the feet of an aspiring celebrity. Any journalist who can deliberately dupe his readers into thinking that my screen role is my true personality should be jailed for character assassination and more. It's slander. You're a discredit to journalism as I know it."

His face contorted. "You think I'm corrupt?"

"It's no less than what you think of me," Desney rebuffed.

"What I think of you!" Wade laughed. "I think you're just like any other two-bit, upscale actress. Big-headed, a showoff with a big ego. Just because you have a pretty face does not mean I have to say nice things about you."

Desney gasped, protectively pulling her thick brown coat over her bodice as though the cashmere coat were concealing her person from further attack. "The very least I expect is that you write honestly. You know nothing about me."

"I know enough."

"You know nothing," Desney insisted, not quite managing to eliminate the resentment in her voice.

"Look," Wade said warily. His every manner indicated that he was not going to endure the conversation for much longer. "Your last role on screen was kissing and bedding Matt Doran in the sentimental Caribbean love story, *The Earl of Black River.* Before that, you played a mistress in *Serenade in Sepia,* a hooker in *Seventh Ave-*

nue, and a spurned lover in *Casino de Paris.* You went two months without work earlier this year, before you landed the role in March as Cinnamon Walker, crackhead and general loose woman in Britain's leading ethnic soap. You've been in that role six months and—"

Desney interrupted him uncomfortably. "Are you trying to suggest that I seek out and play roles that are demeaning to me as a black woman?"

"You said it."

"How dare you," Desney snapped. The casual arrogance in which he held himself frazzled her further. "That's not true. "I've played a police officer, a contralto singer, a student nurse, and last year, Ophelia at the Hackney Empire—which went on Broadway. And if I play my cards right, I might just land a part in *Porgy and Bess* next year summer. So you see—"

"You've backtracked," Wade admitted rudely. "You started playing good roles in the theater and then took bad ones on screen. Why were your good roles never publicized?"

"They were," Desney reeled. "By *decent* magazines, but your research department just chose to overlook them. I suppose you were digging for less favorable information to spice up your story. So," she paused. "Does that mean I now get a retraction?"

"No," Wade said bluntly. He fished his hand into the popcorn bowl again and extracted a handful. Popping each one into his mouth, he munched as he spoke. "Now you're going to tell me I'm dangerous."

Desney shook her head in despair. *Why bother,* she told herself. This man wasn't going to give her any slack. Nonetheless, she looked at him head-on and flinched inwardly at how attractive she found him. Such striking looks deserved a warm personality to fit, she mused. What a shame Wade Beresford did not possess one that was the least bit appealing.

Curiously, she felt compelled to know why he was so hard-nosed, though her better mind told her just to get the hell out of his office. What was the point of dealing with someone who was hard as nails, with every piece of wall space in his office littered with framed covers of *Bribe,* a reminder of how successfully his unscrupulous magazine promoted sleazy journalism at its worst. Surely it had to be a waste of time, and yet she couldn't ignore the sudden rush of anger that forbade her to just walk away.

"I'm wondering if you have a conscience," she pounced. "I mean, if you knew that you had done something wrong, wouldn't you try and fix it?"

Wade froze. Something in his eyes, a flicker, suggested to Desney that she had zoned into an area that hit a nerve. "Are you attacking me?" he jabbed.

"You stacked the deck," Desney challenged. "I just want to reshuffle it."

"You want me to play?"

"What I want is for you to deal fair," Desney prompted firmly. "Or don't you media people know how to do that?"

His dark brows furrowed, his green-brown eyes blazed, and Desney instinctively took a step back. Wade Beresford looked like he had just bounced back twice as dangerous, sword in hand and ready to strike. Judging by the way he was gazing at her, she realized he was the kind of person whose strengths were inseparable from his weaknesses. The notion that she had so far twice suggested that he had no idea how to do his job with integrity, nor any respect for the subject matter of his articles had obviously touched a chord of vulnerability that he was attempting to camouflage with an iron-cast stare.

His expression was a dead giveaway. Wade Beresford appeared hurt. But he was quick enough to foil his emotions. "Look," he began, depositing himself in his wire-mesh chair, appearing uncomfortable as he spoke. "I don't do retractions. But . . ." He paused. "If you can talk your co-star, Frederick Fitzgerald, into giving *Bribe* an exclusive feature about his rumored departure from the show, then maybe I can see my way to putting you both on the front cover—in a loving embrace, of course. It'll help you win back your fans."

Desney clenched her teeth. "Forget it," she seethed.

"Take it or leave it," Wade offered, reaching toward his bowl of popcorn.

"Pop one more of those into your mouth while I am trying to sort out my professional life in here, and I'll ram every one of those popcorn pieces down your throat myself," Desney said evenly. She braced her hands against the cold steel surface of his desk, finding herself gazing into equally cold eyes. "From the moment I walked into this office, you've refused to give me any courtesy. You have a chip on your shoulder about actresses, and for some reason, you've chosen to pick on me. And if you think I'm going to be swallowed into some sexist deal to give Frederick Fitzgerald a lucky break after I was given three pages of rumors, then you're sadly mistaken. If this is a man's club, then you can go get Frederick Fitzgerald yourself."

"A man's club," Wade repeated, notably catching the dark smudges under Desney's brown eyes that were evidence of the stress she was under. "You've got something against men?"

"You're a man, aren't you?"

"My birth certificate says male," Wade nodded, confused.

"And men *in extremis* harm others," Desney concluded.

"I don't think I've ever killed anybody," Wade began uneasily, "or done anyone—"

"You may well have just killed my career," Desney interrupted. "I don't take crack cocaine in real life. I've never engaged in substance abuse. How do you think people are going to react by your misleading them into believing that I'm a crack slinger? Don't you realize just how hurt I am by all this?"

Wade blinked and then shrugged his shoulders. "I sell magazines," he began. "And you're a celebrity. You're public property. You wanted to be famous. Well, it takes people like me to get you there. Now, I'm really busy. If you don't mind leaving . . ."

"You're throwing me out?" Desney gasped in disbelief, clutching at her coat collar to dispel the blow, her fingers curling into tight fists.

"I'm asking you to leave," Wade clarified. "Unless, of course, you've changed your mind about the deal I just offered you."

"The only deal I'm interested in is you doing my reputation justice," Desney answered angrily. "Until then, you can take a running leap. Catch Frederick Fitzgerald by yourself, if you can."

"Okay," Wade shrugged again, putting his feet up onto his desk and crossing them at his ankles. "Tell me what you think of this. If I promise to re-write an entirely honest feature about you, will you then convince Frederick Fitzgerald to give me an exclusive?"

Desney leaned back on her heels. "How are you going to write honestly about me when you know nothing about my life?"

"I'll attach one of my sub-writers to you twenty-four seven to follow you throughout your daily routine," Wade explained casually. "We'll even say what you ate for breakfast."

"I want you to do it," Desney suggested arrogantly. "What?"

"I'm willing to accept if *you* do the hard work," she

jibed. "I want *you* to shadow me twenty-four seven. If I eat cornflakes for breakfast, I want *you* to tell your readers whether I sugar them or not."

"Why are you—"

"It's the only way you're going to learn that your subjects are real people, with feelings," Desney interrupted. "Take it or leave it."

"I'll leave it," Wade drawled casually. "Have you finished?"

"Yes, I'm done here," Desney relented, her spirit, which was never far from her, suddenly pushed to the fore. "You're nothing but a literary bully. I thought you'd want to find that vocation you've missed."

She saw his eyes glint. "What's that?"

"To become a responsible, conscientious journalist," she replied, compelled to push him to the limit. "The type that win Pulitzer Prizes. Guess I made a mistake."

She gave an insolent shrug of her shoulders, cast Wade one last thundering glance, and then turned on her heels toward the glass doors she had earlier forced her way through.

"Wait!" Wade was out of his mesh chair in an instant. He crossed the room just as quickly, and the sudden blaze of fury in his face told Desney she had gone too far. "You want a shadow? You've got one," he threw at her through gritted teeth. The words were hardly off his tongue when he grabbed her wrist.

Thrown into surprise, Desney brought her arms up in an attempt to break his hold, but that only enabled Wade to tug her into his arms. She could smell the fresh tang of his aftershave blended with his natural scent; it tingled her nerve endings, knowing she was so close.

She had not been so intimately near a man in a long time, except while on screen playing Cinnamon

Walker. And Wade had no intention of letting her go. When their eyes met in silent combat, Desney realized he was acutely aware of just how loathsome she found his behavior to be. His features had suddenly softened.

He knew he was overstepping professional conduct to have her interlocked against his hard-muscled frame, and Desney could also sense the brief tremble of his body, making her wonder whether she had affected him in some way. It wasn't so unlike the tremble in her own limbs. She felt marked by it as his voice spoke, so precise and challenging.

"Twenty-four seven, I'll be your full-time stalker," he purred into her right ear, his accent menacing. Even his warm breath had her earlobe tingling as his threatening tone became more intense. "Wherever you turn, I'll be right there behind you. And by the time I'm done, I'll be telling my readers the color of your lingerie."

Desney felt her heart shudder at the suggestion, though she knew Wade was not intending anything lurid. It was more of a dare—that he was going to accurately map out every facet of her life. "I suppose that means . . ." she weakly protested, struggling to break out of Wade's hold, "that I won't know when you're behind me until the knife's in my back, right?"

At the exact moment of her pulling away, Wade thrust her from him. "You'll know when I'm there," he proclaimed firmly. "I'll see to that."

"Note pad and pencil?" Desney goaded, shaken, but determined not to be overpowered by his steadfast gaze.

"Ready to start at oh-nine-thirty hours, tomorrow," he declared.

Desney's mind went blank. "What's happening then?"

"You tell me," Wade replied. "Because that's when I'll be latching on to your tail."

"I . . ." Desney was at a loss for words. "My diary for tomorrow is very busy."

"Good."

"I'm on set in the morning, and we'll be shooting until well after lunch."

"Even better," Wade continued. "It'd be interesting to discover whether you're as spoiled, unprepared for success, and surrounded by idiots and leeches as all the other actresses I've met."

He seemed to be enjoying the fact that she had inadvertently admitted him into her life. "I'll have to get you a visitor's pass, and I'm not sure that the director will allow someone from the media on set while we're shooting," she wavered, ignoring his disparagement of her profession.

"Not my problem," Wade intoned lightly, turning to make his way back toward his desk. He instantly dug his hand into the popcorn bowl and picked up a handful. "You've reshuffled the deck, and I've decided to play." He turned and faced Desney head-on. "So just tell me when and where you want me to meet you"—he tossed a kernel of popcorn into his mouth as though it signified a single score point—"and I'll be there."

Desney felt her innards reel as she caught the satisfied expression of victory in Wade's eyes. "Okay." She nodded slowly, tugging her coat for dear encouragement. "I normally go for a morning jog. How does a three-mile run suit you?"

Wade flinched, but Desney knew he would not back down. "Fine."

"Then I'll see you around six o'clock, outside Marble Arch Station."

"You want us to meet at oh-six-hundred hours?" Wade sounded out in the same military manner he was accustomed to hearing from his father, the alarm slowly becoming evident across his face.

"You have a problem with that?"

"No," he lied.

"Good." Desney now felt like the one who had scored a match point. Hands braced on the doorknob on the way out, she couldn't resist tossing one last glance at Wade Beresford, before smiling sweetly. "About my lingerie." Her voice was filled with candor as she caught him reseated in his chair. "The color would be white."

Wade's brows rose inquisitively. "Would be?"

"If I found occasion to wear them," Desney said. "As it happens, I don't." With that final remark, she sailed out of his office and down the corridor as if the floor beneath her were the still waters of a lake. But little did Desney know that she had just caused the first ripple.

Two

Wade Beresford, resplendent in a jersey sweater, Nike trainers, and a pair of jogging shorts that was tugging at his mid-section, turned over his Lexus keys to Tony Barbieri, who seemed to disapprove of his choice that morning. He stood patiently outside Marble Arch Station, awaiting the arrival of Desney Westbourne.

Oxford Street wasn't quiet, as it seemed to attract the lure of early morning commuters intent on making their breakfast appointments on time. The considerable flotsam, both animate and otherwise, surprised him somewhat, though he had to confess it was not his practice to be on the streets of London at 6:00 A.M.

He didn't normally roll into his office until 9:00 A.M., and even then, he expected Tony to be on top of everything. Wade rather liked the feel of driving leisurely in the morning, along the country lanes of Surrey into central London. At this time of year, when the autumn leaves were changing from green to brown, yellow, red, and orange, he would often take in the landscape and scenery that surrounded him.

He liked to view the oaks, stark and brown, shedding to reveal their bony arms to the world. Italy seemed not as green as England, for he could not recall a season of such vibrancy, when he could hear the soft crunching of leaves beneath his shoes, or walk on top of them when they seemed to carpet the ground, as he did in England.

Right now, though, he was feeling the chill of a dewy Friday morning. His breath looked like smoke rising in the cool air. Damn! Why ever did he decide to meet Desney Westbourne at such an unearthly hour? Had he gone mad, or was it the simple fact that the woman had suddenly intrigued him? Or was it more in curiosity than satisfaction that he rose to her bait?

He had never shadowed a subject before. In literary terms, that's exactly what Desney was. He couldn't really understand why he had agreed to do it, either, unless perhaps it was the way she wrinkled her small nose in frustration, and the way her well-marked frown seemed to enhance her girlish features.

He had to admit, she was extremely beautiful. Not a mark was evident on her walnut brown complexion. Her velvety brown eyes were astonishing, too. But he found her smile—what little he saw of it before she finally left his office—to be adolescent, almost what he would expect to find on the face of an eight-year-old child. He couldn't decide whether she was a baby or a lady, and that wasn't quite like him. He had never been indecisive before.

And there was a birthmark, too. Or at least it looked like one, the size of a dime, hardly noticeable on her left cheek, near the lobe of her ear. It was mud colored, a sort of dark brown. Had she been born with it? He wanted to know. Suddenly, Wade found he wanted to know everything there was to learn about Desney Westbourne. And not out of any selfish aim in making the woman a brief adornment in his bedroom, but more because she had accused him of not having the attributes she most valued in a journalist.

How dare she ridicule him that way? A sudden surge sprang from the pit of his stomach as he pondered the bruising he had felt at her remark. He'd show Desney Westbourne, Wade decided. He would prove to that upstart so-called actress that he had all the makings of a journalist and more.

Which was exactly the reason why he was running in place now, trying to warm the chill he could feel in the tips of his fingers. Wade looked at his watch and frowned out loud when he realized the time read 6:03 A.M. *Isn't that just like a woman to be late?* he seethed. Miss Desney Westbourne, soap queen, couldn't even be bothered to make it on time.

His breath suddenly ejected in a hot flurry. Wade knew he was already becoming impatient. It was one of his worst attributes. That, and his well known code words: zero tolerance. At the office, his staff knew it, too. Tony was the only one who could abate him when things did not run as smoothly as he would like. As a child, his mother, Ruth, had sweetly ignored him until she decided he had calmed down.

Dear sweet mama. A half-smile ran across his face. The only time Wade visited Italy now was to do business or visit his mother, an old lady now nearing sixty-four. She and his father were among the few Afro-Caribbeans who had migrated to Italy after the Second World War with his grandfather, Joshua Beresford. His own father, Seth, fought on the side of the British, but he had made Italian friends during his service in the army and had chosen to settle there when the troubles were over.

He and his sister were raised in Verona, in the northeastern corner of the country. What he remembered most were the landscapes of hills and mountains, which changed gently, though dramatically with the seasons around Lake Garda, Italy's largest lake. His mother always loved the water. He could only imagine that it reminded her of Isla Catalina, the small village in the Dominican Republic where she had been born and raised as a child.

It was probably his mother's wistful musings along the water's edge of Lake Garda, where she would often paint pictures for the visiting tourists, which had first sowed the seeds of his impatience. He and Lenora, his older sister by two years, were simply forced to sit and watch her mix the watercolors she applied to the treated paper, bought at the bustling market in Piazza Erbe. The market still evoked echoes of trading from the Roman epoch. Other times they joked to one another about whether the Dolomite Mountains actually reached the stars at night, kissed the clouds by day, or sheltered Lake Garda from the gods as it nestled in the foothills around the mountain itself.

But while Tony and even Lenora could abate his frustration, Wade felt certain that Desney Westbourne would not. His watch now read 6:09. The chill in the air was beginning to rest on his throat and he ejected an involuntary cough to smooth away the discomfort. Damn that woman, his mind reeled again when he thought about having shaved his five o'clock stubble. He had never done that for anyone, least of all a woman.

Wade always waited until he reached the office before reaching for the electric razor in his desk drawer, which he would apply to his face while reading the morning newspapers. That was how things were with him. A leisurely drive, a leisurely shave, even a leisurely drink of coffee in solitude, within the confines of his warm office.

Now, he was clean-shaven, freezing, and had forgone coffee to make the fast drive to reach Oxford Street for 6:00 A.M. He had even dragged Tony out of bed to drive his car the rest of the way to his office. All this for some two-bit actress who had decided to show up late.

I'll show her late. Wade's temper boiled over just as he caught the distant image of a woman running toward him. His watch read 6:11, but for some strange reason, the eleven minutes disappeared from his mind. Every facet of his brain was immediately filled with shapely brown legs, plump backside, rounded hips, slim waistline, bouncing breasts, firm shoulders, slender neck, and then the familiar face that offered a wide, panting smile. His eyes had worked the full length of her without his knowing it, until Wade found himself facing Desney Westbourne.

"Sorry I'm late," she apologized immediately, gazing at the mobile phone in her hand, which she promptly attached to a band around her waist. "I jogged all the way from home."

Wade breathed deeply of the moist, cold air. She was dressed in Lycra, every part of the fabric hugging her like a second skin. He saw the thin line of flesh between her jogging shorts and vest top, and marveled that not an inch of fat bulged from it. This woman was fit. Sensually . . . wholesomely . . . sexually fit. His mind silently screamed out every word. He hadn't noticed this about her yesterday when she forced her way into his office.

What could possibly have changed between then and today? His mood? The surroundings? What? Territory—that's it, Wade decided. In his office, he had the advantage, and he had made her feel small and inadequate. Now they were both standing on a public sidewalk—equal, even with the passersby who knocked against them. Earlier his superior ego hadn't allowed him to pay attention to what lay beneath the thick brown coat she had been wearing, not that he could have seen anything by way of her figure.

But now, even her face looked . . . healthy. He could see the red blush of blood beneath her brown cheeks, in full bloom from the jogging. And it was fresh-colored, too, which let him know that she was not wearing makeup. Her hair was pulled back into a tight knot at the back—nothing fancy, yet it made her look more girlish than he had thought of her before.

Wade was alarmed to find that his pulse had suddenly quickened at the sheer sight his eyes beheld, though in the wisdom he'd acquired about women in his thirty-four years, he could not pinpoint what was causing the reaction. His mind drew a blank when he hesitated, and then croaked, "It's all right. I haven't been waiting long."

Did he really say that? Wade couldn't think. Surely this couldn't be the same man who had been about to spit fire if Desney had kept him waiting much longer. He gazed at her more deeply before he realized that this goddess had caught his reaction.

Desney was aware of the stare. It wasn't unusual. She had seen this kind of look before, but coming from Wade Beresford it seemed unreal. On awakening that morning next to Poxy, her favorite soft toy, she had pictured his determined face in her head. The dark brows, square jaw line, short forehead, and deep, provoking eyes had stayed with her while she showered, dressed, and ate a bowl of cornflakes.

When she had left her Hyde Park Gardens apartment at daybreak to make the jog toward Oxford Street, she felt a flurry of apprehension, not knowing whether she could stomach the man this morning. Yesterday she had taken a bellyful of his insolence, which wasn't the best way to spend the only free day in her busy schedule.

On leaving his office, she had thought him the worst person she had ever met. No one had treated her that way before. No one. And she didn't believe in the aphorism, either, that any publicity was good publicity. This man had damn near ruined her career. She had yet to measure the repercussions, if any, now that twenty-four hours had passed since he had run the story in *Bribe*.

Could she really believe he was going to make amends? This man, who now appeared even more handsome in his jogging shorts and jersey sweater, revealing knobbly knees and hairy legs that made her lips curl into a smile. "Are you ready?" she asked, adding some gaiety. While she was receiving formal courtesy, Desney did not want to break the ambience.

"Sure." Wade ran in place. Something inside him felt ready for just about anything this woman chose to deliver. "Let's go."

Desney raised a brow. It struck her anew how very different he was—not at all what she was expecting. "This way." She led the way ahead, hardly believing that Wade Beresford, the man who only the day before had her stewing in anger, possessed the nerve or the stamina to keep pace with her. At first she decided to take it steady, turning the bend onto Marble Arch and following the road down. She turned briefly to check Wade's profile, seeing nothing awkward nor any sign of discomfort. But she asked anyway, "You okay?"

"Don't worry about me," Wade puffed, throwing her a monkey grin, his eyes sparkling expressively. "I'm made of the good stuff—hard as a rock."

Desney shrugged, though she felt incredibly aware that there was something about Wade Beresford today that invited touching. "You Italians are full of it," she challenged. "Okay. Let's see what you can do."

Her pace quickened. Wade was aware of the sudden gain in speed. His ego rose to the bait, and he took off like a fox across a corn field. He heard his subconscious protest the stupidity of his actions the moment he took chase, but his ego wasn't going to let this one go. Desney was not going to show any mercy. He had already decided that. But he was the stronger sex, wasn't he? Everything that encompassed male pride was at stake here, and they both knew it.

He felt the sweat against his long legs as they propelled him, jogging side by side with her in silence. After a while, encouraged that he was keeping pace, Wade's eyes turned to Desney, and she returned the stare and curled her lips. "I heard you were difficult to work with," he mocked. "Any truth in that?"

"Not unless you want to believe it," she retorted.

"I'm not sure what to believe," Wade breathed. "Matt said you were murder off the set."

"Matt Doran!" Desney sighed. "I might've known."

"Not keen on the man, then?"

"No."

"Any reason?"

Desney tossed Wade a deriding look, not wishing to go into detail. "Haven't seen the man in two years," she explained. "Besides, I prefer a gallant buccaneer with whom my heart will be safe rather than a man like Matt Doran."

A dreamer, Wade thought.

"A little bird tells me Matt will be taking over for Frederick Fitzgerald," he announced as they cornered a bend. "So your heart—"

"What?" Desney stopped suddenly in her tracks, hands on her hips, her heart racing with instant anxiety. "When did you hear this?"

"You didn't know?" Wade gloated, jogging on ahead.

Desney watched him for five troubling seconds, wondering whether he had heard the same rumor about Frederick's contract as she had, before tagging along, her eyes narrowing suspiciously. "No." Her voice was raised, annoyed.

Wade sported his wide grin, not detecting how uneasy Desney had become. "I think this should be an interesting story. Matt Doran and Miss Desney Westbourne."

"Don't push it," Desney warned, slowly panting out each word with a cautionary tone. "We were only lovers on *The Earl of Black River.* Don't make anything more of it than that."

"Would I ever?" Wade chuckled, deciding he would establish a level of comfort by stretching his strides as the momentum of the jog set in, his smile widening as he took the lead, triumphantly in control of the game.

He was enjoying this interrogation. His confident strides ahead didn't seem to bother Desney, which puzzled Wade, and he wondered whether his questioning had frazzled her somewhat, slowing her down at the mere mention of Matt Doran. She seemed suddenly quite content to lag behind, taking things easy, building up a steady pressure as they went along. But it wasn't until they had bridged the turn into Hyde Park that Wade suddenly realized he had underestimated the situation.

The turnabout was a complete surprise. Desney moved on ahead, her strides pulling her easily past the entrance to the park. Wade felt the pressure build the instant his body attempted to keep up with her. His chest felt like a jackhammer was drumming against it while his legs tried to hold the pace.

The ground felt harder beneath him because of the spicules of ice embedded into the path. They would not even begin to thaw until the autumn sun was well up. His cold arms protested against the elements, as did his entire face—his jaw muscles contracting invol-

untarily and his brows scowling—being more accustomed to cutting any sort of distance by car than by
foot.

When he finally felt his muscles weighted by the
sheer stress of running, Wade's pace slowed and his
eyes rolled in surrender. "Wait," he panted, un-
ashamed at throwing in the towel so soon. His smile
disappeared as he said in a voice so weak that Desney
hardly heard him clearly, "You're going too fast."

She paused to look behind her, only for an instant.
Three seconds tops. "Don't try to bluff an old pro,"
she teased. "I thought you were made of the good
stuff." She was off again at full speed.

Wade puffed and took to his legs again. He tried to
measure his strides against Desney's but quickly realized that her long, leggy movements were beyond anything that he could compete with. Even the way she
wiggled her butt, its graceful pace and rhythm, looked
more athletic than seductive.

In other circumstances, he would have enjoyed
watching that behind move. But not now. He had to
stop. Wade called a halt three minutes later and bent
over to catch his breath.

His heart was racing double time like a skier on ice,
his breath heavy and gasping, his limbs now protesting
in pain. His lungs begged for oxygen and he obliged,
quickly inhaling the frosty morning air, feeling the
chill inside as it went down.

Wade couldn't do this. For the first time in thirty-
four years, he suddenly realized he was physically unfit.
A park bench caught his roving gaze and he sat down
to steady his heartbeat. He took another gulp of air
and then peered into the distance to see if he could
find Desney.

She was like a spot on the landscape, too far off for
him to even recognize her outline or even shout her

name. *The good stuff.* Wade scoffed at himself in disgust and wondered where he had lost it. Perhaps it had dwindled away in his twenties as he acquired the taste for fine food, sweet desserts, vintage wine, and popcorn.

Then he saw the spot in the distance still and begin to enlarge gradually. Desney had realized he was no longer behind her. Before long, he could see every part of her figure re-form: her legs, her arms, her pleasing curves, the full shape of her body, and at last he was able to identify the face that had challenged him.

Desney waited until she was within shouting distance before she yelled, "What the hell happened to you?"

Wade stared at her, his forehead wrinkled in exhaustion. "I'm dying a slow death trying to keep up with you," he gasped.

Desney looked on in mild concern, then mocked, "I suppose that means your first paragraph about me will tell your readers how fit I am."

"You'll get no argument there," Wade conceded.

"Good." Desney took the seat next to him, but rather than remaining still, she tapped her feet on the floor, one after the other.

"Don't you ever stop?" Wade asked.

Desney glanced sideways at him; he looked exasperated. Even seated, he seemed to tower over her. "Oh, how the mighty have fallen," she mocked.

"Don't worry, I'm not about to fall at your feet," Wade retorted.

Desney's chin rose in challenge. "Should I be expecting you to?"

"You're accustomed to immediate idol worship from men," Wade answered, still gasping for breath. "It must be quite a disappointment to find one who is not falling for your drop-dead gorgeous looks."

"And you've based this view of me on what?" Desney chimed, disbelieving Wade's barefaced audacity in turning a compliment so easily and smoothly against her.

His dry tone showed not the slightest concern that he was being rude. "In your line of work, it goes with the territory that women like you are man-eaters."

Man haters, Desney almost hastened to say, but held her tongue, instead tossing Wade a challenging glance, her feet still tapping on the cold ground, though now in annoyance. "Tell me," she said. "Theoretically speaking, does this mean that if I happened to want to kiss you, you'd take it as an act of offense?"

"Damned straight I would," he intoned harshly.

"Then don't worry," she added smoothly. Her feet were tapping harder than ever, more by way of dispelling the rush of frustrated fascination Wade aroused in her. "Should the opportunity ever arise to kiss you, I'd make sure that, as an actress of course, it'd be the most brazen display of female emotion I'll ever perform. And by the time I'm done, you'll be uneasily wondering what exactly it is I do for an encore."

"Sitting quite still would be a start," Wade suggested, unperturbed, though deep down he felt in denial of something.

Desney looked at her feet, then smiled knowingly. "My energy level is intimidating to you, isn't it?"

"No," he lied.

"Well, I don't stop," she smiled. "Fact number one about me is, at thirty-one, a girl should always be on the go."

"How many facts about you are there?" Wade inquired.

"Plenty." Desney's lips widened into an intriguing smirk as she told herself that Wade Beresford was no better looking that the average Egyptian god. "What's a fact I should know about you? Or don't you media types like to be interrogated?"

"You can ask me anything you want," Wade defended.

"Okay. What's the capital of Peru?"

"About me," Wade chuckled.

Desney chuckled, too. Her laugh was clear and bell-like. A good run always lifted her spirits. And she also felt elated at seeing Wade Beresford dragging every last vestige of air into his lungs. This man was indeed conquerable after all. "I know you meant you," she smiled. "I did wonder, which part of Italy you are from?"

"Verona."

"Is it nice there?"

"Sure. Great for tourists."

"So why are you here?"

"I can earn more money in England."

"Slandering people."

"If you say so."

"You're proud of it, aren't you?" Desney couldn't resist aiming that one. Over the years she had conducted most of her interviews with a good degree of control, keeping strictly to questions on her professional life. The obvious productions were feel-good features from those who managed to get an interview. But those who did not provided scandalous, muck-raking coverage, often without her prior knowledge, merely picking up gossip from hearsay.

It had been hard because in England, she was one in a tiny pool of black actresses, having gained most of her early work in the United States. Luckily, she had emerged there at a time when corporate America was beginning to realize and exploit the commercial viability of African-Americans.

Michael Jackson became the king of pop; Oprah

Winfrey, the highest grossing female earner in the land with her talk show that ran coast to coast; Eddie Murphy took Hollywood by storm; while "The Cosby Show" displayed middle-class blacks for the first time on TV screens. And Michael Jordan signed a deal with Nike that would allow him to assume the role of the most famous player in the history of basketball.

The opportunities that had been open to Desney in the eighties and early nineties were healthy inasmuch as they helped mold her into the actress she had become. And when she returned to England four years ago, it had been to forge a career in the theater and challenge herself in more constructive roles. The plan had worked for a while until her financial situation began to dictate what parts she should take.

It was in March when she got her biggest break in England and Kemet Productions suggested to her agent that she screen test a part. When she landed the role as Cinnamon Walker, her popularity and fame rocketed overnight. The role was not only challenging but raised controversial issues that plagued the youth of England. Everyone suddenly wanted an interview, and she had declined many. But none had quite attacked her as viciously as the coverage she had received in *Bribe*.

"I'm proud of my magazine and the strides I have made to build it into what it is today," Wade replied in earnest. "It wasn't easy. It never is at first when you are trying to find the investment to put into a project."

"But things are made easier when you target a person, right?"

Wade's shoulders drooped, wounded. "I said I would make amends, unless you want to pull out of our deal."

"I'm sorry." Desney backed down immediately. "It's just that you media people feel such a sense of entitlement. You like to throw around the 'we made you' slogan and then tear a person down when you want to. But I don't think people really want that."

"What do they want?" Wade asked, intrigued.

"Real stories. The truth," Desney said earnestly. "It's a wide world out there," she aimed the pun. He laughed. "And of course you're here shivering to prove to me that you see my point. Look," she stood up and flapped her arms like a butterfly in mid-flight. "This is what you do to warm yourself."

Wade gazed up at her and crinkled his lips. "I don't want to look like no pigeon," he said dismissively. He glanced at his watch. "In fact, what's next on your schedule?"

It was Desney's turn to stare. "You really do intend to shadow me, don't you?"

"A deal's a deal," Wade said slowly. "Frederick Fitzgerald, remember?"

"Well, I would normally do another mile before going home to shower and change; then I generally head straight down to the set."

"So where would that be and at what time?" Wade asked.

"Why don't I pick you up, outside your office?" she suggested. "Say, ten o'clock."

"Ten sounds fine."

"Good." Desney agreed seconds before her mobile phone rang.

Removing it from the band around her waist, she apologized to Wade and quickly spoke into the mouthpiece. "Hello?"

"Desney, it's me," Frederick Fitzgerald announced nervously. "I need to talk to you."

"Fred, I'm jogging," Desney grimaced. "You should know my schedule by now."

"You have to talk to the producers about next season's contracts, Desney," he implored her in earnest, overriding her remark. "There's a rumor going around and—"

"I'll talk to you later," Desney cut in. "Bye."

She switched off the phone and replaced it in the band before eyeing Wade suspiciously. "That was my costar," she told him pertly. "He's worried. Does this have anything to do with what your little bird told you?"

"Probably," Wade said, refusing to elaborate. "You'd better go and finish that mile."

"But—"

"I'll take a rain check and catch a taxi to my office to change," Wade continued. "So you—"

"Fine," Desney interrupted, surveying his reaction. She knew she wasn't going to get anywhere, and so she turned on her heel, deciding that she wasn't going to wait around for him to be heard.

A quick wave and she was off, disappearing into the park, her figure merging with the skyline on the horizon. As Wade watched her go, he knew he was too long in the tooth to read all the signs. Desney Westbourne made him feel young again. And that was an admission he didn't want to make.

Three

Desney followed the furious Tony Barberi along the wide corridor that lead directly into Wade Beresford's private executive suite. His sudden stopping caused her to bump straight into him, but rather than helping her to regain her balance, he pulled away as though touching her would constitute some danger, leaving her to sort herself out.

"He'll be ready in five minutes," Tony grunted, opening the glass doors to usher her inside. "Just take a seat." He turned on his heel and left her in an instant.

So much for common courtesy, Desney thought as she took the nearest seat in the small lobby area that adjoined Wade's executive suite. In the distance she could hear running tap water and the shuffle of footsteps, yet she was unable to see Wade anywhere. She thought Tony would at least have offered her coffee, but it was obvious the man didn't like her one bit. *Media types,* she tossed her head. *Hard as nails.*

At least her morning run had helped improve her mood. She had only caught a slight recap of the morning news on the radio as she dressed after her shower. There was no mention of the coverage in *Bribe,* and the morning paper she had grabbed from a newsstand while on her way to Wade Beresford's office made no mention of his commentary either.

Maybe she had escaped a media backlash. It was the only thought that ran through Desney's mind as she parked her car and made her way up the elevator at *Bribe* magazine. That, and seeing Wade Beresford again.

Her full-length mirror reflected an image that morning of a tall, slender, elegant female with short, straight, neatly combed hair. Her navy dress was deceptively simple. Knee-length coverage, low neck, a polka-dotted jacket to match, and both belying expensive price tags. The cosmetic arrangement on her face was easy on the eye, too. Just enough to bring out an even-toned complexion, though she could never camouflage the birthmark by her left ear.

She wondered whether Wade had noticed it, or whether he would find her appearance more . . . normal than that of an accomplished actress vying to reach the heights of eternal fame. After all, he thought she was stuck-up, though Desney knew that she was not. She had friends within and—mostly—outside her professional circle, and they were all gracious and genuine people. Like . . .

She suddenly remembered her friend and agent Cheryl, and more precisely, Cheryl's party. *My word!* Desney felt her heart skip. The party was this very night. Was it possible that Wade Beresford would insist on tagging along? Having him follow her to the studio that morning was the least of her worries now. Desney didn't relish the thought of introducing Wade to her friends, let alone to her work colleagues. He may start plying them for information, and she didn't want to subject anyone she knew to that.

The sound of tap water stopped, and Desney heard the click of a lock before she saw Wade materialize from a wooden door close to the side of his steel desk. He saw her instantly from across the room and smiled.

Desney wavered a smile in return, though her mind conspired not to tell him about her friend's party the moment she caught sight of him.

"I hope I haven't kept you long," his Verona accent queried politely, as he glanced across at her. He paused for measure, digesting her appearance carefully. Desney noted the darkening of his eyes moments before he strode toward his desk and pulled a gray jacket from behind his wire-mesh chair.

"No," she admitted, swallowing hard, aware that goose bumps had formed on her arms at Wade's brief adoration of her. She liked it. She liked that he had registered her female prowess. It spoke to the primitive core of her being—the part of her that desired him, though she would never admit that to herself.

Wade's stylish locks hung loosely around her shoulders, not yet pulled back into a ponytail. She wanted to know what it would be like to run her fingers through them, but stoically she withstood the tremor that shot through her at the mere thought. She shouldn't be thinking such things—not of an unscrupulous media mogul whose only interest in her was to sell magazines.

"How was the rest of your run?" he asked.

"Just fine," she answered freely, clearing her throat, forcing herself to dispel all amorous thoughts about Wade Beresford from her mind.

Wade placed his long arms into his jacket and fixed it about himself neatly. He then snugged his blue tie against the clean white shirt beneath and straightened his shoulders to contemplate Desney. "I'm ready." His gaze was brooding as he regarded her from across the room.

Desney rose to her feet, realizing that he was keeping his locks loose. It made his appearance seem so becoming, she had to make herself think of something else besides the shallow ache at the pit of her stomach—the one that reminded her over and over that she was indeed attracted to the man.

She watched as he reached for a small microcassette recorder on his desk and placed it into his breast pocket. Saying nothing of it, she turned and marched toward the double glass doors. "W.O.B," she said loudly as they walked through, repeating the inscription she noted painted on one glass door.

"Are you curious what the 'O' stands for?" Wade asked, following quickly behind.

"Not really," Desney rebuffed, telling herself that she shouldn't sway to his charms.

Wade flinched. He hadn't expected that, especially when he was thinking how exceptionally agreeable Desney's appearance was. "Distrust is stronger than trust," he said calmly.

"You said it," Desney agreed. "And until I read the draft proof on what you're going to write about me, I'm going to settle on distrusting you." Desney heard him chuckle. The sound needled her and flushed out an insensitivity that was not normally part of her nature. "I'm surprised you find my life funny," she added. "By rights I should be charging you to do this."

They were on their way to the elevator, but Wade seemed unperturbed by the comment. "I wonder about you actresses," he said coolly, shifting the subject.

"Why?" Desney was curious.

The empty car arrived and they both entered. Only when the doors slid shut did Wade continue. "Well, you actresses with your carte blanche expense accounts expect men to pay lobster prices to wine and dine you, when they're only getting fish sticks."

Desney gasped. "I beg your pardon?" She was appalled and offended.

"And always saying that you don't mind if there's sex before marriage, or after for that matter, as long as it is not instead of," he finished, uncaring of the expression he saw forming on Desney's face. "Actresses, you are all fools, do you know that? You all just want to be exploited and used."

"And you would know, would you?" Desney retaliated at full steam, disbelieving that he could judge her so readily.

"I have sowed a few wild oats," Wade divulged, his modest accent deepening suddenly.

"You sound like you can qualify for a carload the way you're talking," Desney admonished angrily. "How dare you place me in that category!" She was beginning to wonder what made up the fabric of this man's character, why his views should be so tainted. It didn't deter the attraction she felt toward him, much as she loathed herself for it, but it did make her think.

"You are an actress," he remarked quite candidly, his modest accent sounding almost apologetic. "I don't know. Maybe you can prove to me you are different."

"I intend to," Desney declared, folding her arms beneath her breasts to affirm the point. "And the first thing you're going to learn about me this morning is that I am not difficult to work with, in spite of what Matt Doran may have told you."

"We will see," Wade baited her with a chuckle.

The doors slid open, and Desney marched out of the elevator toward her car, hands clenched as Wade's sarcasm and idle laughter trod on her fraying nerves. "We *will* see," she replied, heading straight for her Honda parked in one of the visitors' spots. She ignored the insolent shrug of Wade's shoulders as he followed closely behind.

* * *

"You're late!" The director's voice bounced loudly against Desney's ears as she arrived at Elstree Film Studios in Hertfordshire and entered the chaos on the studio floor. "We started rehearsals twenty minutes ago," James added, his manner far from pleased.

Desney's eyes narrowed as she noted him read 10:18 A.M. on his watch. Though her delay had been caused by the slight detour she'd made to collect Wade Beresford from his office, she put on an innocent face and lied. "I got held up in traffic."

James Wallace, a tall, bulky, balding black man dressed in faded jeans and a yellow T-shirt, walked purposefully away from his camera and toward where she was standing. "It's a Wide World" was big, splashy, and generously budgeted. It was also his baby. He was the creator, director and senior writer on the soap and hated disrespect for punctuality in any of the cast members. His vision was to have a gravy-bowl ensemble of disciplined actors who would revolutionize his soap by doing their jobs as instructed.

After all, the storyline had broadened to accommodate most of them, moving from subplots about unknown half-sisters, adopted cousins, stolen babies, and secret love affairs to ghetto hustling, gunrunning, and drug addiction with its spiraling affects on the two core families the viewers cared about. It was well written and it touched hearts.

Principally about the Palmers and the Walkers, the show had taken a decisive turn when Cinnamon Walker, the youngest daughter of Alberta Walker, had returned from her travels with a drug problem. Dr. Khumalo, the resident doctor, was a sympathetic character, agreeing to help her kick the habit. But they had begun a secret, tortuous affair that threatened to ruin the doctor. It was a storyline that worked.

James had steered the writers to finding a niche in

the marketplace that had never been tapped before. People who did not otherwise watch black characters on TV—IT consultants, doctors, college professors, and ministers of parliament—programmed their VCR's to tape the half-hour, twice-a-week episodes; and though Desney was now considered a major player, having successfully become the resident substance abuse junkie, she knew this did not make her indispensable. There was always room for a replacement.

James looked directly into her face, narrowing his dark eyes curiously. She had been due at ten o'clock in the rehearsal hall, a bare vinyl-floored room with folding chairs and a couple of tables for cast members to place their scripts while they went through the takes before filming. He inclined his head slightly and contemplated Wade. "Who is this?" he demanded suddenly.

Desney swallowed and began the polite introductions. "James, this is a friend of mine. He—"

James held up a dismissing hand. "I don't want to hear the details," he bellowed, checking Wade over rather quickly. In the brief three seconds of scrutinizing, he seemed to approve of Wade's presence, as though the gray jacket and blue pants, along with the evidence of a clean shirt and smooth shave, were enough to qualify him for being on the studio floor.

"Just keep him out of my way," James barked. Turning quickly, he yelled at the lower echelons of staff. "Kevin, check the lighting. Claire, get Desney a copy of the script, and Pete, go and find a visitor's pass and a cup of coffee for this . . ." James looked at Wade again, then added, "friend of Desney's, whatever his name is."

As he left, Desney whispered to Wade. "You'd better sit over there." She indicated a vacant area where a few wooden boxes were piled. "I'll be right back."

Wade looked around him before sitting on top of one of the boxes. As Desney departed, his green-brown eyes began to take in the large theater, which looked like the interior of an old warehouse and was where the filming for "It's a Wide World" often took place.

Above him, he could see the tall ceiling, littered with a brigade of neon lights of all shapes and sizes. Above the lights were small windows, which he deducted were used more for ventilating than letting in the sunlight. On the floor were wires and cables that led to cameras, lights, and sound equipment.

All around were varying sections of rooms bearing wallpaper designs, elaborate curtain arrangements, sofas, plant pots, fire-surrounds, and entrances and exits, all partitioned off by wooden separators—obviously the various sets for the stable of characters. Clearly, money was being spent on props the viewers could see. The executive producers upstairs were obviously not shy about putting their investment into the soap.

From his vantage point, Wade felt like he were a boy watching a stage play, and that anytime now, a mechanical carousel beneath each room would turn and display the next room ready for the entrance of a fresh burst of characters with an equally new scene.

He began to pinpoint those he knew from among the cluster of bodies that busied themselves with arranging the sets for the takes that morning. The first familiar faces were the doctors and nurses who worked at the imaginary St. George's hospital. Then he recognized Shirley Lamas, who played the Spanish teacher. As his gaze moved westward, he saw the corner shop owner, the butcher, the baker, the murderer, the suspects, the residents and then Desney's costar and leading man, Frederick Fitzgerald.

Wade's monkey grin was planted on his face in an instant when he thought of the bargain he had made with Desney Westbourne to get that all-important interview for his magazine. He was at the point of wondering whether it would be wise to go over and introduce himself to Frederick Fitzgerald when Pete Hinchcliffe, James's young attendant, arrived with a steaming cup of coffee and a pass.

"You didn't say how you liked it," he said apologetically, handing over the Styrofoam cup. "So I've made it light, with one sugar."

"That'll do fine," Wade accepted.

"Your first time on set?" the young man asked, taking it upon himself to pin the visitor's pass directly onto Wade's breast jacket.

"Yes," Wade admitted.

"Well, watch out for Shawnee Van Osten," he warned. "She's Dutch. And very pretty, but—"

"But?" Wade raised a large, journalistic brow.

"Since she got interviewed on that TV show *Black On Black*, she's been walking around here like she's queen of the place."

"Right," Wade nodded, raising his other brow. "What do you think of Desney Westbourne?"

The young man's face lit up and his shoulders straightened. "Now she's got prospects," he began, digging his hands into his trouser pockets. "Not too vain, does the job right. Nothing like Miss Shawnee Van Osten at all."

"You like her?" Wade asked.

"Yeah, she's nice." Pete's smile widened. "Of course she doesn't notice men like me, but I got her picture stuck up in my room and she's autographed a photograph for me, too, which I keep by my bed."

Wade glanced at Pete. He was a little on the thin side, ashen cast, spectacled and just adolescent enough to be growing his first mustache. "How old are you?" he asked curiously.

"Twenty-two."

"Twenty-two," Wade nodded and took a long sip of his coffee. He remembered that age very well, only in his day, he had a crush on Diana Ross. Boy, was he beginning to feel his age! It was one thing being outrun by a woman that morning, but it was quite another to find that that same woman had admirers twelve years his junior.

"I'm her biggest fan here," Pete enthused. "I try to protect her, you know, from the press hounds. Right now I'd like to get my hands on that bastard, Wade Beresford."

Wade choked on his coffee. The hot stuff splattered all over his face.

"Are you all right?" Pete asked, completely surprised. He reached over and gave Wade several pats on his back.

"Fine, I'm fine," Wade nodded, reaching for the handkerchief in his jacket pocket. He could sense Pete standing over him in an imposing manner as he wiped his mouth quickly, and he thought on how best to change the subject. "Am I okay sitting here?" he asked.

"Sure, no one's going to bother you there," Pete answered, digging his hands into his trouser pockets once more. "By the way, I didn't get your name?"

"Otto," Wade replied, instantly bringing his middle name to mind.

"You're foreign, right?" Pete said. "I can tell. You've got an accent."

"Yeah." Wade began to feel nervous. "Where's Desney?"

"She'll be in wardrobe, you know, for her take on set," Pete explained. He eyed Wade curiously. "Which country you from?"

"Me?" Wade laughed, surprised by the inquisition. He could sense something about this young man that was clearly protective of Desney. In his view, he was being checked out. "Shouldn't you be doing some work or something?"

"James told me to get you coffee."

"You know," Wade handed Pete the half-filled cup. "Would you mind getting me another coffee. That last one went down the wrong way, and I can't talk very well on a dry palate."

"Okay." Pete took the cup and left.

Wade felt like he wanted to leave, too. There was nothing he would have liked better, for he knew at that point that he was like a lamb among wolves, primed to be slaughtered.

Only Desney knew who he was, and he had yet to gauge her reaction if she thought about introducing him formally later. He decided to go and find her dressing room and perhaps suggest that he wait in the car. He was not used to shadowing a subject. He should never have decided to take her on.

But as he was about to weigh the pros and cons of confronting Desney in her private dressing room, she appeared, dressed in new apparel and stage makeup, with a brown wig covering her own locks of short, black hair.

"How do I look?" she asked when she saw Wade sitting, nervously rubbing his hands against his knees.

"Desney!" He rose to his feet. He hardly recognized her in costume, and though he knew her face from the TV screen, she seemed entirely different up close.

"We're going to shoot in twenty-five minutes," she informed him with a smile. How she loved the way he looked at her! Even in costume, Desney felt the goose bumps again. "I have to go straight to rehearsal. I hope you won't be bored."

Wade grimaced, not quite wanting to leave, yet beginning to feel like he was imposing. "About this interview," he began. "Maybe we should—"

His sentence was aborted by Pete's timely arrival. "Sorry for the wait, Otto," he interrupted kindly. "There you go, another hot cup of coffee."

"Otto?" Desney eyed Wade and laughed.

The way she threw her head back made Wade's heart tremble. "I didn't want him to know who I am," he whispered discreetly, realizing his voice sounded hoarse. "So I gave him my middle name."

"Otto!" Desney howled even louder, tossing Wade a humorous velvety brown gaze. She wanted to speak, but she couldn't stop laughing. She continued to do so as she made her way toward the set, raising a hand to gesture that she wasn't intentionally being rude.

Wade sat forlornly down and stared at Pete. "It's a private joke," he explained curtly. "You wouldn't understand."

Four hours, three coffees, and a sandwich later, Wade finally watched Desney leave the studio floor. She looked exhausted. Without having worked any lines himself, he felt equally beat. His fatigue, however, was due to the slew of people who had approached him throughout the takes, asking questions, showing him around, and generally prying about his acquaintance with Desney.

He had seen the dressing rooms, wardrobes, and studio floor. Makeup and green room. Rehearsal hall and production offices. The executive suites were off limits—no surprises there. And although he thought himself nosy by profession as the gossip columnist for *Bribe* magazine, the probing and inquisition he had endured while seated on his wooden box reminded him that other people were no different from himself.

He had been pegged as the lover, the neighbor, and the bodyguard, and then the neighbor got dismissed in favor of his being a long lost brother. In the end, he had left them all with the notion that he was a distant cousin.

And once that had been resolved, it wasn't long before another chummy cast member, Miss Shawnee Van Osten, dug in her claws and tried reeling him in. She wanted to see him later, but he was hardly in a mood for socializing. As he watched Desney approach, his only thoughts were of going back to his office to figure out whether Tony had handled the workload without any hiccups.

"I'm beat," Desney said, glancing over at Wade.

"You look it," he answered, standing up and brushing down his jacket. "Is this what your mornings are like every day?" He had seen that she was gifted in her performance, but he still had everything to learn about her, about the way she burst into life the moment the cameras began to roll.

At one point during the shoot it was an effort to take his eyes off her. There was something about the way she handled herself that made his wandering gaze stray back to her time and time again. Yes, the talent was definitely there, and so was his attraction toward her.

"It depends," Desney began, "on whether I shoot in the morning or afternoon. And sometimes I have an all-day shoot if we have a big plot to get through— those usually happen around Easter or Christmas."

"Well, I hate to rush you," Wade exclaimed, not wishing to, but knowing he had better before his body began to speak to him more loudly about this gorgeous woman. "I need to get back to my office."

"You've learned enough about me by watching the

filming?" Desney asked, slightly disappointed. It resonated in her voice, but Wade failed to notice the tone.

"I've been talking to the other cast members," he declared. "Most of them speak highly of you."

"And that's enough for you?" Desney said peevishly, not caring whether he noted her tone.

"Well, I'm assuming the rest of your schedule is free from here on in," Wade breathed lightly, folding his arms against his chest. "You've said nothing to me about anything else that you're doing or that I need to see, unless . . ." he paused, his mouth forming a wry grin, "you want me to be at Cheryl's party tonight."

Desney gasped. "You know about that?"

Wade opened his mouth, about to speak, then paused suddenly. His eyes zeroed in on her. "You didn't want me to know about the party, did you?" he stated, narrowing his brows. "What are you hiding?"

"It's not what you think," Desney wavered, now slightly nervous that her wild imaginings about him being there might actually come true. "My agent's a little unstable right now, and she might be—"

"Apt to say things she oughtn't," Wade chided. "Seems I've just changed my plans."

"I've got an appointment for some publicity stills at four o'clock and then one with my hairdresser at six," Desney relented, wondering whether she should avoid being pulled into the situation of him escorting her. "So don't change anything on my account."

"Oh, don't worry," Wade smiled. "I'll be Miss Shawnee Van Osten's escort."

Long moments passed before Desney spoke. "You're going with Shawnee?"

"She invited me to come along with her, which is more than you did," he remarked.

"I . . ." Desney felt positively sick. Shawnee was the show's token beauty, and she had a presence that radiated far beyond her nurse's uniform. Her banter on set was often seasoned with sleazy one-liners, and a jealous trait in Desney made her feel that this was competition she would rather do without. "My agent's only holding this party to try and please her boyfriend, although in my view, it's some kind of game she's playing with her estranged husband. I didn't want to add to the numbers in case she makes a fool out of herself and you take advantage of it."

"That's very thoughtful," Wade intoned, carefully absorbing the concern on her face. "She must be a close friend."

"She is."

"Good. Then I'd enjoy meeting her."

"She's very loyal to me," Desney panicked. "She's not going to tell you anything you needn't know."

"That's what all good friends say before they sell me the secret negatives," Wade replied.

Desney rode out Wade's determined look. Finally, she said, "Do you think you can take a taxi back to your office. I need to think about whether you're going to afford me any privacy at all."

Wade felt a soft note of pain in Desney's voice, and this time he felt his body respond. Without conscious thought, guided only by a compulsion to allay her fears, he pulled her steadily toward him by her wrist. Her head was downcast and she looked completely vulnerable against him, but something inside made him feel he had to say something to reassure her. "I promise you, I'll act like a professional."

Desney felt the teasing strokes of his fingers against her own and enjoyed the deep sensations that ran along her nerve endings. But stoically she repressed them.

"You have the nerve to evoke the word 'professional' to me," she bit back harshly, feeling that he was probably toying with her. "You're just a wolf out for the kill. When I see Cheryl, I'll remind her to sell you the closet videos, too."

Without another word, Desney left the studio floor. She refused to acknowledge Wade's guilty expression and she was neither surprised nor concerned when he didn't follow her down the corridor that led back to her dressing room. That was the answer she needed, right there. Wade Otto Beresford did not care about her feelings at all. Nor would he ever.

Men like him simply had no concept of feelings. She did not know whether it was because they were starved of motherly affection as a child, or whether it had something to do with a missing gene leaving an emotional void that could not be filled by compassion, understanding, or even love.

Whatever the reason, she felt hurt. Wade just wasn't paying any attention to how serious she was taking his portrayal of her life. She hadn't admitted anyone into it for a long time. Fifteen months ago was the last time she had been intimately involved with anyone, and even that was a mere passing fancy to take her mind off the stress and strain of working on a film. It had lasted four months before she ended it. The thought of anyone getting too close just did not sit well with her after that.

Desney knew it was because she was too much of a perfectionist. A man was always lacking in something. And of course in her world, they had to have good teeth, good looks, a good body, and a good job. She wasn't going to leave anything to chance. If there ever came a time when she wanted a mate, he had to possess the correct attributes to run on her track in the fast lane.

Wade Beresford had already fallen at the first hurdle. He was too . . . full of himself. That was it. And he wasn't physically fit, either. Work needed to be done there. But he had good looks and good teeth, and he didn't have so much a job as a career—and a thriving one at that. But he lacked something more. Desney couldn't quite put her finger on it, but she felt certain she would make the discovery soon—perhaps at Cheryl's party tonight. *Damn! Why did Shawnee have to invite him?* she wondered.

Storming into her dressing room, Desney began to remove her clothes, her thoughts racing over why Wade had ignored her throughout almost the entire shoot. Unusual, she mused, slipping out of her shoes. Why should he be so reluctant to glance her way? Her brows narrowed with confusion as she also recalled that whenever he had caught her eyes, he pondered on her, wistfully and ever so briefly, before quickly shifting his gaze to someone else.

She disliked it immensely. It was a further reminder to her that she was just some newsworthy aberration, and that once splashed across the pages of his magazine, she would soon be forgotten in favor of the next subject.

Desney shivered as she got back into the clothes she had worn earlier. It bothered her that she should care at all that Wade had failed to give her his attention. He's just another man, she tried to tell herself as she removed her wig and sat to fix her hair at the dressing table. But deep down she realized that her ego was feeling a little hurt, too.

She was lonely, but so was everyone she knew, and it had never bothered her before. It had never bothered her because she had always thought that Mr. Perfect would arrive when she was successful, making money, and doing the things she had always dreamed of. Now that that lifestyle was with her, where was the person she should be sharing it with?

Desney looked at her reflection in the mirror. A kindly face returned her gaze. She smiled at it, reminding herself that she was indeed a good woman. Someone like Wade Beresford did not need to write the things he had about her. Did not need to ignore her as he did. Should not have continued to behave in such an ungracious manner. It surprised her also that he did not even insist on being introduced to Frederick Fitzgerald, who had also ignored her entirely on set. What was going on?

Some inner instinct warned her to be wary of the man. She planned to be on her guard tonight.

Four

"Long time, no see!" Before Desney could get through the door of the fifth floor penthouse apartment in Docklands, London, Cheryl Carlton's arms were wrapped around her in an exuberant bear hug. She smelled of musk and was in a far heartier mood than when Desney last saw her. Cheryl stepped back to get a better view, then added, "Look at you and that figure, girl! Keep looking like that and I can get you more work."

Desney made her own swift appraisal. "You're not looking too bad yourself."

Cheryl's height was fully extended by three-inch heels, above which she wore one of her famous full-length georgette dresses over a well-endowed body that digested far too many cream cakes. But the weight didn't show so much beneath the unusually colored russet fabric, for Cheryl's glowing brown skin, generous heart, and husky voice were nature's gifts to compensate her zest for food.

"Come on in," Cheryl said with her familiar sharp laugh as she took Desney's coat and scarf and hung them on a wall peg.

"No handbag?" she asked Desney.

"You know I've never been much of a lady at parties," Desney returned with a smile. Most of what she needed often fit in her coat pockets.

"C'mon," her agent said. "Let me show you off to my friends. Maybe I can hook you up with some future work."

She immediately ushered Desney down the hallway and into the main sitting room where she was thrust into the crowd of a dozen or so guests who milled about bearing white wine in tulip glasses.

"My contribution," Desney offered, handing over the vintage bottle of red wine. Desney didn't recognize anyone but her host and Carlo Vicetti, the boyfriend. No one from the cast was there.

"You remember Carlo," Cheryl nodded to the young male model she'd been dating for two months. He was chatting easily, slapping men on the back, flirting with their wives and occasionally throwing back his head with a roguish roar of laughter. Cheryl blew him a kiss across the room, then added cynically, "He's kissing ass over there, then he flies to Vienna again next week for a fashion shoot with another photographer."

"Cheryl, what's going on?" Desney asked, detecting the absent tone in her agent's voice.

"Gerald, my darling estranged husband will not be coming tonight. He's changed the locks on our penthouse in Kensington."

"You still have this place," Desney reminded. "And Carlo. Do you really need—"

"Yes," Cheryl interrupted. "He reminds me that I'm feline."

"As opposed to canine."

"I have a terrible bite these days," Cheryl admitted. "It's just loneliness. I just want to be loved again. Is that so bad?"

"No," Desney chirped, reluctant to accept her own predicament. "I just think you should be careful, that's all."

"Let's do lunch," Cheryl forced a smile to her features.

"That would be nice," Desney agreed, distracted by a burst of laughter across the room.

"And it's time I started finding a male suitor for you," Cheryl joked. "There's a good selection in here."

"Cheryl!" Desney nudged her in the side.

The doorbell suddenly peeled again and Cheryl was once more thrown into her role as host of the annual Black Screenwriters' Utopia Party, which she held every year. Desney smiled as she looked about her, digesting the little groups that were dispensing topics of interest, admiration, or compliments with one another.

There was no music. Cheryl had never been a party queen but instead, as a mover and shaker and a born conversationalist, instigated snippets of dialogue here and there, thereby encouraging her guests to work their way around the room making contacts.

Soon that very room was dense with bodies, spilling out through the French doors onto the balcony and into the dining room where an elaborate buffet was set, into the kitchen, the hallway, and to the door where further new arrivals caused Desney's heart to skip a beat.

With a tulip glass now in her hand, and having regrouped among a cluster of men on the balcony who had simply introduced themselves as the 'boys from the BBC,' she watched as Wade Beresford and Shawnee Van Osten made their timely arrival.

She knew Wade would probably be far more familiar with the guests than she was. Most of those she had already spoken with were strangers, including members of the fashion and TV circuit, models, designers, photographers, magazine writers, and stylists—lots of insiders of the cosmetic business. There were also producers, casting agents, production assistants, directors, and executive producers—insiders of the television industry. Not quite Hollywood, but close enough.

Her self-defined image as an actress made her feel uncomfortably at home among them, but any hopes as she had of being rescued by Shawnee or even Wade quickly vanished.

When she caught Shawnee linking her arm through Wade's and heading directly toward the dining room, Desney felt her body react beneath the lime green Atelier Versace low-cut dress with its revealing panels and halter neck. Either she was seen or not seen—she wasn't sure. The lack of knowledge only heightened the sinking feeling that Wade was with Shawnee and not with her. But the thought immediately skipped her mind when another arrival caught her eye: Matt Doran.

Cheryl's party was obviously a milestone that had made it onto his filofax, she decided, as he staggered into the sitting room. Then, much to Desney's discomfort, he headed straight in her direction. *Oh no*, she screamed mentally. *Not here, not now.*

"Well, well," Matt crooned suavely, easing his way past a thickset businessman and perching one foot on the threshold of the balcony, the other still rooted in the sitting room. "I'm beginning to think that my luck is in."

"Hello Matt," Desney swallowed, discreetly removing herself from the group to join Matt at the doorway. "How have you been?"

"Couldn't be better now that I've seen you," Matt smiled, leaning his back against the frame of the French doors. The glazed appearance in his eyes gave Desney all the tell-tale signals that he was mildly loaded.

He was dressed quite satisfactorily in a pin-striped

suit and freshly pressed pale blue shirt, his tie slightly askew. He was also fully conscious of her, she saw, but the look of searching on his face sent her gaze following his to see that Wade Beresford, with a meticulously observant expression, was looking at no one but her!

She hadn't noted his re-entrance into the sitting room, though they could see each other quite clearly from where she was standing at the French doors that separated the balcony from the room. Desney's suspicions were raised instantly.

Her brain was calculating whether this could be one of Wade Beresford's setups. After all, she had heard about them—that he was often an avid spectator of the human cortege wherever a pre-determined combination of volatile people had the tendency to explode. It would be just like him to wangle a juicy piece of gossip at a party such as this, a satirical piece ideally designed for the consumption of *Bribe*'s readership. But her heart said differently. The fast beating of her pulse told her that her person had attracted his attention.

Nevertheless, Desney watched as a scheme ran through her head, quashing any impulse she felt to cut Matt Doran short. "Are you here with friends?" she probed quickly.

"No. Thought I'd hook up with you," Matt suggested.

"I'm sorry," Desney tried to eject a level of sweetness into her tone, not wanting to attract such undesirable company or force any sort of conversation. "I'll be leaving at any moment."

"So soon?" Wade's voice adopted the pretense of journalistic cool as he entered the balcony from across the sitting room.

He had seen Desney the moment he arrived, imprinting her slim figure, glamorously attired in a lime

green ankle length dress, into his mind as he followed
Shawnee to the dining room. But every sense he possessed wanted to return and partake of the angelic view
he had glimpsed on the balcony.

He wanted to smell her, touch her, see her, taste
her, and hear her husky voice close against his ear.
The compulsion was strong enough to force him away
from Shawnee the moment she engaged herself in a
conversation. Now that he was facing Desney in the
flesh, Wade didn't know what to do. He told himself
to simply remain cool.

But Desney disliked the calm facade she saw in Wade
Beresford. Something rather impolite rose to her lips,
but she swallowed it with a sip from her tulip glass and
offered him a deriding look instead.

What else could she do? He looked so handsome in
his pale blue suit, with just a white T-shirt underneath
the jacket. No shirt. No tie. Just an air of casualness
that was probably a ploy to put people off their guard.
His hair was loose, too and made him look roguish;
her senses quivered at his very closeness. *I have to keep
my composure,* her mind warned.

In that moment, she realized positively that Wade
knew nothing, and so she fielded his inquisitive persona with an introductory smile. "Matt Doran. I'd like
you to meet—"

"We've met," Matt drawled, shaking Wade's right
hand.

"Oh, of course," Desney recalled from earlier that
morning. "I believe you told Mr. Beresford that I
was . . . murder off set?"

Matt chuckled with embarrassment and Desney
scolded herself for warming to the dimpled smile that
won Matt the admiration of female fans across the
country. "What I really meant to say was that we caused
so much sexsation on screen," he ventured cheekily.

Desney felt a natural aversion to that, but she could not deny that Matt spoke quite truthfully. *The Earl of Black River* had been a national success, attracting twelve million viewers, and earlier that year had gone on general video release.

They had been Lady Connie and Earl Bernart, their storyline a romance of historic proportion set in Spanish Jamaica. He, the young, dashing earl and she, the naive daughter of his enemy, starred in an all-black production in which love and family respect were tested to the limit. She was his challenge as the forbidden fruit to the roguish, domineering predator. The rape scene was to show his true love for her, but to honor her virtue, there had been a duel between him and her screen father, Sir Reginald Oldfield, in which the earl had been killed.

Matt's fame had been assured ever since. The story was as good as Matt Doran was good-looking: his short, black hair shaved close to his scalp, the dusky brown eyes, heavy-set brows, and baby-soft chicory-hued skin that had never seen, in his twenty-seven years, the growth of stubble. Only the thin line of a mustache above his pink lips was present, enhancing his charismatic dominant character, which many women found hard to resist. It was an attraction of a different sort, less endearing than what she could see in Wade.

"That we were," she admitted reluctantly, tossing Matt a steady look, aware that rumor suggested he was going to make a guest appearance on "It's a Wide World" to boost its ratings. "But, as they say, time moves on."

The journalist in Wade quickly took charge, taking mental note of the glances that passed between Desney and Matt. He studied them as coolly as he possibly could and found himself suddenly feeling afraid of something. The physical setting—the moon in a starlit sky, the eerie magic of a fifth-floor balcony being swept by a soft night breeze, the picture of a man and woman looking at each other with a hint of hostility and yet with a sprinkling of hope—moved him to decide that it could only take a man like Matt Doran to catch Desney Westbourne in marriage. And yet, oddly enough, something did not feel quite right.

Matt Doran was tall, black, and handsome. Fit, too, and under forty years old. Hell, he was under thirty and possessed a spa full of the right kind of charm that could woo a woman like Desney into his bed. So why had he never been a running contender?

"So where is the man who is keeping your mittens warm?" Matt began, oblivious to the clench in Wade's teeth that signified his recognition of the charm going down.

"I don't know if I've met him yet," Desney answered, transferring her gaze to Wade. "Or am yet to meet him," she added, catching the brooding glint in his green-brown eyes, and detecting for the first time the small curls that she could just glimpse at the back of his neck.

Both men looked at her, so obviously intrigued that Desney was prompted to take another sip from her wine glass. Men could be friendly when stroked, she thought, but she had to remind herself that they could also be deadly when provoked.

She was aware of Wade Beresford silently watching her, his gaze seeming to crawl about her features, measuring the amount of mascara applied to the length of her eyelashes, detecting that her eyebrows had been freshly plucked, noting that she only wore a thin layer of powder to tone out the smooth complexion of her walnut brown skin.

He was not to know that earlier that evening, she was completely undecided on what image she should project. She had dressed in the only item in her wardrobe that would show a neat, reserved, attractive young woman, her short black hair brushed into a loose chignon at the back of her fine-boned neck. It was the impression she wanted that night. She did not want Wade Beresford to have any wrong ideas about her.

But now, as she stood facing Matt Doran, Desney felt she could hardly restrain herself from trembling beneath his teasing, mocking gaze. She was aware, too, that Wade detected the technique. After all, the ruthless, unscrupulous nature of the man was the same as Matt's. Both might chase her, she realized suddenly, even though at that precise moment Wade was inspecting her with undisguised derision. She had witnessed this typical kind of behavior before with men who plainly found her feminine beauty intimidating.

"You sound like you crave some kind of dependency," Wade assayed. Desney knew that this was his way of trying to gain some kind of control of the conversation.

"Desney would never be totally weak with anyone," Matt laughed, digging his large, brown hands into his trouser pockets, behaving as though he could see inside her head.

"Not even if she was feeling some kind of emotional void without a man?" Wade said, almost unpleasantly.

"Desney has an old wound in that particular void," Matt replied, so candidly that Desney almost began to feel that she wasn't entirely present. "She needs someone like me to heal that wound."

"I'm quite happy to nurse it myself," she snapped, attempting to take stock of the situation before managing a fortifying swallow from her glass. She contemplated Wade's expression over the rim. Matt had obviously downed a couple of vodkas and orange juice, and was at risk of providing Wade Beresford with information Desney had no wish for him to know.

Matt had a tendency to say exactly what was on his mind, and it was often difficult to avoid a predicament when he was around. But any hope of escaping the matter was soon dashed. Desney was totally unprepared for what Matt said next.

"A swindler, that's what she said," he began, his indiscretion now in full swing. "He took Desney for nine thousand pounds and played her like a well-tuned piano." He turned toward Wade and added thoughtlessly, "She never knew where all that money went. Cleaned her right out, so he did."

A cold shiver shot down Desney's spine and her eyes closed, as she prayed he would not say anything more. "Of course I felt so guilty," she heard him slur, her mind dazed as he continued. "Being a man an' all. To do something like that to a fine, upstanding woman like Desney Westbourne. He was—"

"A weasel," Desney shot back, her mind so stunned, she hardly realized she had spoken. All she could think was that Matt Doran had gone mad. She hadn't wanted anyone to know about that part of her life. Not ever. And not coming from him.

She stared at Matt, then risked looking at Wade Beresford. He was standing back on his heels, his mind calculating, obviously working at full tilt. This was not the kind of news she wanted him to know when he had promised her a re-write in his magazine. The humiliation was almost too much to bear.

But to walk away now would indicate some form of admission that she had been terribly hurt. Of course, it had been an unforgivable sin, and she had never thought she would be reminded of it again. And Matt's habits had always extended to believing he had the right to say anything he wanted, to whomever he wanted, whenever he liked, without pausing to consider the consequences of his actions. Silence was not one of his virtues, especially when he had been drinking.

"C'mon baby." His attentions were now on her, his voice having risen enough that some considerate person decided to put on music to dim his bawdy baritone. "Don't be like that. We're gonna cause another sexsation when I start shooting next week on *It's a Wide World*. They tell me I'm gonna be Nick Palmer."

That was the last reminder Desney needed to push her over the edge. "One of these days," she gasped, scarcely believing that he was confirming what Wade Beresford had told her earlier that morning, "you are going to walk around with an atom bomb of information that is going to explode in your face."

"Desney!" Matt crooned.

It was Shawnee's timely arrival that broke the disturbance. "They say three is a crowd, but four is plainly impossible," she smirked. Shawnee, looking elegant as usual in a pale blue, low-necked chiffon dress that displayed all her womanly curves, was carrying two glasses in her hand, one of which she handed to Wade. "What's going on, Otto?" she asked, noting his sympathetic gaze at Desney.

"Otto!" Matt chuckled, his voice growing more sluggish. "This is Wade Beresford from *Bribe* magazine."

"Wade . . . what?" Shawnee broke out, flushing to her hairline. "The guy who wrote the piece about Desney?" She gave a husky little giggle. "Why, you sly fox," she aimed at Wade. "I thought it was downright unfair what you wrote about Desney."

This was more than Desney could bear. "Isn't anything sacred around here?" she said, then walked from the balcony, through the sitting room, and down the hallway to the main door. She confronted Cheryl on her way out. "My coat," she wavered, about to reach for it on the peg where Cheryl had placed it.

"Are you leaving already?" Cheryl was aghast. "It's only eleven-thirty."

"I have a breakfast appointment," Desney lied, feeling the tears tugging behind her velvety brown eyes. She heard a burst of laughter from the sitting room and decided that she was the center of the joke.

"I'm sorry I invited Matt," Cheryl said, suddenly understanding. "But he is on my books—"

"I know," Desney said. "I have to go."

"Who could you be seeing so early in the morning?" Cheryl queried, reluctant to see one of her best clients leave so fast without her knowing whom she would be meeting.

"Me."

Desney swung around to find Wade Beresford behind her, his arms outstretched with her thick brown coat, urging her to put her arms into its sleeves. She did so and pulled the cashmere around her, aware that his voice had been friendly, full of sympathy. For some reason, she warmed to the sound of it.

"So you're both leaving?" Cheryl intoned, her brows raised curiously.

"Cheryl, this is Wade Beresford," she introduced, watching as they acknowledged each other. "From *Bribe* magazine."

"Pleased to make the acquaintance," Cheryl smiled wryly.

"I'll call you next week about that lunch," Desney added on a final note.

Another peel of laughter from the sitting room had Desney out through the door in an instant. By the time she reached street level, walking ahead of Wade without so much as a backward glance, the warming effect of his voice had faded and her animosity began to surface.

"That man had no right," she seethed, stupefied by the entire ordeal, her voice dimming the sounds from Cheryl's party. "How dare he." She stopped in her tracks and turned to find Wade Beresford only inches behind.

"I thought you two were old friends at least," he offered sympathetically, standing directly opposite her.

"I prefer to reserve judgment on that until I see him sober," Desney choked, her shame at even knowing the man causing tears to tug at her eyelids. "And you had no right, either," she attacked.

"What?" Wade was completely taken aback.

"To be there," she snapped. "I suppose the fact that I'd once been conned will find itself among the pages of your illustrious magazine?" Desney blinked away the tears before adding, "Woman cheated out of her inheritance. Great headline, don't you think?"

A mask seemed to cross Wade's face. "I wouldn't do that," he finally admitted after a few seconds of thought.

"No?" Desney said tearfully. "Doesn't sound like the Wade Beresford I know, feeding off the ills and woes of others."

"Look," Wade began, his tone carefully pitched. "Not all reporters are jerks. You've obviously gone through something bad and—"

"I don't need your pity," Desney said, her voice suddenly weakened as memories flooded her mind. "It was a few years ago and I'm over it now. So don't pity me."

"I'm sorry," Wade said quietly.

"Can I have that in print?" Desney chuckled tearfully, pulling her coat about herself as though she wanted to hide beneath it.

Wade looked about him and felt the chill of the autumn air, annoyed that the street was still quite noisy for that time of night, and that the usual activity of night-clubbers and pub crawlers intruded on his conversation with Desney. He realized that she was clearly upset, more so by her attitude toward him than by anything that had happened in her past.

And she had been right. The old Wade Beresford would have gleaned that piece of information as vital evidence in exposing the real Desney Westbourne. But to his discomfort, he was also aware that he didn't really know this woman at all. And wasn't that why she had invited him into her life, so that he could discover the genuine human elements that lay beneath that beautiful walnut brown exterior that had dogged his dreams of late?

He needed time to think, but he couldn't let Desney go just yet. Not while she was feeling so hurt and in need of calming down. "Why don't we try and bridge this gap over coffee?" he asked suddenly. "I know a great place on Kensington High Street."

Desney looked into Wade's face. She could hardly make out his features for the tears that threatened to fall. She guessed that he was trying to make amends. And her better judgment told her to give him the chance to do so. After all, he had followed her from the party to see whether she was all right, so there was no question that he felt partly responsible for the way she was feeling presently. Yet she still felt so suspicious of the man. Was this his way of trying to probe for more information now that she was vulnerable and not up to par?

"I think I'd rather like to go home," she finally responded, gladdened that her voice sounded more in control.

"Okay." He took a step back. "You'll be driving, of course?"

Desney nodded.

"Then let me at least walk you to your car," Wade insisted. "At this time of night, a girl can't be too careful."

"I'll be fine," Desney opposed. "My car—"

"I insist."

Desney drew in a long slow breath. "It's just over there." She pointed fifty yards down the street.

They didn't hold hands, but rather kept a comfortable distance that was neither formal nor intimate as they made their way toward the car. After a short while, Wade gave her a sideways glance, then asked, "You went to drama school I take it?"

"Italia Conti Stage School," Desney said a bit defensively, "here in London." She glanced at him briefly, attempting to measure the seriousness in his face, but deciding not to read any further into it. "I did a lot of stage plays, dancing and singing, that sort of thing," she added as they continued walking. "You're already familiar with the highlights of my career."

"Yes," Wade nodded absently, his hands dug firmly in his trouser pockets, unsure how he should proceed with the conversation.

She looked at him again, noting the aloofness in his tone. It suggested to Desney Wade's lack of interest in the tangible parts of her life, and so in a fit of honesty she admitted, "I always hoped I would be famous one day—not out of vanity or self importance as you seem to think, but because I happen to enjoy acting. I love the level of expression it gives me, and I didn't appreciate what you said about actresses only wishing to be exploited."

Desney felt the sudden restraining pressure on her arm as Wade detained her from going any farther. As

he turned her to face him, she saw that he was hurt
by her remark. The telltale signs were in his eyes, in
the furrow of his brows and the pursing of his lips that
almost seemed to tremble as she looked up into his
face. Desney was aware also of the flicker of guilt that
flashed briefly across his face but was just as quickly
lost when he blinked and caught hold of himself.

"You confuse me," he told her quietly.

"Me?" Desney was surprised. "In what way?"

Wade contemplated her for a brief moment against
the backdrop of the night. The cool breeze was just
enough to whip up a flush of color into Desney's
cheeks, and as he looked at her he knew that she was
unlike any woman he had ever met. She did not know
how ethereal she appeared, her brown cashmere coat
drawn around her body, the collar hugging at her neck
and earlobes where her unconscious nestling against
the soft fabric made her seem so vulnerable to Wade.

The image was so different from what he had seen
on the screen, where a more feisty, cheeky, and out-
going woman was projected. But the woman facing
him now had a sense of pride and ambition, virtues
he had thought would make her egotistical and pre-
tentious, whereas in fact she was none of these things.
How could he have been so wrong?

"My first impressions are normally correct," he
found himself saying. "But you don't behave like an
actress."

Desney couldn't believe the chuckle that escaped
her lips, but it came nonetheless. "And how should
an actress behave?" she asked.

"They're usually like—"

"A bitch?" she concluded. "Black, intelligent, truth-
ful, caring and humorous with fur coats, manicured
nails, piles of makeup and an entourage?"

"Something like that," Wade nodded. He glanced

sideways again, and this time Desney realized he had traveled to some place in his past.

"I prefer to be myself when I'm not working," she explained, pulling him back to the present time. "No falsehoods, no pretense."

"I like that about you," Wade declared. "It's . . . sweet."

Desney felt a simple smile break across her lips. "You're being kind," she said. "It's . . . this is not like you."

She risked looking into his eyes and caught a sign of something that made her retreat one step back. She had seen a flicker, an amorous flame that seemed suddenly ignited by the moment. After all, they were standing on a darkened street, facing one another, with a starlit sky above their heads. She had been in such settings before, but they were artificially erected for the TV screen and were designed for wooing.

But Desney had no wish to be wooed by Wade Beresford. It would be a disaster. They were from two different worlds. His conformed to standards that she detested: prying into people's lives, divulging their details for all and sundry. She, on the other hand, believed in privacy, sanctuary, and the idea that one's business is one's own and nobody else's. How could she possibly become attracted to someone who was so totally opposed to those views?

She needed to be in the haven of her car right now, and pulling away from Wade seemed the logical indicator to warn him that her thoughts were firmly set on getting there. But her will to increase the distance between them was stubbornly refused. On her retreat, Wade simply advanced a step forward and, to her chagrin, pulled one hand from his trouser pocket and placed it against her chest. Though her coat provided full coverage from the elements, it didn't prevent him from feeling the tremors beneath the cashmere.

"You're afraid of me," he told her matter-of-factly.

Desney's eyes widened. "Why . . . why do you think that?"

"Your heart is beating so fast," Wade breathed.

"I know."

"And I'm causing that?"

Desney nodded. She had little choice. From the moment Wade had looked at her in his state of confusion, she had known that something about the mood between them had changed. There was a tension now—an awareness that something needed to happen, but she knew not what.

There was also a magnetism. It wasn't a strong one. Nothing that she would attribute to chemistry or the first throbs of wild passion, but rather a pulling together. And it was not out of curiosity, but of some miracle that seemed borne from an understanding she could not comprehend.

When their eyes met, she knew that Wade knew it, too. His hand warmed her immensely, and a wonderment filled his face with a glow that took her breath away. The thought that this moment could be happening between her and Wade Beresford seemed too unbelievable to be true, but not for the man who had now taken his other hand from his trouser pocket to put one of Desney's in his own.

"My heart is beating, too," he confessed. "Feel." And he took her right hand and placed it against his chest.

Desney felt the strong tremble against his jacket. Each thud ran up her fingers, up her arm and to her shoulders, and from there they transmitted to her own chest, where the rhythm kept time and measure with her own. The miracle seemed ever more remarkable, that two people could be enthralled in this way.

"Wade." Suddenly Desney wanted to break free. Surely if anything were to happen now, it would only compromise his research for *Bribe* magazine. "My car is over there," she reminded, swallowing hard on what little moisture was left in her mouth, telling herself she didn't really want to know what those tiny curls at the back of his neck felt like. "Perhaps we should—"

Her words broke off in startled surprise when Wade instinctively caught her face in both hands and turned it up toward his lips. Desney's eyes widened, her pupils equally black and dilated as those that reflected like pools into hers, full of apprehension and excitement. His warm palms were clammy against her cheeks and his fingertips pressed softly on her temples like feathers tickling her skin.

"I'm not going to rush you," he whispered against her lips. "Nothing is going to happen here tonight unless you want it to. I can wait."

Desney smiled. "I'm glad."

Wade's eyes deepened. "Why?"

"Because if you wanted to sleep with me tonight, that would mean that there wouldn't be a second night."

"And you want a second night with me?" Wade whispered.

Desney heaved a ragged breath. "What I want is—"

"This."

The unsaid words were swiftly and sweetly obliterated in a softly bruising kiss. Desney reacted as she knew she would, accepting the mere brushing of Wade's lips, allowing her own to part even as his tongue delved into her mouth for a brief, arousing taste of her. Then, as quickly as the intensity of enjoyment began to rise, she pulled away, apprehensive of the odd expression in Wade's dazed eyes.

"What?" he whispered, his breath hoarse, her face still cupped between the warm fingers of his large brown hands.

"My heart," Desney rasped, every nerve ending now sensitized. "I need to know—"

"Yes," Wade nodded, miraculously tapping into the confines of her mind, returning his lips to within inches of her own, his head bent, fully intent on claiming them once more. "Your heart will be safe with me."

Desney held onto the brief intensity of the moment, unyielding to his tantalizingly close proximity to her. "You're not wondering," she wavered, unsure.

"About what?"

"Whether that kiss was a brazen display of my acting abilities?"

Wade's fingers tightened softly around her cheeks, his forefingers tickling against her earlobes. "If that was acting," his voice pulsed against her breath, "then it's time I tasted the encore."

The moment their lips met again, Desney couldn't resist. As much as she wanted to, as much as she told herself that she should not be kissing a man whose ethics she despised, she simply could not help herself. Her body desired it, her mind accepted it, and her soul was in full need of it.

Everything spiraled into darkness. The busy street, the distant sound of Cheryl's party, even the unexpected arrival of Matt Doran on the balcony flew from her muddled thoughts. Only the feel of pulsing lips ruled her world. And Desney ravished them like a woman who had never been kissed, sinking fast and freely into a whirlpool of feelings that engulfed and washed her anew.

Time had no measure. Space had no time. When a few wolf whistles from passersby finally penetrated through to them both, it was Wade who first pulled away, though he rested his hands against Desney's shoulders and licked his lips to savor the seasoning of salt and moisture against his mouth. "That deserved applause," he smiled.

Desney looked around her, embarrassed, observing the lewd winks by young onlookers enjoying the show. "Our audience approved," she said, moments before one of them shouted in recognition of her.

"Hey, it's Cinnamon Walker."

"Let's get her autograph," another enthused.

"I have to go." Desney pushed Wade away and reached for her car key inside her coat pocket. "I have to go," she repeated, already making strides toward her car. "Fans can get very aggressive."

"Wait!" Wade rushed after her, feeling suddenly helpless as they reached the silver Lexus, knowing she would not be inviting him in with so many people in fast pursuit behind them. "When do I see you again?" He felt alarmed at how pleading his tone sounded as he watched Desney root herself behind the steering wheel and slam the door shut.

Within seconds, he was swallowed by a small crowd as the electric windows rolled down and the car's engine started. "I'll call the magazine on Monday," Desney assured him, noting the arrival of a cluster of more bemused onlookers. "I promise."

"What about this weekend?" Wade yelled after her. "I'm supposed to be tailing you, remember?"

"It'll have to be Monday," Desney said in a loud voice.

Those were the last few words that registered in Wade's mind as the car came to life and sped down the blaring street amid the bustle of excitement. Wade stood on the empty sidewalk and watched as the crowd looked after Desney's car like birdwatchers seeing a rare species.

As it disappeared around a bend, an old drunk with a bottle of whisky in his hand couldn't resist inquiring as he ambled on by, "VIP was it, mister?"

"Yeah," Wade acknowledged, nodding, unable to deny the pounding beats of his heart. "A very important person to me."

Five

The alarm went off just after ten and played the usual Saturday morning pop chart. Desney reached an arm out from under the sheets where she lay curled up against her favorite soft toy, Poxy, and turned it off. She wanted to pretend she hadn't heard it, but she had a lunch engagement that morning she couldn't get out of.

"Damn." She sat up in bed. Her hair was dishevelled and her mouth felt dry. She stifled a yawn between her teeth and was about to pull away the covers when the telephone rang. She didn't want to answer that, either.

Her mind was a mishmash of mixed feelings as the terrible truth pounded in her head like a dull ache: She had *kissed* Wade Beresford. It was a complication she could well do without. What a terrible mess. She fell back against the pillows, her eyes closed while she tried to think.

The shrill of the telephone didn't make it easy. And no amount of thinking could possibly undo what she had done last night. Still, it wasn't as if they had slept together. It had only been a kiss. One long, lingering kiss. And her only consolation—if she could call it one—was that a horde of fans had arrived and aborted the risk of their taking the kiss any further.

Desney opened her eyes and grimaced at the phone.

She would have to ditch the shadow, which meant she could forget about Wade completing his feature on her. End of story. End of mess—if only it could be that simple.

The impatient ring prompted her to sit up again, irritated at the intrusion. She wasn't in the mood to talk with anyone. All she wanted to do was forget that she had kissed one of London's most feared journalists, and the revelation that she had enjoyed it. *Damn that infernal noise,* she hissed to herself as her hand reached for the telephone while she considered what Wade's thoughts of her must be now.

Desney drew in a sharp breath and picked up the receiver, holding it to her ear and speculating what Wade's last memory of her must have been. *Loose woman with flagrant conduct* sprang to mind. He was probably at that very moment making designs on taking her to bed.

She shouldn't allow him to, her common sense said. Mustn't. He was a man who had decided that she was like all the other actresses he'd met: spoiled troublemakers, unprepared for success and surrounded by idiots and leeches, she told herself harshly. Just because he was being nice to her now, it shouldn't exempt her from the opinions he still held true.

And just because he looked so wickedly handsome last night when she had longed to touch the small curls she could barely glimpse at the back of his neck, it didn't mean that they should begin a . . . fling, either. Yes, that's precisely what it would be. A brief, meaningless romp that would end in tears. Hers.

"This is your early morning call." Desney gasped at the familiar voice that suddenly came through the receiver.

"Wade!" She was alarmed. Her thoughts raced. "How did you get my number?"

"Cheryl was more than accommodating," he explained, his mildly accented voice sending thrills through her body. "You left your scarf at her party."

"You went back?" she said, aware of what scandal could already be cascading around her head.

"I had to get my coat," Wade explained. "Cheryl knew we had a breakfast appointment, so . . ."

Desney grew heightened. "Where are you?"

"On my mobile."

Desney felt a shudder run up her spine as she imagined his wide monkey grin. "And exactly where are you with your mobile?" she asked.

"Outside your apartment," Wade concluded. "Look through your window."

Desney bolted from beneath the covers and counted to ten to calm herself. She was dressed in her silky pajamas and her bare feet were cold against the expanse of decorative ceramic tiling that stretched all the way to the split-level window overlooking the main street.

She reached it a few seconds later, carrying the telephone in her hand as she poked her head through the curtains and saw Wade outside his car, leaning casually against it. He looked so incredibly handsome, even from a distance, that Desney had to catch her breath up short.

"I don't believe this," she breathed, stifling another yawn between clenched teeth. "Why didn't you just come on up instead of standing out there on ceremony?" She threw him a wave.

"Cheryl didn't give me your apartment number," Wade returned the wave. "She just asked me whether I was seeing you at Montgomery House, which I happen to know is at Hyde Park Gardens, so I said yes, then—"

"Cheryl realized she'd let my address slip," Desney

finished, annoyed that her agent didn't have more sense. Then again, Cheryl's mouth always had a habit of running away with itself. "Well I'm sorry," she began. "I can't see you today. I'm busy."

"I'm coming up," Wade said suddenly.

Desney was immediately horrified. "No, you're not." She rushed from the window directly to her dressing table, using one free hand to attempt to fix her tangled hair while the other still held mercilessly onto the telephone.

Wade wasn't deterred. "I'll buzz every apartment number on the intercom system until someone lets me in," he persisted.

"No." Desney caught her reflection in her dressing table mirror and realized that she didn't look so bad. Maybe if she washed her face, she thought, it would help soften the dark lines from lack of sleep that were visible beneath her eyes. Maybe if she dressed first, she could forget about last night and remind herself that it was a new day. Maybe . . . She couldn't think. "It wouldn't be a good idea for you to come up," she told Wade finally. "My neighbors might think—"

"Your neighbors." Wade chuckled. "You're playing Britain's number one hussy on *It's a Wide World* and you're worried what ordinary folks might think about a reporter coming to see you on the weekend?"

"You're not just any old reporter," Desney said, rushing over to her elaborate wardrobe and fingering her way through the racks of clothing. She was stalling for time and she knew it. By keeping Wade talking on the phone while she selected a simple multi-patterned velour blouse and a plain black skirt to match, she had time to get dressed just in case she decided on letting him in. "You have a reputation," she continued, slipping out of her pajamas. "And besides, I'm having second thoughts about this interview we agreed on."

"So you do have a secret you don't want me to find out," Wade suddenly affirmed. "Is there a man in your bed?"

Desney paused after slipping into her skirt and stared at the phone, disappointed. "Why are you here?" she asked suspiciously.

Wade detected the sudden change in Desney's tone. It came down the receiver like an icy chill reaching all the way to his bone marrow. He looked up at the window, but she was no longer there. She was inside her apartment, which he could obviously see had security measures that would prevent anyone from entering her lair unless she wanted them to.

Since she was a well known actress, he supposed it was a wise precaution, and he suspected now more than ever that Desney was the type of woman who guarded her privacy as carefully as she did the mysteries of her life. And from her reaction to Matt Doran the night before and her cold shoulder that morning, Wade knew he had stumbled onto something.

"I need to find out whether you sugar your cornflakes for breakfast," he said, keeping his tone quite amicable. "That's a major secret I'd like to know," he added with a deliberate chuckle.

Desney seated herself on the edge of the bed and thought for a moment. She felt unsure. Last night, she had allowed Wade to kiss her. It hadn't been intentional; it just happened. All her instincts told her it was meant to happen. But now, in the light of day, she could see all the hazards of allowing him to be close to her again. A soap star with a jaded journalist was like dynamite with a lighted match.

And of course someone would get hurt. She could hardly imagine that someone to be Wade. He was the type that would bounce back, probably more dangerous than ever. And a celebrity such as herself could hardly be expected to instruct her lawyer to take out a gag order against him if he later chose to reveal all the torrid secrets of their affair in his magazine.

No. She would have to put that one kiss behind her. She would have to find out how long he expected to tail her, then get him out of her life as fast as he had entered it. She would have to pretend that everything about her had been an act for his benefit. And for her own self-preservation.

"Desney?" His voice infiltrated her thoughts.

"Apartment 343," she said decisively, though inwardly she wondered what she was doing.

She clicked off the phone and placed it on the bed. Looking at the clock, which read 10:14 A.M., Desney quickly slipped into her blouse and sandals and made a dash for the bathroom. She had just enough time to rinse her face when the sudden loud squawk of the intercom made her jump.

She rushed to the grilled pad on her wall and pressed the release button that would allow Wade into the building. "Come on up," she said.

She gauged that for him to make the distance from the lobby and up the stairs to her apartment door would buy her ample time to put the kettle on and make a calming dose of chamomile tea which she needed right now. A quick stir of sugar and Desney had just raised the hot cup to her lips when the knock on the door came hard and sudden.

"No jogging this morning?" Wade asked on entering. He eyed the cup in Desney's hand and then added, "Or have I just woken you?"

"I'm allowed to sleep late on Saturdays," she snapped, closing the door and following Wade into the sitting room. "So you won't be able to stay long."

"Your scarf." Wade held up the loose woollen wrap as he stood in the center of the room and looked about him. Placing it on a nearby sofa, his hands dug into his jeans pockets and he surveyed Desney's retreat as if he were a real estate appraiser.

With the sun shining through the window, Hyde Park looked more prepossessing than usual and so did he. Desney registered his clean-edged profile, and the strength of purpose in his jaw made her send a reminder to her brain that she had valid reasons for keeping him at bay.

But Wade's physical attraction was too strong to be set easily aside. Dressed simply in faded jeans and a white T-shirt, his black ringlets pulled back into the usual ponytail, and the cleft in his chin widening slightly as he threw her a grin, Wade seemed more handsome than ever. Sinful, carnal, potent. Even the sun bouncing off his honey-brown skin caused Desney to catch her breath in fascination.

"You live well," he said approvingly, his hands pulling at his jeans until the fabric stretched taut across his thighs, tensing every nerve in Desney's body. "Porcelain statuettes, palm plants, an orange sofa . . . lilac walls?"

"My interior decorator believes in *feng-shui*," she answered, well aware of the unusual coloring of her sitting room.

"So," Wade said, glancing directly at her. "Why didn't you want to see me?"

The question came so suddenly, Desney took a step back. "I told you," she explained, her voice hardly calm as she lounged casually against the wall, gently sipping her tea. "I'm busy today."

"Nothing to do with the fact that I kissed you last night?" he probed unashamedly.

Desney coughed and stared down into her cup. "I've been kissed a thousand times before," she said, taking the statement no more seriously than she was sure it was meant to be taken. "I don't see why kissing you should be any different from the rest. It's all an act and I'm good at it."

It seemed the perfect remark to make, Desney convinced herself. It was obvious to her that, at his age, Wade could make love to a woman with such expertise, he probably had standard movements all mapped out. She had decided she wasn't going to be baited.

But Desney was surprised when Wade stood back confused. "You've changed your tune," he chided, the blow catching him unawares.

"It's not my tune," Desney conveyed, deciding this was the moment to tell Wade about her misgivings regarding his proposed feature on her.

"What was that about last night?" he asked.

"Last night," Desney began, refusing to be deterred, "was about me performing like actresses do. And you surprise me," she continued, unable to stop herself from measuring the breadth of his shoulders and the rippling musculature that was visible to her roaming gaze. "You seem to be changing the tune to suit the piper."

"Me?" Wade was dazzled.

"Weren't you the guy who told me it must be quite a disappointment to find that there's one man out there who is not conforming to my drop-dead gorgeous looks? I assume you were referring to yourself?"

"Yes, but—"

"And wasn't it you who said women like me were man-eaters?"

"I know, and—"

"He who pays the piper calls the tune."

"That was before . . . before I got to know you better," Wade explained.

"Does that mean you've now considered that I am

accustomed to complete idolization by men?" She dared to look directly into his green-brown eyes.

Wade was silenced. He glanced at Desney, undecided on where she was coming from. Desney didn't know either. All she knew was that she liked being on one side of the fence with Wade Beresford, the enemy, at the other. Anything other than that would be a disaster, especially where her heart was concerned.

"Why are you behaving like this?" she heard him ask. Wade ran a finger across his forehead and thought perhaps he should take a seat.

Desney decided to remain standing, her back still against the wall as he reclined his tall build into the cushions of her sofa. She felt she had more control that way. "You're a reporter," she said. "One minute you behave as though you hate me . . . hate actresses on all counts. And the next, we're soul mates. A girl in my position is bound to think that something is afoot."

Wade raised a brow. "You think I'm leading you on? For what?"

"For me to drop all my guards. For me to tell you everything about my life, including the things I hold most dear," Desney pressed on.

"Now wait a minute." Wade's emotions were roused. "You were the one who wanted me around to tell my magazine readers about the real you. You were the one who invited me into your sorry little life to watch you jog, act on set, chin-wag at parties, and whatever else you will be doing—a manicure, a back massage, another date at the hairdressers, I expect."

"My sorry little life?" Desney wanted to explode. She pushed herself from the wall, placed her cup on a nearby coffee table, and stood over Wade, staring down at him, her hands defiantly on her hips. "My life was doing quite fine until you came into it."

"Correction." Wade stood up and towered over her, majestic and imposing. "You mean until Matt Doran came into it."

Desney's shoulders shrunk back. "What do you mean?"

"I thought I had full tabs on you," Wade conceded. "I even began to like your soft, vulnerable nature and the way my arrogance seemed to bounce right off you. But I saw the way you looked at Matt Doran last night."

"He's—"

"Someone from your past," Wade broke in. "I can tell."

"We worked together."

"There's more to it than that," Wade acknowledged. "I know from the frown on your face every time I mention his name." He traced an unsteady finger across the lines on her forehead. "See?"

Desney regarded him with outward calm, though an inner turbulence shook her. The moment Wade's fingers ran down her cheekbones, she put her own hand over his and stopped the downward motion. "Don't," she whispered.

"You don't have to tell me about him now, but I would like to know," Wade finished.

"So you can add it to your gossip column?" Desney jabbed. "What about your past? Why is it that you don't have a wife?"

Wade stepped back, seemingly offended. "She was like all the other actresses I've known. Just out for a piece of that F.A.M.E."

Desney's eyebrows rose. "Meaning?"

"Far Away from Marriage Effect," Wade replied, tight-lipped.

"I'm sorry," Desney backed down, feeling a little ashamed at her outburst. "I just don't like you knowing too much."

"Look," Wade reminded, his tone bordering on the sympathetic. "I only came here to see—"

"Whether I sugar my cornflakes or not," Desney finished. "Yes I do."

"And because I wanted to see you again," he concluded. "I'm not the big bad wolf you think I am. I do know about life's journeys. I've lived through a couple myself."

Desney was curious. "What do you mean?"

"Our journeys give us the lessons in love and allow us to meet the people we have to leave along the way until we eventually find that special person who will give us our strength and wisdom."

"That's a bit heavy." Desney was shaken. "I suppose you're going to tell me that we're on the same journey?"

"Maybe we are," Wade admitted softly, catching the bewilderment in her eyes.

"I don't think so." She refused to be swallowed into his psychological blabbering. "I'm on a different journey."

"No you're not," Wade returned tersely.

"Then I'm at a different stage of that journey," she clarified with a harsh note. "I'm not ready to receive or give that much love."

"You did last night," Wade reminded.

"I told you what that was about," Desney rasped. "It was an act. I'm good at that, remember?"

"So you did." A part of Wade advocated retreat, but his combative spirit still waxed on. "I live and learn," he finally intoned, pulling his car key from his jeans pocket. "I guess I'll have to broaden my feature on you to include your remarkable dramatic abilities. I must say it's worthy of the stage. I can't see any scope for male complaints there."

Desney was sorely tempted to swear. How dare this

man behave as though she was ready to give up anything and everything for the sake of a good performance! Didn't he think that she had any principles at all? If he had set out to rile her, he had certainly succeeded.

"You should know," she countered scathingly. "You were the one who authenticated my faultless technique in acting last night."

His eyes held hers, then Desney saw Wade's face grow angry. "Stop this," he lashed out, lunging forward to pull her against his tall, muscular frame. "Why are you doing this?"

"I don't want us to get close," Desney finally relented, trying to inch away from Wade. "This idea of you interviewing me, I don't want to do it anymore. I don't want you as my shadow, watching my every move. Most guys are content with me the actress, but you want to get into my soul."

"We made a deal," Wade said, annoyed. "You reshuffled the deck, remember?"

"And in hindsight, I think it'd be wise if I don't play this . . . poker game," she objected. "You journalist types thrive on the knocks that go on in other people's lives and feed off them like parasites."

"That's my job," Wade implored, inching one step forward, easing into the space Desney had vacated.

"Don't you see?" she cajoled, tearful. "There's nothing to love in someone like that. You're . . . hard as nails."

"And you're soft like a cushion," Wade struck back, advancing further until he was within inches of her again. "You're not like I expected. You're warm, affectionate, and I wish I'd never said any of those bad things about you."

"Then why—"

"Let's just say I underestimated the healing power

of time," Wade answered. Again Desney saw that flicker in his eyes that transported him to some place out of her reach.

She shook her head, confused. "I don't know who's the bigger mystery, me or you."

"Why don't we work that one out over lunch."

"I can't," Desney apologized, reminding herself that she was expected at Tottenham Court Road by 12:30.

"Look." Wade reached out and caught hold of her wrist. "I don't want to fight with you." Anticipating some degree of opposition, he pulled her closer to him. "The real reason why I'm here is because . . . I want to kiss you again."

Desney tried to pull back, her heart beating like a jackhammer against her rib cage, but Wade kept a firm hold. "This is going way off the scale," she breathed, bedazzled. Her feet felt weak under her, and it was a battle to keep them still.

"I believe in looking forward, not back," he said softly.

"Yeah, right over the edge of a big cliff," Desney answered, her senses aware that the grip on her wrist had begun to ease to a more gentle hold, though it in no way lessened the feeling she had of being on a precipice, about to fall at any given moment.

"Is it so hard being on the edge?" Wade asked. His voice was gentle and Desney was struck dumb with the soft, lingering tone of it. "On the fringe, you can feel that rush of passion. It's like thunder in your ears, the crash of waves washing over your soul, and the beating of tribal African drums against your heart." His soothing voice was beginning to warm her. "And when the night falls, your heart cries out into the moonlight for a love to find you. That's the edge we all want."

Desney was captivated, hardly aware that Wade had

pulled her into his arms until she felt his warm hands around her bottom. She heard his car key fall to the floor against the Afghan rug under their feet, felt the squeeze of his fingers against the fabric of her skirt, and when his head dipped and she could feel the tip of his nose against her own, a stretched thread of tension inside her snapped.

Her head lifted and his wet lips engulfed her like a blaze of fire, pulling the sweet essence of her desire into him in slow, persuasive movements. Desney weakened instantly. Wade's coaxing persistence, his tenacity in claiming her so greedily, the relentless, devouring mouth, robbed her of the resolution she had made to remove him from her life.

Wade was kissing her with complete abandon. There was something intimately soothing about the strength that smothered her and caused her to tip her head back to accept the power that emanated from the man whose burning tongue was inciting her so easily. The craving Desney experienced was new. All new. She was driven to move closer into Wade, where he absorbed her as if she had become vaporized, his senses inhaling the morning scent of her hair until he gasped against her lips before ardently taking them again.

Desney was swayed by the surge of his desire. Her hands moved up into his hair and ran along the long black ringlets of his ponytail. She followed the trail down to the softer curls at his nape. At last, her fingers were on them. They felt silky, like down against her fingers, the feel of them sending ripples along her veins.

Her body yielded, moving mindlessly against his, the heat of their kiss deep inside her. Sweet inebriation seemed to sweep her away, leaving her unaware of the bewildered moan that left her lips until it echoed back across the room.

"Wade . . ." she whispered, her heart palpitating in a frantic plea.

"You're on the brink," Wade breathed into her mouth. "You've been there since the moment I met you. You were right there on the border only last night when I kissed you. We both were. And today," his eyes captivated hers, "we go over the edge."

He took her lips again and Desney melted. A moment later she was on the sofa, melding with his strong, soft kisses. Desney twisted into Wade's embrace and straddled his thighs as she felt his fingertips stray past the bottom edge of her velour blouse to touch the satiny texture of her walnut-brown skin. Her belly trembled as he urged her closer.

His other hand grasping her hips, Wade brought Desney down firmly onto his bulge, a painfully sweet sound leaving the back of his throat as he felt the intensity of the movement ripple between them. She felt so good against him. The back of her hand smoothed the hair at the side of his face; she bent toward him, placing a sizzling kiss just beneath his Adam's apple.

"Hmm." Desney ran her fingers through the black ringlets of Wade's hair close to his scalp, massaging his head, bringing him closer to her, forgetting her vow not to let him get close.

"Hmm," Wade returned, as his tongue lazily traced the delicate line of her jawbone in slow, tempting strokes.

"Wade . . ." Desney sucked in her breath, all thoughts of keeping him at bay, of holding him as a mere trifle in her affections, scattering the leaves from her desire-drugged mind.

"I'm right here, baby," he whispered hoarsely. Then his mouth pressed heatedly against her own once again, and his fingers nimbly delved beneath her skirt to tug gently at her panties.

Desney made a slow animal sound, a blend of agony and yearning, as his warm fingers trailed down the length of her bare thigh. Wade's feather-light strokes tingled her warm flesh.

Her deep pining urged Wade to bring one hand to a breast and fondle her hardened nipple. He moved the other hand to her buttocks, teasingly pulling at her panties. The heat was getting to Desney.

His roaming fingers enticed her to rub against his arousal. The frisson was electric. He thrust forward as their kiss deepened with scalding intensity, the silk of Desney's panties making contact with the zipper that threatened to burst forth the passion it concealed.

A scorching breath escaped Wade's lips. And then his hands stilled in an unyielding grip on Desney's thighs. He rested his damp forehead against her heaving breasts, while he tried to calm his breathing. He had no thought of the moment ending, but a low warning sounded at the back of his mind nonetheless, telling him that this reckless game he was playing should stop and now.

"Desney," he managed between a lick and a nibble on her earlobe, a final gesture that he was calling a halt.

Desney looked at him through drowsy eyes, then remembered something. *Thunder. Waves. Drums. Moonlight.* "Hold on a minute." Her voice had peaked as she leaned back and rested her bottom on Wade's knees. "What you said just now, those were Matt Doran's lines in *The Earl of Black River.*"

Wade sat up on the sofa and faced Desney head-on, his hand lazily running up and down her spine. "I know," he admitted, his voice husky and raw. "You see, I don't believe in mutually accepted delusions or bouts of false security. I don't go with play-acting, either. If life is only going to be about performances with you, then you've got a long way to go. Without love, there is only existence."

"You . . . sanctimonious, self-righteous . . ." Desney jumped up from Wade's knees. She stood up on shaky legs and faced him, feeling that some inner part of herself had just been sorely tested. "I'm beginning to think that the events of the last three days are working havoc on your mind. You need to take a couple of steps back. What was this? Some kind of screen test?"

Wade reached for his car key on the floor. "You needed to hear that about yourself," he began, having retrieved the key and now standing before her. His gaze leveled on Desney as he wiggled the key between his fingers nervously. "I don't want an act. I want you," he stated firmly.

"Go to hell," Desney rebutted, feeling the hot sting of shame rush into her face. "That was cold and brutal. The chill isn't so nice from where I'm standing."

Wade drew his brows together in an impatient frown. "If you thought I was being cold, then maybe it's time I left before I start teaching you a few things in your bedroom they didn't teach you at drama school. The next move is yours."

"I think I'll call security," Desney retorted, heading straight for the grill pad on her wall.

"I won't count that as a move," Wade countered.

"I do," Desney returned, now acknowledging the truth in his actions. "Your story on me was about as out of place in your magazine as you are in my apartment, and I'm now of the opinion that you actually believe the things you wrote about me. Let's be honest," she heaved. "Sex sells. You're not here because you want to discover the real me. You want notoriety and I'll be damned if I give you any more leverage into the private areas of my life. Now get out."

Wade stared at her, the sting of her words pinching

him to the core. He shook his head in disbelief, his chest taut as he looked into Desney's vulnerable face. "I'm sorry you see it that way." His voice trembled. "I guess I can't expect to get everything from one person." He glanced back before striding to the door, knowing Desney would stay exactly where she was for several minutes after the door had closed.

Only when he reached street level did Wade begin to ponder the question that dogged his sharp mind as to what should cause such a beautiful woman to behave this way. What was Desney Westbourne hiding? He was more determined than ever to find out.

If Wade could have seen his own reflection, his face would have appeared as impassive as stone. He felt like a voyeur as he watched Desney leave her apartment building and walk across the road into a private taxi-cab. He was curious why she wasn't taking her own car, and felt even more compelled to follow her as he started the Lexus and began to edge slowly down the road from where he had parked, out of sight.

He was troubled, grappling with an emotion that he didn't recognize. It was borne from the moment he became physically aware of Desney Westbourne's body. He classified it as an unmistakable sign of the withering of his spirit, for he often felt sapped of his strength and emotionally drained whenever he was near her. He had never experienced this feeling before—with anyone.

As the taxi broke full-speed into traffic, he slammed on the gas and instinctively followed. He was already beginning to feel uptight. Teaching Desney a well-deserved lesson in her apartment wasn't something he had planned. He felt bad, not so much for having deliberately picked a line from *The Earl of Black River*, but more from the fact that Desney's kiss had meant a lot to him, even though she seemed to have treated his delivery of it so casually.

He had never kissed a woman that way before, either. In fact, the last time he enjoyed the pursuit of a nubile female in the way he was enjoying tracking Desney was at the tender age of twenty-one, when life was so free and simple and women were less impossible.

Desney would be high-maintenance, though he had thought she would be worth his special attention. Maybe it was his interest in her as a subject that was confusing him so, but he had actually believed that he could get close to her. Now his brain was telling him differently. What would be the point if the woman didn't know the difference between reality and an act? He didn't want a puppet. He didn't need someone in his life who couldn't transmit her real, true feelings. If there was ever going to be anything between him and any woman, Wade told himself it had to be genuine.

So she deserved it, he told himself in retribution as he shadowed the taxi cab around a bend in the road. *She needed to know that about herself,* he thought, going back over what he'd told her. In any event, it was done now. He wondered whether his story on her would ever be finished. Would she allow him to get close to her again? More importantly, what could he do to salvage the situation?

He cruised with his mind on autopilot for a while, thinking that it would be best to calm himself. His concentration on the road helped. The taxicab seemed oblivious to his close following. He tailed it all the way to a quiet back street just off Tottenham Court Road, and when he saw the vehicle begin to slow, he broke away and pulled in three cars behind, cutting his engine once he reached the curb.

Wade couldn't believe what he was doing. This was all new to him, following a subject. But Desney Westbourne was becoming more than that. His curiosity about her was now insatiable. As he watched her pay the cabby and found himself reaching into his glove compartment to pull out a pair of sunglasses, Wade began to question his infatuation with her as he slipped the shades over his eyes.

He dipped his head as she glanced around the street. It was just a little after 12:30, and the sidewalk was full of residents and shoppers going about their business. He heaved a sigh of relief when she did not note his car, though he felt certain she had seen the silver Lexus. Maybe she had decided it wasn't his, he thought as he poked his head up again.

Desney was dressed in her cashmere coat. He couldn't tell whether she had changed clothes again, but her hair was finely combed and swept back with clips, making her seem quite elegant even from this distance. Her legs were shapely and brown, the calves set off by the three-inch heels she was wearing. She carried a small brown leather handbag under her arm, which surprised him, for he had never seen her carry one before.

Then he leaned over to catch sight of the building she was entering. That was when Wade's mouth fell open. For a brief three seconds he struggled to find a motive for her being there. Then it dawned on him. Could this be Desney's secret? Was this why she had suddenly kept him at bay and had been so cold and distant when he saw her again that morning?

The sign read: BLACK DRUG WORKERS FORUM. Beneath the sign was the addition: REHABILITATION CENTER. It wasn't well known. He knew of no celebrity that had ever gone there. Nonetheless, that wasn't the argument going on in Wade's mind. What had begun to niggle him was the idea that he'd become emotionally attached to a recovering drug addict. His first female attachment since . . . Teadra Lopez. And with this he realized that his first feature about Desney Westbourne in *Bribe* magazine wasn't so far from the truth after all.

Six

It was early Monday evening when Frederick Fitzgerald briefly knocked, then burst through the doors of Desney's dressing room after a long day on set, every line in his face creased with worry. A cloud of acrid blue smoke hovered above him as he puffed impatiently at his cigarette, his mahogany brown skin looking almost as gray as the smoke from lack of sleep.

"Have you heard?" he said angrily. "Bastards! It's official."

Desney remained completely still in her chair, the red lipstick poised at her lips as she contemplated Frederick's reflection in the mirror. His lanky body hung like a man flogged with sticks. The white doctor's uniform he wore while playing Dr. Khumalo seemed to drape over his thin, lofty frame, giving it an unusually decrepit aspect. At forty-seven, Desney realized that for the first time, Frederick was beginning to show his age—more from stress than anything, she decided as she listened to his moaning.

"I'm going to be axed," he protested in disbelief. "I heard the rumors, but I thought they were only that."

Desney turned from her dressing table. She was in no mood for this. Her weekend had been as foul as the weather: cold, damp, autumn turning to winter.

But the chill that really gnawed into her bones was caused by the way Wade Beresford had treated her.

The truth was dawning on her, too, and she'd felt the pain of knowing that he was right. She should not have behaved as though her whole life was some sort of act. Behavior like that was apt to ricochet and affect others, and Wade had simply let her know how her masquerading of her feelings hurt him.

Still, she had gotten her own back, she thought. She had given him a taste of the same treatment he gave her in his office—with one exception. They had kissed. How could she have allowed such a deliciously wicked thing to happen after the oath she had made to herself?

The thought made her grimace as she carefully fixed her gaze on the man who had chosen to invade her private space. "Who told you a story like that, Fred?" she said in denial. "James hasn't—"

"James has," Frederick blazed. "The double-crossing bastard. He promised me another season when my contract was up for renewal, but now he tells me those dinosaurs upstairs are looking for an African god."

Matt Doran, Desney suddenly thought, alarmed. "Did James say who was replacing you?" she asked.

"No," Frederick spat out vehemently, exhaling more smoke as he plopped down in a chair by the door. He crossed his leg over the other knee and rested his elbow on the top knee, tossing Desney a cautionary glance that said he trusted no one. "Have you heard anything?" he jabbed suddenly, his dark brows knitting almost together.

Desney thought immediately of Wade Beresford and what he had told her the week before, but held her tongue. Seeing that she had not seen Wade since his visit to her apartment on Saturday, she thought it would hardly be wise to enlighten Frederick on a matter she knew very little of—especially since James himself had not yet told her anything official.

"I think there's been a mistake," she hedged, turning back toward her dressing table to avoid showing any signs of deceit. "Who could they find to replace a darling like you?" she added sweetly.

"You've always been kind to me Desney," Frederick drawled, exhaling more plumes of smoke into the air.

"We work well together," she acknowledged light-heartedly. "You, the doctor trying to cure me of my crack cocaine addiction, me knocking you out stone sober. Hope I didn't hit you too hard when we did that take."

"No," Frederick said, his tone uneasy. "And you've never tried to squeeze me like the others. Maybe I should try and square it with James."

"That sounds like a good idea," Desney encouraged, replacing her lipstick by her makeup bag and turning to take a good look at her costar, debating in her mind whether she should see Wade or not. "Only then can you start weighing your options," she said.

"Yeah." For a second, a wave of anger swept across Frederick's tired, flabby features. Then he leaned his head against the chair and threw Desney a conniving grin that broke the tension in the tiny room. "A guy like me has got to start making plans. If James is fishing and I'm not going to be catch of the day, then that means my days are numbered," he reasoned. "And after what I heard today, those numbers just got smaller. The way I see it, I've got a lot to lose, so I'm going to have to start talking to my lawyer and have him draw up some papers."

"You don't want to start a war now," Desney cautioned, thinking that maybe she had provided Frederick with more enthusiasm than she intended. "Just tell James what you want."

"Job security," Frederick admitted, rubbing the bridge of his nose between thumb and forefinger. "I knew I'd make sense of it after talking to you."

"Fred—"

Desney was abruptly interrupted by another knock at her dressing room door; a moment later, Pete Hinchcliffe walked in with two dozen ivory-colored roses in a large vase of water. "These just came for you," he smiled with amusement, "and nobody died."

"For me?" Desney's jaw dropped, as she quickly made room on the dressing table for Pete to place the vase.

"The card says anonymous," Pete warned protectively, using his fingers to spread the flower arrangement. "Could be a fan."

"A deranged one," Frederick laughed, catching Pete's raised brows. "Just my two cents."

"I'd expect change with that remark," Pete scoffed.

"Well I'm out of here," said Frederick, standing and making for the door. "I want to check if I have any fan mail before they close the set."

"Only three envelopes," Pete said in a wry tone.

"Three?" Frederick was mollified. "How many did Desney get?"

"Two hundred and six."

"In one day?" Frederick gasped. His brown eyes stared at the two dozen roses, and for a second Desney saw something evil flicker in Frederick's gaze—something of his inner self that made her uneasy. "I see."

As he turned, she couldn't help feeling sorry for him, regretting that she did not have the heart to tell him what Wade—and even Matt—had told her. She had just begun to ponder whether she should have a word with James herself when her dressing room door banged open again and there he was.

"What the hell is this?" He threw a copy of *Bribe*

magazine directly at her red-sandaled feet. Turning quickly to see Frederick and Pete standing there mute, he stormed, "And why didn't you tell me that was Wade Beresford you had on set last week. Shawnee just told me."

Desney screwed up her face, glancing at Pete to gauge his surprised reaction before she gave James a nervous answer. "He promised me a re-write," she affirmed slowly. "In fact, he wants to run the piece with a story on Fred about this murder plot we're doing."

"You're naïve," James railed. "He's priming you to get a story leak." His eyes caught the roses on her dresser. "I suppose he sent you those," he added. "Had they arrived last week, then I would already be suspecting that you've had a conversation in his bed."

"How dare you!" Desney said, looking at the flowers. Though James hadn't missed the truth by much, she felt justifiably hurt. She was abundantly aware of Wade's gifts—the believable, magnetic charm that he laid on so cunningly, making people around him feel comfortable enough to tell him just about anything. She had applauded herself for being on her guard, disclosing nothing of interest to him that related to her professional career. She was alarmed that James could have such a low view of her, that he could actually imagine her to be so silly. "I made a judgment call about the re-write," she began. "Mr. Beresford—"

"Kissed you, didn't he?" James rolled the words around his mouth with such sensual emphasis, Desney was forced to lower her eyes in admission.

Frederick cut in abruptly, a little nettled. "Steady on," he cautioned.

"What are you doing in here?" James said, redirecting some of his ire.

"I came to ask Desney to join me for dinner,"

Frederick lied, noticing how alluring she appeared in evening wear.

"She'll have to bail out of your dinner invitation," James jabbed. "I want to see her in my office in ten minutes. There's someone I'd like her to meet. In fact," he paused to take a calculating look at Frederick, "the producers upstairs have just hired him on a three-month guest contract. We've brought him in to boost sex appeal, and I'll be expecting Desney to show him the ropes."

"Me?" Desney asked, a trifle dazed. "Who is he?"

"An old friend of yours he tells me," James smirked. "Matt Doran."

"Matt Doran!" Desney groaned. "He and I were a match made in hell, and—"

"The devil just hired him," Frederick finished, fixing his hardened eyes on James.

A long, tense silence filled the room as James glared at Frederick before shifting his gaze to Desney. "I'll be putting out an internal memo," he declared, ignoring Frederick's outburst. "No one talks to the media. It's business as usual, you both got that? We've got an explosive storyline coming up and I want it handled very quietly. Understood?"

Desney nodded, too weak to understand anything. At that precise moment her brain seemed wrapped in cotton as she wrestled with whether to keep her dinner date with Wade or to try and reach him to cancel. In any event, she had to make a decision—and fast. It didn't help that she felt so unsure of what she was doing, yet deep inside, so drawn to the idea of keeping the appointment. Why else would she have telephoned Wade Beresford that morning if she hadn't wanted to see him again?

Throughout the day, his face had appeared several times in her daydreams: when she drank coffee during her break off set; while she changed costume for various takes. Even during rehearsals, as she forgot her lines time and time again from fretting over whether she should call him or not, he had paraded around in her mind.

It was an inward battle that she lost at every turn, when the daydreams turned to lust and she imagined herself straddled across him, his virility pressed against her. Finally she gathered enough nerve to have the operator patch through the call, and her voice caught at the sound of his deep baritone.

Her heart had skipped a beat just hearing his voice, simply knowing that he was on the other end of the phone and agreeing to meet her later that evening. He had suggested Floriana's, a popular Italian restaurant in the West End of London. She had never been there, but Wade had told her that the food they served was made in heaven. The restaurant was so old, it was said that Malcolm X had dined there before heading for Oxford to give his famous speech at the university.

She couldn't possibly turn Wade down now, not when she was so looking forward to seeing him—not when she felt such a need to explain herself, and when she felt so helpless to deny the churning feelings the mere reminder of him created inside her body. Feelings that had grown stronger in his short absence, until they spiraled in all directions, making Desney wonder whether she was suffering from obsession. Whatever the source of her emotions, it was enough to spur her on.

"You're a dark horse," Frederick mused, brows slanting in curiosity as he watched Pete and James leave the room. "You didn't tell me that Wade Beresford wanted to do an article on me."

"I didn't get around to it," Desney confessed, her

mind wrangling over whether she had made the right decision concerning Wade.

She had spent Sunday in a hellish sort of mood. Moping around her apartment, tidying up, eating chocolates, and talking briefly with her parents in Grenada before calling Shelagh, her younger sister. She had then collapsed on the sofa, skipping impatiently from channel to channel with the remote control, searching for anything to hold her attention.

It was the usual late-night diet of B movies and music videos, and the 1940s adventure love story put her to sleep with a dream of Wade. They were together on a pirate ship, he a dashing buccaneer rushing to her rescue just as she was to walk the plank, blindfolded and hands clasped behind her back, into the sea of oblivion.

As her courageous knight, he salvaged her life and her honor with his sword and a monkey grin, sweeping her into his arms and kissing her with unbridled passion while the crew cheered him in his victory. And when the sun set, their captured ship drifted into the horizon of an orange-and-yellow sky with them both at the helm, lips pressed together in a luscious kiss. Her heart was his.

She awoke to the blare of rock music. It had been a wonderful, romantic dream, which meant that Wade had gotten into her human system and was beginning to dominate her thoughts. But she held onto the fantasy as dearly as she would an ounce of diamonds, telling herself that one night she would replay that hedonistic vision again. Bored, she had later called Cheryl, thankful that her agent had such an empathic nature.

It was at Cheryl's urging that she had decided to call Wade at all. Her friend knew how volatile she could be and didn't want her to risk any adverse reaction or backlash in the media should Wade get vindictive about her treatment of him.

"You don't need a publicist," Cheryl had warned. "You're selling yourself. That man might just decide to dish the dirt on you after what you've told me. Apologize to him now before revenge tempts him to make a fast buck on your name."

"He wouldn't." She was aghast. She hadn't looked at it like that. Not when she thought of what it had felt like being in his arms, tasting his hot lips against her own, feeling passion pass between them to and fro like an electrical current.

"Who knows what he's capable of," Cheryl cautioned. "You hardly know him personally, but you've smooched with the man, and in my world that qualifies for a kiss-and-tell feature."

"This could be the break I've been hoping for," Frederick's voice infiltrated, breaking Desney's chain of thought as he paced the room in excitement, his own mind working double time.

But Desney wasn't listening. Within seconds she was putting on her coat and reaching for her keys by the telephone. A quick glance in the mirror revealed a woman who was, for once in her life, behaving rather impulsively.

Her immaculately combed hair hung loose, the touch of makeup just enough to accentuate all her features against the walnut-brown of her skin. Her velvety brown eyes sparkled with childish mischief, a reminder to herself that it was indeed early evening and by rights the present time belonged to her and not with James in his office. As far as she was concerned, her contract deemed that she was done for the day.

"Where are you going?" Frederick was baffled. His eye movements shifted to Desney, realizing that she was not paying much attention to him.

"I have a dinner date," Desney answered, her hand now braced on the door knob. "Give James my apologies. Tell him . . ." She looked at the flowers, "that I have a date with Mr. Anonymous."

The wide smile that Frederick threw across at Desney gave her all the reassurance she needed as she fled from her dressing room and proceeded down the corridor toward the break of daylight, where a short ride in her car would take her toward her destiny. But Desney was hardly at the end of the corridor when Matt Doran restrained her with a single large brown hand against her shoulder as he came through the door.

"Going somewhere?" he asked, seeing her dressed, as he was, to meet the harsh autumn weather. He was arriving, however, and she was leaving.

Desney noted that his eyes were glazed and seemed to sparkle with keen interest, his curiosity hardly concealed beneath his blue mackintosh. He was not about to have her leave in a hurry.

"I'm on my way to dinner," she explained, hoping that he would let her continue on her way. "So James will just have to conduct his meeting without me. Congratulations, by the way."

"You heard." Matt folded his arms against his chest and leaned against the wall. "Mind you, you're the queen on this set now, so I guess you'd have to hear first." His eyes groped casually and smoothly along the length of her. "Lucky dinner date, is it? You need a man?"

"I have a man," Desney lied, offended that Matt, in his semi-drunken state, should try to pick her up, let alone think he could meet James Wallace in this state.

It didn't surprise her that he wasn't deterred. "So?"

"Matt, I do one-man relationships, not one night—"

"Why?" He cut in in a forthright tone.

Desney braced her shoulders back, seeing the determination in his eyes. The sight of him leaning against the wall almost barring her exit, smiling devilishly at her, had her extremely worried. "We're not on a film set now, Matt," she began. "I don't use sex to enhance my career."

"When do you use it?" he mocked.

"I don't."

"That figures." He tapped his chin with his forefinger. "Didn't stop you when we were young."

"I don't know what you're talking about," Desney said evenly. "The only thing I remember is that you blackmailed me out of my grandfather's inheritance." She spoke discreetly, looking around her and down the corridor to make sure no one was eavesdropping. "I nearly thought you were going to confess it to everybody at Cheryl's party the other night."

"I didn't mean—"

"Well, I've forgotten it now and I've forgiven you, so—"

"I can't help feeling guilty about it," Matt wavered helplessly. "Love forever, hurt never. I told you that once."

"And you did nothing except hurt me," Desney said, her voice low and pitched to sound inconspicuous. "Now let's just forget it."

"And forget that we were once married?" Matt made the disclosure so casually and flippantly, Desney almost reeled back on her heels in shock.

"Annulled, remember?" She forced the reminder by holding an index finger to his face. "We were young—and stupid. And I paid you hush money until I ran out of money," she cursed adamantly. "We ended the matter when I got you the leading role in *The Earl of Black River.* You're a celebrity in your own right now, so let's leave it at that."

"And what about that certain *coup de foudre?*" Matt smiled, running a sensual finger along Desney's cheekbones.

Desney's brows furrowed at the gesture, though she could not deny the tremor her heart felt. "What?"

"That lightning flash of love!"

"Infatuation," she chided, removing his finger. "It was never more than that."

"We'll see."

"No, we won't see," Desney countered harshly. "Once a mistake, twice a habit. And I've never been a habitual sort of person. And speaking of habits, you have one that needs looking into. Your drinking."

"All that started when you got our marriage annulled," Matt mumbled, his head dipping in what looked like shame. "And when I wanted to sort it out with you—"

"Our marriage was never consummated," Desney affirmed. *Thank God,* a little voice in her head shouted. "My parents were within their rights to get it annulled. We should never have eloped. I just want to forget it ever happened. Please."

Matt stepped back, seeing the desperation in Desney's face. "Are you afraid?"

"Yes," she admitted.

"Of me?"

"No. For you."

He dug his hands into his pockets and studied her. He didn't recognize the woman in front of him. She seemed so in control. "I start next week," he drawled finally. "I won't say anything about . . . us. Your secret is safe with me."

Desney threw him a brief smile. "I have to go."

As she turned to check the corridor once more, she did not see the eyes that peered at her through the crack in her dressing room door, nor did she detect the determined glint in Matt's forlorn gaze as she made to leave. All she knew was that she had a date, and she hastened her feet, not wanting to be late.

Wade Beresford squinted at the restaurant's custom-made matches and then thrust the small packet across the table, his green-brown eyes glancing sideways in anticipation of Desney's arrival. He recognized the level of his impatience as the same in degree as that he had felt while waiting for Desney at Marble Arch Station on that day they had gone jogging together.

But this time, there was an added, disquieting anxiety that coarsed through his loins, and this he had not been aware of before. It was new. He wondered whether it stemmed in part from fear of her not coming.

He had never been stood up before. Women had always been available to him in one way or another. Not that he was really a man of the world. He had lived those days in his youth. At thirty-four he was more selective, discriminating of his choices in women, and not slow to put them in their place either.

Desney Westbourne was different. Clearly her profession was outside the norm, but the difference was not so much in her career as in the fact that she acted so . . . ordinary. Could he have been wrong about her? Sometimes public women constructed images that were mere caricatures of their true selves. His conscience pricked him when he thought of all the assumptions he had made. She wasn't some two-bit upscale actress after all, nor did she behave like a big-headed show-off on an ego trip, either.

A sex goddess she was indeed. Pretty face, lovely behind. In fact, she looked so drop-dead gorgeous, he was already uncomfortably eager in his chair, thinking about whether he would ever discover if she had told him the truth about the color—or the absence—of her lingerie.

The image in his head made him yearn to taste that sweet morsel of lust that had eluded him for some time. He had thought that perhaps it was because he was too busy, had too many deadlines to meet, or was— dared he think it—getting too old for that special kind of intimacy he had often felt reluctant to give.

Deep down, he knew he had turned it off. He had killed his love for women two years ago after dating an actress who hurt him badly. Teadra Lopez was beautiful, too. She had set it off once. But not in the same manner in which Desney Westbourne was setting it off now. Desney awakened that animal instinct that had quickened his nerve endings, making him ache to sniff and prowl, just waiting to pounce with savage hunger. It felt like he was learning all over again.

In fact, the moment he had replaced his phone in the cradle after her call that morning, he had scrubbed his nails, re-shaved his jaw line, added an extra dash of cologne, and had actually considered going home to change clothes, indecisive of whether his navy Hugo Boss suit and a Lacoste polo shirt were okay for dinner.

It was Tony who had delayed him in leaving. Briskly walking into Wade's office, he was suddenly alert to the fact that his boss was getting ready to meet a girl. "Who is she?" he had demanded in a tone that caught Wade's curious attention.

"You know who she is," he said, looking at his wrist watch, and checking whether he had enough time to make the journey to Surrey and back. He did not.

"You're supposed to be running a magazine, or have you forgotten?" Tony said. "Oh well, it's your neck in the noose."

"Meaning?" Wade asked.

"She's going to use you just like the others," he replied. "If you want a hoochie mamma, there's plenty out there. Just don't go chasing this particular pu—"

The profanity came sharply and with emphasis. It was the first time he could ever recall swearing at Tony, but he was not about to withstand ridicule from his assistant editor for a choice he felt helpless to deny.

"I know what I'm doing," he added harshly. Desney Westbourne had been on his mind in great doses from the moment he saw her enter the Black Drug Workers Forum. All Wade knew was that he *needed* to see her again. Simple as that.

"Don't come to me a third time with your self-healing garbage when the shit hits the fan," Tony admonished angrily before storming out of the room.

Wade recalled staring after him, his concentration still sapped as he thought of the annoyance that had marked Tony's face. He was jealous, Wade realized suddenly. His own assistant editor could not bear him being on a date. But why?

The question hung unanswered until a quiet voice asked, "Mind if I join you?"

Wade craned his head upward to see Desney standing there. She was dressed in her cashmere overcoat and the headwaiter was greeting her expansively by name. "Hi!" He couldn't believe that she beheld his gaze. By the time she had seated herself he, too, like half the occupants in the restaurant, was staring at her.

"I almost thought you weren't coming," he admitted finally, absorbing the warm smile she flashed his way.

"You said the next move was mine," Desney explained. "And I wanted to apologize for last weekend."

The smile was real. She was aware that Wade, with his medial mogul instincts, was tuned into her like radar before she even sat down. He was quite magnetic in his suit and polo shirt, his locks loose around his shoulders, and his whole persona exuding masculine appeal. But the allure stopped in his green-brown eyes, which were like a steel door slammed shut.

"It was a surprise to hear from you," he said, straightening the cuffs of his sleeves. "I always eat here." Floriana's had its own A-list of devoted patrons. It had won three rosettes in the AA 2001 Best Restaurants Guide and specialized in hearty northern Italian cooking, evoked by the restaurant's murals of Lake Garda, his birthplace. "You'll like it."

"It's nice," Desney approved, shedding her coat and wishing she could just as easily remove all thoughts of her brief conversation with Matt Doran.

Briefly looking around to acquaint herself with her surroundings, she tried to calm herself. Floriana's was a wonderful recreation of an Italian eating house, lit by ornate golden lamps and decorated with exquisite Roman statuettes and plates of hand-painted porcelain. Where they sat, between a pair of marble pillars, a silken canopy was stretched above their heads. Everywhere in the room hung heavy drapes of silk in rich hues of orange, green, and red.

But the room's interior wasn't what was on Wade's mind as he watched Desney place her coat behind her chair. Even the head waiter couldn't help but stare. She was utterly unlike any other woman in the room, dressed quite elegantly in a low-cut red Vera Wang creation of silk chiffon that clung to her like a second skin. She looked every bit the screen siren with a simple string of pearls around her neck. She wore long pearl drops at her ears, and he noted that they took attention away from the small birthmark that was evident beneath her lower ear.

He was smitten instantly but managed to mask the emotion by gesturing to the headwaiter, who was hovering discreetly nearby and promptly appeared at his elbow with a subordinate in tow.

"Compliments of the house, Miss Westbourne," his Italian accent rang out as he took a bottle of Mumm's champagne from his sommelier and displayed it to Desney for her approval.

Desney nodded and then chuckled as the waiter popped the cork into a towel and began to pour the contents into two flute glasses. Handing one to Desney and the other to Wade, he stiffly and politely awaited their acceptance.

Desney mused theatrically for a moment, allowing the sweet, sparkling bouquet to run around her tongue before she nodded in agreement. "Wonderful."

"Very nice," Wade swallowed.

They were then handed the menus while the bottle was replaced in a bucket of ice and deposited in the middle of their table. "I will return shortly," the head-waiter said.

"I suppose you always get treatment like this?" Wade began softly. "It must feel good."

"Sometimes," Desney admitted, allowing her own gaze to stray across the room, aware that she was being watched from all corners. It put her in mind of Matt Doran, and she felt nauseated knowing that she would have to face him again on set.

Wade clasped his hands together against the immaculate white linen. "So, to what do I owe the honor of us agreeing to dinner?"

"Like I said, I wanted to apologize," Desney stated tersely.

"Well, if it's any consolation," Wade said, a grin spreading across his features, "I'm glad you picked up the phone. I never make a play on the same woman twice."

Desney almost choked on her champagne. "You Italians are really full of it," she chimed, having already apprised Wade of this once before. "I hoped you would be thinking that I'm owed an apology, too."

"I do," Wade breathed, though his mind was working at cross-purposes. He wanted to know more on the matter of Desney's drug problems, but he had no wish to rush into the subject too hastily. He had resolved to keep their meeting formal, and that meant keeping Desney at arm's length—at least until he knew what he was dealing with. "I think I was a little heavy-handed with you on Saturday."

"You were," Desney agreed, absently reaching for the string of pearls around her neck and rolling several of the small, cream-colored balls between her finger and thumb. "I've never been told that about myself before."

"Well, if you remember, I did apologize," Wade said, his brows furrowing slightly as he recalled how she had behaved. "Anyway," he added in a lighter tone, "that's the hurt dispensed with. Let's move on to the making-up."

Desney's brows lifted. "Excuse me?"

"I assume you still want me to do a feature on you?"

"Oh, that," she sighed, relieved. "I thought . . . well, we're not exactly lovers so—"

Wade cut in smoothly, sensing the level of interest around them. "This is strictly business," he proclaimed in a shrewd manner, taking his pocket tape recorder from his breast pocket and placing it by the champagne bucket. "Let's order food first and then we'll begin."

"Begin?"

"Your interview." Wade clicked his fingers and the headwaiter appeared, ignoring several of his loyal diners.

Her hesitation did not go unnoticed by Wade as Desney silently looked at her menu. This was not the Wade Beresford that had walked out of her apartment on Saturday, she thought slightly alarmed. He was Machiavellian, ingeniously in control, a maestro journalist out to get his story. Could this be what Cheryl had been warning her about?

"I think we should start with orsini," he suggested, completely in command. "Pino here will tell you, it's quite outstanding. They're sea urchins. You eat the gonads, apparently."

"Indeed, sir." The headwaiter smiled broadly, his deep accent very pronounced as he turned to Desney. "For a *bella* like you, so pretty, so nice, they will melt like butter on your lips."

"Okay," she muttered, feeling completely hoodwinked into trying the dish.

Wade glanced at Desney, then started studying the wine list. "Do you like red or white wine?" he asked, shifting his gaze immediately to the headwaiter. "Pino, we'll have a bottle of Rosemount Grenache Shiraz. I think that will go splendidly with the pumpkin tortellini, carpaccio of beef, sweetbread with prosciutto and porcini, and octopus salad."

Pino retrieved the menus and disappeared as subtly as a wisp of mist melting into the morning sky.

"So," Wade braced himself for conversation. "You don't mind if we start now while we wait for our food?"

"Do we really need the dictaphone?" Desney protested, annoyed that he should take it upon himself to order on her behalf, but more by how professionally he was conducting their dinner date.

"It's a standard precautionary measure," he explained, giving her a convincing smile. "They're widely used all over. It's to protect you as well as myself."

Desney loathed herself for being captivated by that smile. It told her that he still liked her, and she him.

"Okay," she conceded, deciding not to debate the issue. "Just keep it real."

Wade leaned into his chair and contemplated her. The mirror of his eyes absorbed her walnut brown skin and her hair, a black cascade that spilled almost to her shoulders. He was mesmerized by the jutting V of her breasts beneath the tight bodice she was wearing. "Tell me about your childhood."

Desney relaxed one elbow against the table and rested her chin against the knuckles of her clenched hand, her gaze traveling briefly around the room, aware that others were still paying attention to her.

"It was warm and nurturing," she murmured, a little jittery. While the thoughts of her conversation with Matt Doran were still playing on her mind, she found it hard to field more probing questions. "I'm the middle of three sisters. We were all born in Birmingham, and then when I was eight, my father, a doctor, got a job in a London hospital and so we moved."

Though Wade could see the smile on Desney's lips, he knew that something had crept behind the sparkle in her eyes and he felt compelled to continue their discussion, starting with simple questions. "Are your parents still alive?"

"They're retired now," Desney explained. "And live in Grenada in the Caribbean."

"And your sisters?"

"One studied law; the other wanted to be a singer."

"And you wanted to be an actress."

"When I was ten, my father arranged my enrollment at the Italia Conti Stage School," Desney continued. "I think it was his profession that spurred my ambitions. He was the only black doctor at the North Middlesex Hospital when he started there in 1978."

"You admire him?"

"Very much. My mother, too," Desney added. "She did clerical work at the local post office."

Pino reappeared suddenly with a brigade of waitresses and their food. "The chef would like your autograph," he whispered to Desney discreetly while the food was being placed on the table. "I . . . he would be much obliged." She graciously accepted the notepad and pen, signed, and glanced at Wade.

He flipped off the tape recorder and looked hungrily at the various dishes. "I think we should take a short break," he said. "You'll love the orsini. It has to be tasted to be believed."

Desney felt a bit better the moment the tantalizing smells reached her. It did look good, all of it. For the next hour, as they delighted in the wonderful delicacy and beauty of the dishes, Wade flipped the recorder back on and kept up a relentless barrage of questions, wrapping Desney in the comfortable cocoon of his voice as he delved further into the hidden corners of her life.

"So now we have you in your twenties," he probed, biting into a piece of octopus salad. "What are you doing now?"

"I'm in New York," Desney explained, enjoying the wine, enjoying the eyes that gazed in fascination at her. "I started with commercials and then got a lucky break on a made-for-TV movie. I think it was my English accent that pulled it off. Things kind of took off from there."

"Then you returned to England."

"In nineteen ninety-four," Desney declared, now thoroughly relaxed, all thoughts of Matt Doran at the back of her mind. "Rhea, my older sister, wasn't very well and I had wanted to do theater work. England is the best place for that, so I came home."

"You played Ophelia at the Hackney Empire and

then on Broadway," Wade prompted. "What was that like?"

"An incredible experience. Especially to be nominated for the New York's Critics Circle Best Actress Award. It was a disappointment not to win, but I was the first black British actress to make the list. That's really something."

"It is," Wade agreed, catching the animated laughter that sprang from her lips. "So between doing further stage work, where I think you said you played a student nurse, a police officer, and a contralto singer, what made you decide to take a negative role as Cinnamon Walker in It's A Wide World?"

"Are we going back to you thinking that I've backtracked?" Desney asked, a slight slur now detectable in her voice.

"No," Wade insisted. "I'm trying to piece together how you've strategized your career."

Desney laughed heartily, hardly thinking that Wade Beresford would believe her. "I wanted to champion a cause." She volunteered the information with another chuckle. "Crack cocaine addiction is a serious social problem that is affecting more black teenagers today than ever before. I just thought that by playing the role of Cinnamon Walker, I could help one young mind to learn of the harmful affects it can have not only on them, but on their entire family."

This was the opening Wade had been waiting for. He homed in on the subject, full steam ahead. "How did you research the role?"

"I read books," Desney responded without suspicion of his aim. "The problem is not as huge here as in America, where the statistics are much higher, but it is evident nonetheless. And race isn't the problem," she added, "but it can be more real when it is one of your own."

"You seem to know a lot about it," Wade pressed, hoping to latch onto something juicy.

"Substance abuse is a subject very close to my heart," Desney wavered, the concern etched in her voice. "Especially since I'm in a public position where I can help."

Her gaze skirted around the room where she glimpsed the headwaiter showing off her autograph. Other diners chatted quietly, the odd one or two throwing looks of curiosity her way. She returned her gaze to Wade.

"So tell me," he ventured suddenly. "I've been exhausted by the love life the press has given you, but why haven't I found a slew of lovers lurking in your past?"

"You know there was one guy that I've learned not to talk about," Desney said sharply. "That's enough."

"I was hoping you'd answer the question," he prodded.

"What about you?" Desney turned the tables. "What's your story?"

"Mine's a tragedy," Wade drawled slowly. "You wouldn't want to hear it."

Desney detected the forlorn tone and wondered what nerve she had touched. Just how tragic were the circumstances of *his* previous relationships? Did someone die? Was he hurt badly? It seemed almost impossible that a man with such command as he had could even have a heart to be broken. Maybe this was why she felt he was lacking in something. "You could at least tell me what turns you on in a woman," she taunted lightly.

Wade raised an eyebrow and something in his expression sparkled brightly. "Hmm." It was a devilishly wicked sound. Desney felt a *frisson* of excitement run along her veins in anticipation. "I have a sister. Her

name is Lenora," he intoned, mesmerizing her with
his brooding eyes. "She keeps nice nails."

Desney shook her head, dazed. "Nails?"

"Yeah," Wade chuckled, delighted that his unusual
turn on the conversation had thrown her. "I like
women's toes. She has to have nice feet and her toes
must be on point."

She was completely lost. "On point?"

"A pedicure. I don't date women with bad toenails."

"I can hardly claim you for a buccaneer on a seized
ship, coming to my rescue with a sword and dagger,"
Desney laughed, finding his fetish amusing. "As the
damsel in distress, I would be busted all over. You'd
fail to set me free."

"A dreamer," Wade said softly. "Do you mean
busted as in well endowed?"

Desney laughed aloud. "My mind goes most places,"
she told him, "but even *I'm* having a problem with
that one."

Wade laughed, too. He liked this woman. He liked
her humor. Her imagination. The freedom being an
actress gave her, allowing her to transport herself anywhere and be anyone she wanted. He had already discovered that talent in himself. He loved losing himself
in all the problematic trials of people's lives: their scan-
dals, secrets, lies, and fears. It made him feel he had
become someone else. A voyeur perhaps. That was
what made him feel free.

"Tell me about your parents," Desney prompted.
"What are they like?"

"Mum likes to paint, and she's very tolerant," Wade
said easily. "My father's dead now, but he was in the
army once. Fought in the Second World War. He was
very disciplined."

"You still see your mother?"

Wade smiled. "Yeah. I think—"

No sooner had he spoken than there was an abrupt interruption as a burly woman with red eyes and grubby clothing approached their table and screamed like a mad banshee. "You junkie bitch," she yelled at Desney, her African lingo broken and slurred. "You lick him down, yes. Dr. Khumalo was only trying to help you."

Wade stood up immediately and shielded Desney while the headwaiter rushed over and attempted to apprehend the woman. Panicked, the intruder yelled louder. "May the Lord have mercy on your soul!" she screamed. "Repent, Cinnamon Walker!" Pino called for more help and was able to pull the unbalanced offender away. "Repent!" Her parting words echoed as she was ushered firmly from the building.

"Are you all right?" Wade asked, alarmed, putting a consoling hand against Desney's shoulder. His gaze switched to the door, checking that the deranged woman had been escorted away.

"I feel sick," Desney mumbled, knowing that she was suffering an adverse symptom of panic from the attack. It was one of the hazards of playing a well-known character on a TV soap.

Wade glanced at her, concerned. Flipping off the tape recorder he eyed Desney more closely. "I'd better take you home." His voice was firm. He knew that she had also had a little too much to drink, though she seemed to be holding her liquor well. "Did you drive?"

"Yes." Desney felt a tinge of alarm. She had never drunk so much that she couldn't drive. She wondered whether having confronted Matt Doran and then undergoing Wade's interview had unnerved her so.

"We'll take your car," Wade said lightly, hailing the headwaiter to bring the check. "I'll drive. I can pick my car up later."

"Everything all right, *signorina?*" Pino asked, returning swiftly to their table and helping Desney into her coat.

"Everything's been fine, Pino," Wade assured, handing Pino his American Express card. "Don't worry about it. I'm taking Miss Westbourne home."

"I am sorry, so sorry," Pino apologized, returning moments later for Wade's signature. He caught the brave look on Desney's face and clapped his hands in approval. *"Bella signorina,"* he smiled, as the entire restaurant decided to join him in the applause. "You go home. Mr. Beresford is good man. He will take care of you."

Desney didn't doubt that. As she left the restaurant and walked out into the night and the moonlight that seemed to bounce off the street lamps and into every nook and cranny, she sensed a closeness to him. Perhaps it was the way he held his arm around her shoulder, protective of her as they walked to her car. Or maybe it was of the way he effortlessly steered her unsteady gait as they made their way slowly along the sidewalk. Perhaps it was simply because he had paid full attention to her and what she had to say as they shared a wonderful meal. Whatever the reason, Desney suddenly felt that her dream had just been rekindled. Wade Beresford was her dashing buccaneer, keeping her heart safe.

Seven

As the Honda drove through London, Desney began to sober up. Her dream was fading. In its place was a wolf snarling and showing its teeth, causing her dashing buccaneer to fade into the background. The echo of a woman screaming "You junkie bitch!" resonated in her head and her eyes opened to find traffic lights glaring in her face.

"Oh boy!" she sighed, inhaling deeply from the air that filtered in through the open window. She turned to see Wade, concentrating on the road en route to her home.

"You okay?" he kept his eyes fixed on the road, though Desney heard the note of concern in his voice.

"That woman," she wavered, drawing an unsteady finger across her throbbing forehead. "I hope you know she was a result of your article in *Bribe*."

"What?" Wade snorted, giving her a sidelong glance.

"You, the mercenary press, encroaching on my privacy," she protested. "There should be a referendum on the integrity of journalists like you who believe in tearing things down solely because you have the power to do so."

"She was an obsessed fan," Wade said softly, aware that Desney's voice was free from anger, the tone more in recognition of the consequences of negative press coverage. "You must be used to all this attention by now."

"I get it all the time," Desney admitted forlornly, "but never like that. It was an attack of violence."

Wade glanced at her, noting her open concern, and was convinced. "You're right," he agreed, his eyes returning to the road. "You must feel like you've been stripped of your freedom."

It was Desney's turn to pause. This was not like him to be so accepting of his errors. But uncannily, his admission set off a sneaking fondness for him inside her, where it began to stir slowly. He was re-stacking the deck, she thought. Or was he calling a new tune? Somehow she couldn't quite tell, though she liked the sound of this one.

"James warned me about you," she said, with a bit of a little-girl-lost expression. "You've got a cool act."

Wade immediately picked up the thread. "Why is your producer sweating bullets about me?"

"He thinks you're trying to glean the plot for 'It's a Wide World'."

Wade laughed. "A story leak? Believe me, honey, my only interest was in keeping tabs on you." He looked over at her, a grin playing across his face. "All I need to find out now is whether you told the truth about the lingerie."

Desney gasped as his soft, husky drawl seemed to sing in her ears. She couldn't escape the delicious tingle of expectation that coursed through her body. "You would want to know, wouldn't you?"

"I'm a man," Wade admitted without apology.

"So your birth certificate says," Desney replied.

"Well, are they white, or were you really telling the truth about . . . not wearing them?" His sultry gaze bored into her for two long seconds before he again looked back at the road.

Electric sparks began to fly deep inside Desney and she answered, "That would make matters easy for you, wouldn't it, if I just told you the truth without you having to search for the facts like a *real* journalist would?"

"If you want to be searched, I'm all game," Wade said with a little chuckle.

This time Desney understood him more than she would care to admit. In Wade's universe, they were playing some kind of game—one that involved media politics, press tool tactics, and public interests. The object was to keep the subject guessing, and that meant Wade was still hoping to find a skeleton or two in her closet.

"Yes, you are," she appended suddenly.

"What?"

"You wanted to know if I thought you were dangerous the day I stormed into your office. You are."

"Me?" Wade feigned innocence. "I like cats, I'm good with old people, and I know how to hold a baby gently. Deep down, I'm as harmless as Peter Rabbit."

"Very apt," Desney said slyly, her velvety brown eyes twinkling. "They say he had no friends, either."

Wade chuckled again. "You're very smooth. Moving the subject from your lingerie to me without breaking stride. Maybe I've missed my vocation in life."

"You could still be a good journalist," Desney encouraged. "If you concentrated on real issues instead of—"

"Secrets and lies," he finished the thought.

"Yes," Desney agreed. "People like to keep those to themselves."

"Really?" Wade's tone was filled with disbelief. "But everyone has some kind of story they want to get off their chest."

"Yeah?" Desney was intrigued, feeling it was time

Wade Beresford had a taste of his own medicine. "I'll trade you." His face creased with alarm, and she enjoyed seeing the telltale signs in the set of his jaw. "You can go first."

"I . . ." Wade was thinking, disliking the change in topic, yet unable to fight the pull Desney had on him. "Okay," he began, telling himself he could do this. "I told you my mother's a painter. When I was young, she did a lot of business with the tourists. One day I sold one of her paintings and convinced her she'd lost it."

"You naughty boy," Desney laughed, facing him head-on. "What did you do with the money?"

"That I will never tell," Wade said sheepishly.

"Aah, c'mon," she pried. "You're not being fair." Feeling mischievous, she tickled his knee.

Something in her manner made Wade feel he could tell her just about anything. "I went to a newsstand and bought my first x-rated magazine."

"Kinky," Desney let go with a wolf whistle. "So that was you planting your first seeds toward becoming a jaded character."

"Your turn," Wade said peevishly, hardly believing he was now trading secrets with the one woman who had been on his mind from the moment their paths had crossed in his office.

"When I was sixteen I lost the keys to my parents house," Desney began. "So I broke in through the window and broke all the plant pots trying to get in. Then I told my parents that I'd warned off a burglar and they called the police."

"What did you do?" Wade asked, surprised.

"I carried the story through," Desney admitted. "What else could I do?"

"Ooooh," Wade purred, narrowing his eyes. "I suppose that was you testing out your deceptive acting skills."

They both laughed and Desney sighed with relief, feeling the tension ease after the strain of their confessions. They reached her apartment building and Wade began to pull the car in, parking it at the curb. He cut the engine and released his safety belt. "You don't mind if I use your phone to call a taxi?" he asked. "No strings."

Desney was thrown by Wade's sudden formality. "Of course not." She got out and closed the door. *I'd be happy to have you tie me up any day,* she mused as he followed her to the building's main entrance.

In her apartment, Desney noticed the fine strands of distinguished gray at the temples in Wade's dark, shoulder-length hair as he faced her, telephone in hand, intent on ordering a taxi. She had never studied him in this way before, noting the minute details of all the sharp angles and hard-hewn features, the enigmatic color in his green-brown eyes, the cleft etched in his chin. She committed to memory the face that might almost have been carved from granite.

He seemed distant. Though she had only to look into the depths of his eyes to know that he liked what he saw and had found her presence that night agreeable in every sense of the word, she knew something wasn't quite right.

She could still feel the warmth of the wine inside her as she kicked off her shoes and shed her coat, then made for the kitchen, as parts of their previous conversation came back to her. "Coffee?" she asked, her voice slightly raised. "For the road?"

Wade nodded while still on the phone. Desney smiled as she stepped into the kitchen and switched on the kettle. She tried to formulate her thoughts logically to arrive at some conclusion about Wade's behavior.

First, he had accepted her invitation to dinner, then he had used the opportunity to conduct a very formal interview about her career, and now he seemed in a hurry to get home. She could hardly imagine that this was the same man who had kissed her and whom she had dreamed about with such glamorous, swashbuckling illusions. He appeared so far away from her now.

A sense of disappointment flooded her system. Desney began to wonder if she had done something wrong. A part of her longed to be kissed by Wade again, to experience the pulsing of his lips against her own, but another part of her had suddenly become ambivalent, wary, and cautious as to what was making him so standoffish.

She reached for two mugs from the cupboard and spooned coffee into them. While she did so, she thought of Matt Doran. For a brief moment, she felt panicked, wondering whether Matt had disclosed anything about their past life to Wade. Could this be why he was so distant? Could his knowing that she had been previously married be the real reason for this sudden turnabout in his character? After all, she had not yet told him this juicy little fact. She fleetingly wondered whether this might be why Wade had broached the subject of secrets.

"I take my coffee with milk, no sugar." His voice suddenly broke into her thoughts as he entered the kitchen and leaned against the doorframe, watching as she reached in the refrigerator for the milk. "Any popcorn?"

"Don't you worry about your teeth?" Desney countered. She set the milk carton down and stared at Wade, reading the signs in the hard-drawn lines of his

forehead. They spelled fatigue. He was just tired, she
told herself.

"My teeth are fine," Wade assured her, his gaze
holding hers captive.

He grinned, showing white, even teeth. Desney had
noticed his energy level before and had already decided that his fitness regime needed a complete over-
haul. But aside from what she had heard about the
man, and what she had discovered about him since
they met, she had to admit that she knew very little
else about just what that made Wade Otto Beresford
tick.

Perhaps this was another reason why he was behaving so professionally, so controlled and aloof. After Saturday's fiasco, when she had made certain points clear,
he had come to realize that there was a client-editor
relationship between them, and that she was not going
to allow him to overstep that barrier. What else was
she to expect?

The kettle boiled and Desney poured the steaming
water into the mugs. Stirring the milk in, she handed
Wade his coffee. "How long will the taxi be?" she
asked.

"Ten minutes."

Desney smiled casually and carried her coffee
through to the sitting room. As she sat and watched
Wade's tall body slump into the chair, throwing his
right ankle over his left knee, she couldn't help but
cast him a questioning look. Every fibre in her body
demanded that he be near her, close enough for her
to smell him and feel his warmth against her. But he
had put a gulf between them by taking the other chair.

She thought back to when they left the restaurant,
remembering how secure she had felt nestled against
his shoulders. She also recalled the conversation they
had shared in her car and how they had confessed

their secrets to one another. Wade's detachment from her now simply confused her, though why she was in this blind abyss, she did not know. She had told him that she didn't want them to get close, so shouldn't she be happy to see him honoring her wishes?

"What's the matter?" Wade caught the questioning look.

Feeling the warm rush of blood to her face, Desney said the first thing that came into her head. "I'd like to know what happened—why you didn't get married."

Wade seemed to find the question funny. "Got close to it once," he told her without hesitation. "She let me down."

The one who wanted fame, Desney thought. "What happened?"

"We both wanted different things," he said simply. "I think she wanted independence, success, and a sense of place. I wanted a companion—a friend as well as a lover—and believed I should be the provider."

"You said she was an actress," Desney recalled. "Was she anything like me?"

"No," Wade answered, amused at the thought. "I found myself making plans for us, but she was making plans for herself." He sighed. "Anyway, I didn't feel sure about her, to be completely honest. A man will only find three loves in his life, so he has to be sure about his choice."

Desney stared at him, confused. "Three loves?" She sat erect on the sofa. What could he possibly mean?

"My first love was precisely that," he began to explain. "She was my first taste of scorching, unbridled, mind-altering sex," he added with a wry smile in recollection. "My second love . . . she opened up my world and made me aware of all my possibilities. But my third love, she will enrich my life in a way that will make me feel complete."

Desney was awed. "That's the journey you were telling me about, where you'd left a couple of your experiences along the way?"

"You're getting the drift," Wade said. "Some men like to settle with their first love and others with their second."

"But you're looking for that special love who will enrich your life?" Desney concluded, her brows raised while she sipped her coffee, watching him over the rim of her mug.

"In a nutshell."

Desney sensed a note of sorrow in his modest Italian accent. "Your second love hurt you didn't she?"

He nodded.

"So how will you know when you've found your third love?" She couldn't resist asking that one.

"I'm not sure," Wade answered truthfully, his puzzlement visibly marked across his face. "I think if she's someone who has a sharp sense of who she is, and what she is doing with her life, and feels my soul when we're together, shares my fun, pain, and bad times, and can give deep love to me without sharing it with anyone else, then I will know whether I can fit into her life or not."

"All that?" Desney gasped, surprised at the precision in his answer. For a man who had just told her he wasn't sure, he sounded pretty clear about it.

"All that," he repeated, making Desney aware that he had given this much thought. "So if you're like the other actresses I've known who are just looking for one of those men who's a paragon of athletic prowess, then—"

"I'm not," Desney blurted, shaking her head. "I'm just looking for a considerate man, the type who will see me as his best friend. If he wants to do everything with me and cannot stop thinking about me, then I'd feel more secure about sharing my heart with such a person, and that we're falling in love."

"In love?" Wade's puzzlement grew.

"Yeah," Desney nodded. "When the world feels like a wonderful place and your future looks rosy, productive, and bright, and you feel like you're a part of that person and their life in every way."

"All that?" Now Wade was awed by her precision.

"All that," Desney answered, as if from a long way off.

This further confession plummeted them both into silence. Desney was not sure what was going on, but she was aware that they were both unused to making such startling revelations and deep disclosures about themselves—particularly all in one night. It had to mean something, she tried to think logically, but what? Were they both subconsciously trying to establish that they had a compatibility worth exploring?

"The food was nice at Floriana's, wasn't it?" Wade ventured in an attempt to break the silence.

"Yes," Desney agreed lightly. "They say the way to a man's heart is through his stomach."

"Hmm, I don't know," Wade broached, deciding that he now preferred a little lighter conversation. "I always thought the gift of a good pair of Nike Airs did the trick."

They both laughed and then the mood was truly broken when the intercom buzzer intruded. Desney jumped to her feet, feeling a little bit sad. "That'll be your taxi," she said, looking forlorn. She still couldn't shake the feeling that something had happened, but she didn't know what. She went over to the grill pad on the wall and told the cabby that his fare would be right down.

Wade rose to his feet and placed his coffee mug on a nearby table. "Thank you for a most enlightening evening," he smiled. "I think another two weeks of being your twenty-four-seven should be sufficient for me to start writing up the piece. Then I'd like to interview Frederick Fitzgerald."

There was his formality again. Desney was more sensitive to it than she had been before. "I've spoken with Fred," she said, as she escorted Wade to the front door, trying to blot the image from her mind of him with a bandana around his head, sword in hand, kissing her in the fire of an exotic sunset. "He's looking forward to the interview. I think he's hoping that it will save his career."

"So the rumor is true that he's leaving the soap?" Wade asked, instantly intrigued. His hands dug down in his trouser pockets, and Desney contemplated him warily.

"You knew before I did," she replied. "And you never told me how you came by the information that Matt Doran was taking over."

"They've hired him, then?" Wade was all ears.

"He was put on the payroll today," Desney confirmed. "I've been assigned to show him the ropes."

"Hmm." Wade pondered the information, much to Desney's dismay. She felt ever more wary as to what he might be hiding. "It's time I left," he finally added. "You okay?"

"Me?" Desney's eyes widened before she realized that Wade was referring to the crazed woman who had verbally attacked her earlier that night. "Yes, I'm fine—really," she smiled. "And thank you for the flowers."

Wade paused on the threshold of the front door. "What flowers?"

"The two dozen ivory roses . . . Mr. Anonymous." Desney caught the blank expression in Wade's face.

The revelation came swiftly. "You didn't send them, did you?"

"No," Wade admitted, shaking his head, touching Desney briefly on the wrist. "But thanks for letting me know about the competition." He advanced a step toward her, so close that Desney was aware of his aftershave and the brown specks in the green of his irises. Then she felt the warmth of his breath against her left cheek as he placed a soft kiss there.

It was friendly. A parting between friends. None of the arms-enfolding, hardness-of-his-body, rapturous intimacy that she desperately craved. And wasn't this what she had wanted, to lose her passionate candor and have Wade believe that everything about her attraction toward him had been an act and nothing more?

It didn't feel that way now. As simple as his kiss was against her cheek, as courteous and formal as it had been, a wealth of signals nonetheless ran through Desney's system and met steadfast at the center of her heart.

And as she watched Wade leave, waving goodbye as he threw her a backward glance, something deep inside her began to struggle with itself as Desney managed to get out a muffled word.

"Goodnight." He smiled and her heart warmed. Suddenly she couldn't resist the urge to ask, "How do I find you?" There she was again, reshuffling the deck.

"You don't find me," Wade returned, his voice loud enough to cover the distance down the corridor. "I find you."

"And action!"

Desney moved around the set with her usual expertise, pausing to look into Frederick Fitzgerald's face in his guise as Dr. Khumalo. She moved in close and was able to sense the hot scent of him through his clothing as his grip hardened around her shoulders. Matt Doran was in the background, breaking in his role as Nick Palmer, standing around so that the viewers could get used to seeing his face.

The pace of the day was maddening. It was slow and badly run. There was an air of coldness that came in with the breeze of October, and all the cast members sensed the unpredictable tide of coolness and detachment.

"I ought to wring your neck." Frederick spoke out his lines with ample control for the benefit of the cameras, narrowing his eyes with the practiced ease of a pro. "But I love you so, and you need my help."

"Dr. Khumalo," she implored weakly, searching for the line. "I am weak. I fear that . . ." Desney faltered. "I fear that . . ."

"Cut!"

James's voice sounded like thunder. Within seconds he materialized from behind the camera, gritting his teeth at Desney. "You've forgotten your lines again," he frowned. "We've done this take six times already and you still can't get it right."

Desney swallowed hard, quickly assessing the situation. She felt a sudden, swift stab of conscience. In these past two weeks since agreeing to be interviewed by Wade Beresford, she had been so wrapped up in her private affairs, she had scarcely given the soap much thought.

Wade had filled her every waking moment from daybreak, when she would find him outside the gates of Hyde Park waiting to join her for jogging, to night's end, when she would meet him at Floriana's and then wave goodbye when he walked her back to her car after dinner.

The routine had begun by tacit consent when she had found him outside the gates of Hyde Park the morning after they shared their first dinner together at Floriana's. Desney's hadn't been sure she would ever see Wade Beresford again, but he had said that he would find her, and he was true to his word.

Their meetings felt full of intrigue, like covert operations, him immersing her in her past to discover the slightest trivia about her life, while with her finding it difficult to break through his sullen barrier of reluctance and be forthcoming about anything other than his work. She had wondered fleetingly whether their confessional discussions left him wary of her knowing too much, but she had been no more inquisitive than he had been about her.

Still, he wasn't always brooding. There were times when his moods were humorous, sociable, and even cheeky—especially whenever they moved on to a topic of controversy. Desney was a woman who never claimed to know the workings of a man's mind, but she had found herself enjoying Wade's company—even his probing into her life—and yet she had to tell herself that she didn't know quite where she stood with him.

One morning after he had left her to continue her jog alone, she had run twice around the park, never pausing, never slackening in her step once, just to contemplate this thought. Running. Driving herself until her thighs ached and sweat ran in rivulets down her face, her lungs ready to burst in the pursuit of an answer. Then, running so hard on her way home, Wade Beresford trailing behind in her mind, never quite catching up to the point where she needed to make a decision. She could not. And she couldn't run him out of her system, either.

There was that, and the unbidden excitement of wondering when and where he was going to show up next. They never made prearranged appointments. She could be at the hairdresser's, jogging, or at the supermarket, and he'd be there. But it was tiring. Were they on their way to becoming lovers? Or was he simply trying to be a friend?

It was this question that taxed her mind, leaving her exhausted as she explored all the avenues until she soon found herself losing sleep. The fatigue motivated her to avoid Frederick, who had been trying to catch her attention of late. Fatigue had induced her to be pleasant with Matt Doran, though she would rather have kept him at arm's length. And now, fatigue was causing her to forget her lines.

James Wallace wasn't the most patient of men, and if the tone of his voice was any barometer, it wouldn't be long before her days were numbered just like Frederick's. "I had a late night," she told James truthfully, reminding herself that she had spent it at the premiere of the latest Bond movie, where Wade had been unexpectedly among the guests—probably on a press pass; she wasn't sure.

"Out with that trash reporter again?" James mouthed with disdain. "You're supposed to throw trash out, not sleep with it. And I thought I gave instructions that no one speaks to the media."

Desney was instantly boiling. "Don't treat me like a prostitute, James," she said. "I just take the money that's on my contract and do my job here, on this set."

"Everyone take five," James announced.

Frederick remained rooted as though protective of Desney, and she threw him an appreciative smile in recognition of his support. "I'll shape up in five minutes," she promised James.

"You'll do more than that," James demanded. "I want to know what's going on."

"Nothing." was all she said.

James grimaced ruefully at her evasiveness. "Missing meetings, forgotten lines. Matt Doran's been on set two weeks and you haven't even bothered to show him the ropes."

"Ask someone else to do it," Desney told him tautly. Matt Doran was another person she had chosen to ignore. Despite his sweetness, his attentive off-set manner, his generosity in offering to take her out to dinner, she had declined his advances at every turn, simply offering pleasantness in return.

"I want *you* to do it," James said in a voice that left no doubt. "Your contract isn't unbreakable either."

"What's that supposed to mean?" Desney was peeved.

"Nothing." James pulled back, holding his tongue.

But Frederick was quick to seize the opportunity. "Are we all for the chop?" he drawled. Both he and James were withdrawn and headstrong men, much more interested in fact than conjecture. "I mean . . . no one has clarified my position," he went on. "And I read that the show was up two points last week in the ratings."

"The show's doing just fine," James sighed his manner stern. His gaze penetrated Desney's velvety brown eyes. "I just don't want the media knowing anything ahead of schedule."

"I wouldn't do that," Desney insisted, annoyed that James could even conceive that she would leak the plot line to Wade.

James liked to film "It's a Wide World" two weeks ahead of airing so that he could get feedback from selected viewers and work them into storylines weeks later. It was a tactic that worked well with the soap and it helped them stay in one of the top five daytime slots in the country. How could he even think she would want to jeopardize such success?

"See that you don't." His curt reply stung.

As he walked away, she turned toward Frederick and sighed with relief. "He's a live wire."

"We need to stick together," Frederick said. "A solitary stand doesn't work for anyone."

"I don't want a war." Desney didn't like the implication. "I do my job and that's my lot."

"That's very selfish," Frederick snarled. His tone took Desney by surprise. "After I hung in your corner just now, the least I expected was a united front."

Desney felt overwhelmed. Was everyone going to have a go at her this morning? "I didn't mean to come across like that," she said, trying to stay civil. "We're all just feeling a little freaky right now. There's no need for any of us to rock the boat."

"That's easy for you to say," Frederick attacked with both barrels blazing. "You're not the one who could be out of a job anytime now. I would just love to know what's in the script two weeks down the line," he added suspiciously. "Maybe I'm going to be shot dead or something. I mean . . . after the way you knocked me out in that last episode, who knows, anything could happen."

"If James was going to write you out, wouldn't he have told you by now?" Desney said soothingly, realizing that Frederick was now bordering on hysteria.

"Maybe he has," Frederick persisted. "And you're just behaving like a spoiled little bitch refusing to stand in my corner."

"A spoilt what?"

"Bitch."

Desney gasped. "You mean Babe In Total Control of Herself?" She stared at Frederick in disgust before she left the studio floor. Five minutes! Desney felt more like she needed ten. What was wrong with everyone? Of course, she had no answer to that.

A quick glance at her watch told her it was 11:37. Shooting was to last until 4:00 that afternoon. She wondered whether Wade had already decided to sneak up on her again that night. After the premier, they had shared a glass of wine. He kept his professional manner by offering her a peck on the cheek before departing to his own car.

It would not have felt so unusual had they never kissed so passionately before all this seriousness began. Had they never held each other so crushingly close, nearly giving in to their impetuous lust, not felt that heady rush of wondrous feeling at the touch of each other, then she would think nothing of the aloofness or his level of detachment.

Even after reminding herself time and time again that she was the one who had instigated this, Desney was reluctant to admit it to herself. The withdrawal of his attentions simply fueled her need for him. Knowing that he was no longer there to touch made her imagine him all the more in her mind, his image clear and precise right down to that monkey grin. And his secretive behavior, his withholding of information from her, made her feel she didn't want his extended interview to end until she had completed one of her own on him.

She looked around her. The studio crew were busy in preparation for the next take. Five minutes' sanctuary in her dressing room and a re-reading of her lines should put her back in full swing, Desney thought. But no sooner had she opened the door of her dressing room, than she was pulled inside and the door slammed shut behind her.

Desney was immediately pinned against the wall. The gasp that escaped her lips was quickly smothered with a kiss that felt as familiar as it was sweet. She gave up the struggle as the mouth, warm and demanding, enveloped hers. She was swept into the kiss as if by a soft breeze, but the heady feelings that had quickened her heartbeat when she last was kissed, when Wade had claimed her with such masterly seduction, did not follow.

Something inside her panicked when the invisible thread, taut with sexual energy, did not snap. It remained stretched and trembling with tension. Whoever was kissing her now was an artist, a master of the same art she used on set. Desney's mouth went slack and she pulled away, leaning against the wall. The eyes that looked into hers were dark with introspection.

"Matt!"

"I needed to do that," he confessed, but at the same time shaking his head in the negative. "I don't know what came over me. Maybe it's because we've got that screen kiss coming up next week."

Desney stared at him. "You didn't reach me," she wavered, paralyzed by his attempt. "I'm not sure why you would even want to try."

"I've missed you," Matt said simply. "I always have."

"Matt . . ." Desney tried to be firm, but she knew that it was really all sympathy. "We got married too young. I was only twenty-one, remember? Ten years ago. And when I made a name for myself in America and came back, you started to blackmail me because you were just too lazy to work." She sighed deep and heavy. "You're here now because your love turned to greed. You're trying to save something that is no longer there. We're just friends." And even that, Desney knew, was pushing it.

"You're right of course," Matt conceded. "I just thought . . . I don't know what I thought. I guess I'm just jealous that you're seeing Wade Beresford."

"He's just completing a feature about me," Desney explained convincingly. "That's all."

"Well, you'll do well to stay clear," he replied, adjusting the costume tie he had been wearing for the morning shoot. "He's been jilted twice. I guess a guy like him has the knack of rubbing women up the wrong way."

"Jilted?" Desney was intrigued.

"The second one at the altar," Matt supplied incredulously.

"What?"

"The bride was a no-show."

Desney gasped. Could Matt Doran really be talking about Wade Beresford, the man as hard as nails, the only man who had ever been able to make that thin thread of tension inside her snap? Suddenly, she felt as though she had been given the answers she needed as to why Wade was being so aloof and standoffish.

"Let's just get back on set," Desney swallowed, inching her back against the wall in the direction of the door. "James will be rushing around like a mad hatter."

"At least you showed when we got married," Matt said, holding her back. "Desney—"

"Don't." She was adamant. "You wanted me and you got me. Didn't know you had me, then lost me. I can't go back to something that was never there. And neither should you. I'd be living a lie."

Matt nodded, though Desney realized he probably didn't fully comprehend her meaning. This was just like Matt, so irresponsible, a man who couldn't function unless some woman was right there pulling his strings. She needed someone much stronger, much more in charge of who he was as a person.

And despite her vacillation, Wade Beresford fit that profile in every sense of the word. The only problem Desney had now was how to convince him that she had changed her mind when she had no idea where he was going to show up next.

"Point taken," she heard Matt say. "I feel like a jerk."

"We all foul up every once in a while." Desney tried to keep an air of detachment in her voice and succeeded without effort. "I just want to get back on set."

But the shrill of her telephone deterred her. Desney grimaced as she stared at the handset, knowing that to answer it now would keep Matt stalling around in her dressing room indefinitely until she was ready to leave.

"Could be important," he raised a brow, an impromptu cue that he intended to eavesdrop.

Desney's heart skipped when she heard Wade Beresford's voice at the other end of the receiver. He sounded evasive. "I won't be at Floriana's tonight," he apologized. "A friend of mine is in town. We're going out for a drink."

"That's okay," Desney lied, her heart sinking as fast as it had risen. For the first time in the two weeks since Wade had been charting her life, it never occurred to her that he himself had a life of his own, outside the context of interviewing her. "Maybe I'll see you on Wednesday?"

"I'll call you."

Something about the way he said that gave Desney the distinct feeling she was receiving a brushoff. "It's up to you," fell from her lips before any further thought processes could kick into place.

Putting down the receiver, she turned and faced Matt, tears stinging at the back of her eyes. The reality of knowing she could never have Wade was beginning to sink in. If there was ever an edge of the precipice, where passion and delirium met and merged, Desney felt she had just found it and fallen over in one fell swoop. She hadn't even recognized she was there until she played that stupid act of pretending his kiss was just like the others. An act.

All the others were like the man facing her now. Second best. Desney tried to get a perspective on it as they returned to the studio floor. She told herself that her newly found impression of Wade Beresford was just projection in her head of what she wanted the perfect man to be, and that the real person was far from her imaginings.

Wade Beresford was arrogant, a gossip monger, and she didn't need to be around people like him. Yet after barely two weeks, she was already pining for the man. Another dose of reality revealed that she was alone. She needed affection, and his kissing her had confused her senses.

Like it or not, she had to get a life, and that meant putting awful truths like this firmly and permanently behind her. She would call Cheryl and have dinner with her instead. Maybe her agent and friend could help her get back on the right track.

Eight

"Is this business or pleasure?" Cheryl mouthed while chewing a large morsel of rump steak.

They were seated at Maxim's, Cheryl's favorite English restaurant in the West End of London, a place of densely packed tables, white lilies, and chic clientele. It was a place preferred by the more committed carnivores, plain brick walls and wooden floors, giving the smartly decorated room a rustic edge. The curved floor-to-ceiling window, designed for diners to watch the beautiful people go by, was a picture of the West End overelaborated with nighthawks dressed for the evening's frivolity of London merrymaking. But Desney was in no mood for the jollities.

"You're my agent," she said, tight-lipped. "Can't we just do dinner?" She looked at her plate. It was the chef's signature dish of refined English food: carrots, brussels sprouts, roast beef, boiled potatoes, Yorkshire pudding and gravy. But her appetite was lacking. Still, the wine list boasted some superb vintages, and she downed another gulp of Chardonnay.

"Are you suffering from a broken heart?" Cheryl asked suddenly.

Desney raised her head. "No. It's . . ." She sighed. "I've allowed Wade Beresford into my life to do a re-write for *Bribe* magazine," she explained. "We got unusually close for a while and now he seems to have backed off."

Cheryl was cynical. "You hardly know the man."

"I know."

"And he's told you practically nothing about himself," she went on. "So what is he hiding?"

Desney was alarmed. "You think he's hiding something?" She had suspected this herself.

"Men who withhold information about themselves always are," Cheryl said dryly.

"Cheryl!"

"We've both got something in common," Cheryl reminded her. "We've both been swindled by our first husbands. These days a girl has to be careful."

And of course she was right, Desney mused. What did she really know about Wade Beresford? Aside from the fact that he was from Verona, owned a magazine, and lived somewhere in London, what else could she claim to know about his life?

"You know he got jilted by his second love," she said casually.

"Where did you hear that?" Cheryl asked, surprised.

"Matt Doran."

"That red-eyed ex-husband of yours who had you by the short-and-curlies?" Cheryl gave one of her trademarked chuckles. "Girlfriend, you shouldn't give a rat's ass what guys like him tell you. He's been trying to get you back for weeks. That's why he's working on 'It's a Wide World'."

"How do you know things like that?" Desney was intrigued.

"I'm your agent," Cheryl stated tersely, biting into another piece of steak. "It's my job to know when to listen to gossip."

Just like Wade Beresford, Desney thought. "What if it's

true?" She was compelled to return to the subject of his nuptials.

"Matt wanting you back, or Wade being jilted?" Cheryl asked, aware that they were on two subjects.

"Wade being left at the altar," Desney clarified, her brows raised. "What if it's true?"

"What if it is?" Cheryl swallowed her food with a sip of wine. "It probably happened a long time ago, and it should be no reason for the man to treat you in this way—writing bad things about you, saying he's going to make amends and then doing a disappearing act. You're dealing with a dangerous individual."

"Are you saying I should forget him?" Desney shook her head in confusion. Her mind didn't know what to make of the matter, but her heart was firmly fixed on hanging in there.

"If he doesn't really want you, then there's nothing you can do," Cheryl said, cutting her steak. "You can't force yourself on a man edgewise, not in my universe. But of course, you're not into anything with him yet, so what do I know?"

Desney sighed. "I do pick 'em."

"You haven't picked a man in years," Cheryl chided, her fork poised. "Last time you had a fling was when? . . . fifteen months ago I think, with that small-time actor from—"

"Never mind him," Desney looked down at her plate. The food looked less appetizing than before.

"We both pick 'em," her agent sympathized seconds later. "Remember Carlo Vicetti, my boyfriend? He's cheated on me at least five times now."

Desney's mind reeled at the sudden revelation. "Why do you stay with him?"

" 'Cause I'm cheating on him."

"Cheryl!" Desney's mind was immediately side-tracked. "Who with?"

"James."

"James!" Her mind wrapped itself around that singular word. There was only one person she knew with that name. *"My* James? James *Wallace?"*

"Sure thing," Cheryl confirmed.

"But he's married," Desney reminded her, aghast.

"I know," Cheryl replied. "That doesn't mean he can't have an outpost in my bedroom. In fact," she added, "I called *Bribe* magazine and leaked a little bit of gossip about us being together. Thought it might force his hand a little into allowing us to become a public couple."

Desney was in shock. "You phoned Wade Beresford?"

"I got his stooge, Tony something-or-other—"

"Tony Barbieri," Desney revealed. "He's Wade's assistant editor."

"Yeah, him." Cheryl swallowed another sip of wine. "I told him that James and I were having a secret affair and that Frederick Fitzgerald was walking the plank to make way for Matt Doran. He told me I could get up to ten thousand pounds for supplying him with photos of the affair and another sixteen thousand for syndicated rights. He would, of course, embellish the story."

Desney reached for her wine glass and took a large, fortifying gulp of Chardonnay. This was all news to her. Amazing information. She hardly knew how to absorb it all, though her mind was able to grasp that Cheryl was Wade's source on knowing that Frederick was rumored to be axed. "How did you—"

"Pillow talk with James," Cheryl told her. Seeing Desney's disillusioned face, she added, "I shouldn't have sprung all this on you, should I?"

"You and James." Desney's mind was spinning.

"He needs me right now," Cheryl argued, her tone convincingly pitched. "Or maybe it's me needing him now that my second husband has thrown me out. I don't know why I'm doing this to myself, but James stimulates me. He makes me feel needed. He has got this great storyline he wants to put to the producers and I'm just helping him overcome his crisis of confidence. I'm more than fond of him."

Desney stared at her agent. Cheryl's vulnerability was like a mask across her face, corrupt and yet so innocent. She was a woman searching for love, just as Desney was, only Cheryl was prepared to play the poker game of love with her own deck—and where the stakes were high. Unlike Desney, who had allowed Wade Beresford to shuffle the cards, Cheryl was obviously more in control. Desney had a devilish thought. Perhaps she should play an ace and do something impetuous—like go and give an exclusive interview to a rival magazine.

Public interest in her role as Cinnamon Walker was ripe. *Bribe* had already slandered her. And though Wade had promised a rewrite, could she really risk her career by waiting this length of time for him to publish it? Frederick hadn't yet been interviewed and at the pace things were going, Wade skipping on their usual meeting that night, would he ever?

Dinner over, Desney was still contemplating this contingency plan as she and Cheryl got up to leave the restaurant. The entrance door swept open, and Desney's heart froze as she almost walked into a well dressed couple.

"Wade!" His name came out with a gasp for air. Wade was not alone. The woman who stood at his side was a sultry, sloe-eyed beauty. Her olive skin was flawless, her hair in a short sleek black style trimmed close to her scalp, and she had a voluptuous body clothed in a low cut, melon-colored chiffon dress that made her look like a model straight off the pages of *Today's Black Woman* magazine. It was clear to Desney who the woman was. She had seen her before at a recent Cannes Film Festival, with men orbiting around her like bees around a honeycomb.

"Desney!" Wade's voice was filled with guilt. He turned toward his date. "I'd like you to meet Teadra Lopez."

Desney affected a handshake with one of Spain's most reputed soap actresses. She also quickly reminded herself that they both had once applied for the same role on *Serenade in Sepia*. "Hello." Her voice was weak, nothing like Teadra's firm greeting. "We're just leaving," she told Wade.

Their gaze met and Desney wanted to kick herself. Wade was attractively dressed in a dark emerald green suit with a pristine white shirt and lime green tie, his honey brown complexion highlighted to full affect by the vibrant shade of his suit. His black shoes were polished, too, she noted, and his hair hung loose, tipping her off that this was a date he was taking very seriously.

"Is the food good here?" he asked. His formality was so chilling that Desney was at a loss to answer.

"You'll have a chance to escape with your wallet intact," Cheryl spoke for her instead. "But if you want to feel pleasantly pampered, there is a bias toward regular customers."

"We'll give it a try," he smiled, and Desney wanted to vomit.

"Enjoy your meal," she was able to utter with quiet dignity, a perfect actress ad-libbing her farewell.

At street level she turned to Cheryl, her eyes filled with tears. "He thought I was at Floriana's tonight," she said, feeling ridiculously stupid and naive. "That's why he brought her here. He wasn't expecting to see me." The tears fell. Dumb, foolish, idiotic tears washed over her perfect complexion.

"And there you were, wondering if he could be

yours," Cheryl said cynically, pulling Desney into her arms and rubbing her shoulders in soothing companionship. "You've fallen in love with him, haven't you?"

Desney felt the full weight of the pain. She couldn't answer.

But Cheryl didn't need to hear the admission. "I guess now you have your answer to what he's up to," she simply told Desney. "Kill the rewrite now. Don't let him pull you into doing another interview. And hang up if he phones."

At that precise moment, Desney decided that the cards in the deck weren't worth playing.

Frederick Fitzgerald dragged at his cigarette as he picked up the telephone and called Desney. He had an urgent matter to discuss, and he wanted to do it now. He glanced at the luminous hands of his watch in the gloom that wasn't yet daybreak. Half past four in the morning.

He was still in his bed but hadn't slept all night. He knew Desney would be awakening soon, because they had a morning shoot and she liked to take a jog first. And so he dialed her number, feeling well within his rights to take this liberty in order to save what he could of himself.

The ringing intruded into Desney's sleep. At first she thought it was the intercom buzzer and wondered whether it was Wade wanting to explain himself. But as she blinked her eyes and saw the familiar dark shapes of her bedroom and the gray streak of pre-dawn light that was trying to invade through the curtains, she switched on her bedside lamp and muttered to herself as she picked up the receiver.

If there was one thing she had learned over the

years, it was that bad news tends to come in the middle of the night. "Yes."

"Desney, it's me," Frederick chimed.

"Fred?" Desney sat up against her pillows and moved a strand of hair away from her forehead. "What is it? What's wrong?" She sensed the worst.

"I need to talk to you." Desney could hear the pleading in his tone. "It's about you and Matt Doran." Her heart panicked at his last comment.

"Fred, it's four-thirty," she reminded. "Can't this wait until—"

"No," Frederick interrupted, his voice now bitter. "I'm looking for some concessions here."

Desney was alert to the menacing edge to his tone; something was most definitely wrong. "Concessions?"

"Yes," Frederick snapped. "First off, I want you in my corner when I go and tell James Wallace to go to hell."

"Fred—"

"Listen to me," he said, his voice rising to a point that now had Desney on her guard. "Second, I want you to convince the producers to get me another contract on *my* timetable. And last," he paused and the silence felt frightening. "I want Matt Doran fired."

Desney stared at the telephone in disbelief. She simply did not have the power to do all those things, even as leading cast member on "It's a Wide World." Why Frederick should even believe that she could was beyond her comprehension.

"Fred," she began quietly, in a soft tone she hoped would appease him. "I don't make those kinds of decisions; you know that." She tried to be kind, thinking that Frederick had been drinking. "I can talk to James, but even you know how tough he can be."

"I don't want to hear any excuses," Frederick lashed out suddenly. "I've got the story on you and Matt

Doran and how you two little lovebirds got wed. I'm sure this Wade Beresford would love to get an anonymous tip about that, or better still, I might just provide him with a transcript of the little conversation I overheard between you and Matt in the corridor outside your dressing room—just to spice up that feature he's writing on us."

"Frederick!" It was the first time Desney recalled addressing him by his full name, so great was the outrage that flooded her body. "I—I'm—"

"At a loss for words?" Frederick jeered. "Well, don't worry about it. I'll speak for the both of us. You have two weeks to get James and the producers upstairs to change their minds or my transcript is gonna grow legs, and it'll be walking all the way over to *Bribe* magazine for a tidy fee."

"You . . . *bastard!*" Desney felt the hot flurry of angry tears behind her eyes. "I've never done anything to hurt you, Frederick. I always thought we were friends."

"Even friendship has its price," Frederick proclaimed harshly. "And when a man's back is against the wall, he's got to start calling in his favors. Two weeks, Desney. See you later on set." The phone clicked dead.

Desney replaced the receiver and stared dazedly at the dark, flowered wallpaper in her bedroom. This couldn't possibly be happening—not when she had just about given Wade Beresford all the information she wanted him to know, and certainly not after she and Matt had agreed to keep their annulled marriage a secret.

She bolted out of bed; she would have to forgo jogging this morning. She decided to make an early visit to Elstree Studios instead. She remembered Matt Doran telling her that he would be on set early before taping started, to familiarize himself with the new props. Maybe he could help her think of what they should do, seeing that Frederick Fitzgerald wanted him fired. In any event, she convinced herself while quickly struggling out of her bedclothes, he deserved to know that their conversation had been overheard by an enemy.

The Honda pulled into the Elstree Studios parking lot at precisely 6:43 A.M. Desney cut the engine and walked briskly from her car and through the side entrance that said STAFF AND CAST MEMBERS ADMITTANCE ONLY. After clearing security she made her way immediately to the studio floor.

She was dressed in black trousers and a black sweater, wearing her cashmere coat and black gloves to protect herself from the harsh elements of a mid-October morning. Her hair was tucked under a brown woollen hat; there had been no time to style it in anything more pleasing.

This is so hard, Desney told herself as she hurried down the corridor to her dressing room. She wanted to warm herself and gather her bearings before attempting to find Matt Doran. She wanted to believe that everything would be all right, that Matt would find a solution to dealing with Frederick; but by the time she reached her dressing room, Desney felt more dismal than ever. Her thread of tension was stretched taut as a wire.

Her eyes caught a fresh vase of ivory colored roses, looking pretty and fresh among the clutter of wigs, makeup, costumes, old scripts, shoes, leftover snacks, and cheap jewelry. Immediately she conjured up an image of Wade Beresford, and her heart sank into the pit of her misery. He hadn't sent the flowers. How she wished he had! And who had sent her fresh ones now? The emptiness of knowing that they were not from Wade but only from "Mr. Anonymous," made the misery even more unbearable.

Everything was going wrong. Just when she thought she had dealt with one thing, something else had to happen. Frederick's timing could not have been worse. She took off her coat and placed it on her chair, putting her keys by the telephone. She wanted to blame someone. Anyone would do. Wade Beresford would have been the perfect culprit, but he could not have imagined that she was being blackmailed yet again. First there was Matt, trying in his adolescent manner to wangle a lucky break in his career, and now there was Frederick trying to save his. Didn't these men have the slightest bit of integrity?

It seemed ironic that both men, having ample talent to carry them through without stooping to coercion or blackmail, did not believe they were skilled enough to play in the arena among the competition like anyone else. And Frederick! Desney wanted to scream. She had always been good to him. How could he or anyone turn around a friendship in this way?

The tears were there, brimming behind her eyes again. It was hurtful—all of it. Being a good person had only gotten her trampled on. *Well, no more,* Desney resolved, her mood now bolstered. She would find Matt Doran, and together they would oust Frederick Fitzgerald before he had a chance to take any gossip to Wade Beresford.

With that resolve firmly planted in her mind, Desney left her dressing room and walked the length of the corridor and through the swing doors to the studio floor. She pulled her woollen hat off, forgetting to leave it with her coat, and held it in her hand while she looked around.

It was dark. No one was around. The expanse of the empty studio floor reached out to her with an eerie, haunting quality. Desney felt peeved. At the very least, she expected to see Pete Hinchcliffe running around making sure the director's chair was in place, that the cameras had enough film, that minor details such as James Wallace receiving his morning coffee were handled. But even James wasn't around and it was rumored that he was always the first to arrive, long before even the producers congregated upstairs to approve or disapprove last-minute script changes.

Desney grimaced and started to return to her dressing room, but as quickly as she turned, she heard a noise. It was a choking, gasping sort of sound. And it came from the direction of the corridor she had just walked down. Desney's primal instincts were heightened instantly.

"Hello?" She ventured timidly. There was no answer. "Anyone there?" she announced her presence with a much firmer tone. Still no answer.

Desney looked quickly around her as she heard the sound of feet running away. It was a heavy tread. She hoped it was one of the security guards wondering who was there, but somehow she couldn't convince herself of that.

"This isn't a joke," she bellowed.

There was only one light on set and it cast a dark, macabre shadow on everything round about, making even the cable wires underfoot seem like vipers wriggling in all directions. It would be hard for her to see if there was anyone else close by. Certainly if there were, he would be shadowed, perhaps as she was, standing there in the hope that her eyes would become accustomed to the gloom eventually. Then Desney heard a door slam and she jumped.

"That's it!" she raged, making straight for the corridor that would take her back to her dressing room, picking her way through the maze of cables and ladders that surrounded the sets. She was frustrated at not having found Matt, and a little scared that no one was around. At least if she returned to her dressing room, her makeup artist would be arriving shortly and she could talk shop with her until the rest of the crew arrived.

The decision implanted in her mind, Desney pulled the double swing doors open and immediately fell over. Her last recollection was a blow to the head, the distant sound of voices, and the world tilting up at her as she hit the floor.

The world began to hold still as Desney felt strong hands helping her to her feet. She was still disoriented and a little dazed, but as she focused, she found herself peering into a pair of green-brown eyes.

"Where am I?" she asked, looking about to find herself the center of a group of concerned onlookers. There was James Wallace, and Shawnee Van Osten, Matt Doran, Pete Hinchcliffe, Shirley Lamas, and Wade Beresford, who was holding her firmly around the waist.

"You're at Elstree," he informed her, heavy concern marked in his voice. "I found you on the floor. We've called the coroner."

"The coroner!" Desney looked at Wade in alarm. "You thought I was dead?"

"Not you," Shawnee interrupted, her expression weakened in shock. "For Frederick Fitzgerald. He's—"

Desney's mind spun. "What?"

"We think it's murder," Shawnee gulped.

"I . . . I," Desney tried to take it in, but her legs felt weak. "I just spoke with Fred this morning." She glanced at Wade, aware that he was practically holding her up. "What are you doing here?"

"I'm your twenty-four-seven, remember?" he whispered, his grip tightening around her waist. "Just as well I followed you here. The murderer might have gotten you, too."

Desney couldn't keep the sarcasm out of her voice. "Are you telling me you saved my life?"

"I think you'd better sit down," Wade suggested. "Are you hurt? Are you in any pain?"

"No." Desney looked around her and realized she was still in the corridor. "Where's Frederick? How . . ." She turned abruptly in Wade's arms and gasped when she saw the rigid body lying cold on the floor with a white cloth covering the corpse. "Oh my—"

"We're not allowed to move him," James explained, "until the police arrive to check for evidence."

"They're not here yet?" Desney wavered, alarmed.

"We just found you, two . . . three minutes ago," Wade filled in. "You were out like a light."

"That means the murderer could still be here," Desney panicked, rubbing the back of her head. She pulled away from Wade, noting the flicker of reservation in his face. "I need a glass of water."

"Let's all go to the green room," James said, his tone a little nervous, but still businesslike and firm. "We need to discuss what we're going to release to the press."

"Is that all you care about?" Desney bridled, pointing at Frederick's cold body, her head a daze. "A man is dead over there."

"And I have a soap to put on air without the costar," James reminded her harshly. "I need to discuss plot changes with the scriptwriters right away. We're going to have to break Matt in sooner than I expected, so the last thing I need right now is to discuss your inability to deal with the situation."

"Back off!" Wade turned on him. "She's just been hit on the back of her head. It could've been fatal."

"I don't like dealing with tosspots," James said, glaring at him.

"Wade . . . please," Desney pleaded, attempting to calm the situation.

She glared at James and then at the others, who looked away uneasily. Of course, in their world, James felt he was right. There was no room for compassion on a soap—not when twelve million viewers were waiting to see their next installment. In her profession, there was just a chilling acceptance of the fact that the world revolved and life had to go on.

On the other hand, she couldn't help but see Wade's point of view, too. As she watched Shawnee and the others follow James to his office, she turned to find Wade waiting quietly for her, his gaze holding hers, checking that she was indeed all right.

"Hooray," she conceded, a flurry of tears now prickling her eyelids. "You were right. I am surrounded by idiots and leeches." She pushed open the door of her dressing room and went in, standing forlorn, the tears now washing down her face. "This is a selfish business, isn't it? Too much thanklessness, pushiness, and greed."

Desney sensed that Wade had followed her in, closing the door quietly behind him. She felt his warm hand rest on her shoulder and she heard the commiseration in his voice when he spoke. "Frederick probably didn't feel anything," he said calmly. "The blow to his head was quick. You don't know how lucky you are."

"I do." She crumbled. Wade squeezed her shoulder. Suddenly Desney felt bitter, as if a rush of recent

memories clouded her head. "What are you doing
here anyway?" she asked.

"Just seeing that you're all right," he ventured.

"All right?" Desney wiped her eyes as though the
display of tears made her appear pathetic. "My twenty-
four-seven is asking if I'm all right. I'm surprised you
got past security."

Wade stepped back, Desney's words throwing him
like a hard punch. He knew immediately why she was
on the verge of exploding. He hadn't expected her to
see him last night with Teadra Lopez after leading her
to believe that he would be at their usual spot at Floriana's.

But the call from Teadra came unexpectedly. She
was in England and they needed to talk. He felt he
owed her that. He also knew he owed it to himself to
discover why she had left him as she had done. But
none of this had anything to do with Desney. Clearly,
however, he could see that she had taken his breaking
of their dinner arrangement personally.

"I came in with Shawnee," he began, seeing the
hurt in her velvety brown eyes. "I wanted to explain
about last night."

"Really?" Desney retorted. "Whether it matters now,
who knows? It can't bring Frederick Fitzgerald back,
can it? I suppose this changes the complexion of your
article, now that we have a corpse on our hands." She
was blustering and she knew it, but Desney wasn't sure
that she wanted an explanation.

"Teadra Lopez was my ex-fiancee," Wade broke in
before Desney could ramble any further. "My second
love. We needed to talk."

His voice was calm, soothing, but it did nothing to
settle Desney's nerves. Her insides felt like they were
high on something, her thread of tension stretched

almost to the breaking point. She was shaking her head, disturbed at being pulled into the discussion.

"Your personal business is your business," she breathed, walking toward her dressing table, placing her hands against the back of her chair for support. "Talking is good, though," she agreed, nodding. "I was only talking to Frederick this morning; he was threatening to blackmail me. Secrets—we all have them."

"Desney?" Wade finally realizing that she wasn't paying too much attention to what he had to say. He felt more determined to make her understand. "Teadra and I were never a secret. We fell in love once upon a time, and there was an occasion when I asked her to marry me. I thought it was what we wanted."

"Did you know I was married?" Desney threw out, turning to face Wade head-on, fresh tears now glazing her eyes. "We were young and he was the wrong man."

Wade was silenced for a moment, his mind taking in the new information. Then he acknowledged her statement with a nod. "You made a mistake like we all do," he said finally.

"Don't try and rationalize it!" Desney yelled. She calmed herself with a deep breath. "It was annulled before we could consummate it. My parents took over and sent him on his way."

"They did the right thing," Wade declared softly. "Sometimes doing the right thing is the only thing. That was why I needed to talk to Teadra. She . . . she jilted me at the altar on our wedding day and I never did find out why until last night."

"At least she didn't try and blackmail you," Desney spat out, her hands fretfully rubbing the back of the chair, her mind unsure what she was saying. "Mine did." Her voice was trembling. "My . . . first love swindled me out of the money my grandfather left me, just to advance his career. I didn't want anyone to know. I wanted my secret kept so it wouldn't spoil my own career, but all it did was get me into trouble."

"You don't need to blame yourself," Wade drawled slowly, the weight of the conversation now beginning to burden him. "Blaming yourself isn't the answer. I did a lot of that and eventually discovered it just ate into my psyche when the fault wasn't even mine. Teadra left taking the secret with her. It hurts. It always hurt."

"I should never have given him any money," Desney chortled, her voice weak with emotion. "I was left broke—my parents never knew, of course. I just kept paying him until I ran out of money."

Wade could see that Desney was rocking on her heels, the grief now lining her face, tears washing down her cheeks. He wanted to hold her but stopped himself. His compulsion to explain seemed more important than taking her into his arms and kissing away her tears. He didn't feel he deserved her affections until he could validate his own reasons for distancing himself from her, for seeing Teadra, and for regularly seeing Desney beyond the time required for a journalist to research a subject.

But this subject had grown on him in more ways than he cared to admit. Her childlike smile warmed him; her velvety brown eyes made him lose himself in her world, the normality about every facet of her life was extraordinary considering her stature as a gifted, talented actress. She was different. He stood in awe of how liberated she was. And even though he had yet to discover why she visited the Black Drug Workers Forum, he felt certain it could never tarnish his newly constructed picture of her.

"You can put all that behind you now," he told her. "It's over."

"It's never over," Desney sighed, using the back of her hand to wipe away more tears. "Fred's dead and it's all my fault."

"It's over," Wade repeated. "I knew it was over with Teadra when I saw her last night, when she told me that . . . that she'd aborted our child. She told me that it would have gotten in the way of her career, that she wouldn't have been able to travel if a job came up in TV or film. I don't know if I can ever forgive her, but I do know it's over and deep down, so do you."

Desney heard his words, but somehow they had trickled off elsewhere, certainly not into the part of her brain that needed to make sense of what he was saying. "I forgave him," she muttered weakly. "I thought, if I could forgive him then I'd always be a stronger person for it. I'd excel, and I did. The last thing I expected was for him to return to haunt me with my past. To have people like Frederick find out." The tears fell again. "That's why he's dead."

Something inside Wade grew in concern. Suddenly, his distraction about explaining himself dwindled into what Desney was trying to say. "Desney." He stepped closer to her now, standing inches behind her, replacing one hand on her shoulder. "Are you saying that the secret of you having been married caused Frederick Fitzgerald's death?"

"Yes." Desney turned and faced him, looking up into his green-brown eyes. The depth of understanding she saw in them penetrated to her heart. He was listening, she told herself, though only her subconscious picked up on this. Her mind was still otherwise engaged on getting matters out into the open. "Frederick told me he was going to take the news of my annulled marriage to you. I came here to tell Matt Doran, but I couldn't find him. And then someone hit me and the next person I saw was you."

"Matt Doran?" Wade asked curiously. "Did you expect him to help you?"

"Of course I did," Desney railed on. "He was my ex-husband. I thought if we both tackled Frederick then—"

"You were married to Matt Doran?" Wade stepped back in shock. Learning of Teadra's confession last night, and now this, propelled his mind into uncertainty. It seemed that being a gossip columnist for his own scandalous magazine was not enough to prepare him for digesting all this hard evidence. "I thought you two were just lovers on *The Earl of Black River.*"

"I got him a part in that and then he left me alone," Desney replied. She looked down at her feet, her limbs shaking with trepidation. "Then Frederick found out and now he's dead."

Wade was silenced. He didn't know whether what she was telling him amounted to a murder rap. "Who else knew that you had a secret marriage?"

"No one. Only Cheryl, my agent," Desney said, her tone still far from relaxed.

Wade looked around Desney's room and saw the fresh flowers on her dressing table. "Get your coat," he said firmly. "We're leaving."

Desney stepped back and did precisely that. While she did so, Wade walked over to her dressing table and picked up the card attached to the vase of ivory roses. "Same admirer?" he asked, reading the inscription: MR. ANONYMOUS.

"Yes," Desney answered, thankful that he seemed to be taking charge. In her present state she felt confused and unsure of her universe.

"Hmm." Wade replaced the card. "We'll go to my place," he told her. "I think you ought to have a brandy, calm down then go over everything with me again. We'll wait until we hear what the police have to say before you give them a statement."

Desney paused at the door, some filtering of information in her brain rising to the forefront of her mind. "About your baby," she suddenly interjected, "I'm sorry. You didn't deserve that. She didn't deserve you."

Wade nodded, a weak smile forming on his face. She'd heard, he told himself, although how, among the chaos of events which were swirling around them, he couldn't quite fathom. What he had expected was a reconciliation discussion that could draw him closer to Desney Westbourne, but it had turned into an examination of past hurts, broken dreams, blackmail and now murder.

There were hidden depths at every juncture. He decided he couldn't nor shouldn't expect to be able to solve all of them. Teadra's disclosure had still yet to sink in to the point at which he knew the real pain would strike. But in some way, Desney's trials were helping to lessen the blow.

Male instinct prompted him to place a hand at the small of her back as he led her down the dressing room corridor toward the back entrance door that would take them to the parking lot. He looked back and saw Frederick's body still covered and realized that Desney needed protecting right now. As a man well versed in media politics, he knew she had to get her facts straight.

Desney didn't dare look back to see whether Frederick's body was still lying on the floor. She was just grateful that Wade was right there behind her, his hand steering her along. She was aware she needed calming. Staying on set that day would not help anyone. They approached the end of the corridor where the green room was located. The door shot open and

James leaned himself against the door frame, his manner agitated.

"You walk off this set today and I'll sue," he said when he saw that Desney was ready to leave.

"I'm taking her home," Wade said firmly. "Or have you forgotten she took a nasty knock on the head."

James looked squarely at Wade for the first time. "Want her all to yourself, do you?" he goaded him, a stealthy look creeping into his eyes. "That's why you're on my set, sniffing for a story leak. I don't want you here again. You got that?"

"I ought to thump you just on general principle," Wade said, steering Desney along. "But you're not worth it."

"Whether I'm worth it or not," James declared harshly, pointing his finger at Desney. "She's not leaving here until the police arrive."

By the time Desney got to Wade's house, she felt shattered. It wasn't yet noon and she'd lapsed into a sullen silence, a drawn look on her face. Staring at the carpeted floor, her hands were clasping and unclasping, so that when Wade arrived with a glass of brandy, he was forced to still her fingers before placing the slightly warmed drink between them.

"Drink it slowly," he advised, taking a seat next to her.

Desney sipped it gratefully, before exerting a deep sigh of relief. "This feels like a nightmare," she said at last. "It feels so unreal."

"Yes," Wade agreed. "Not quite the story I was expecting to get, either."

Desney glanced at him alarmed. "You're not going to print this in *Bribe*, are you?"

He chuckled. "Not even I would stoop that low," he

said, resting his hands on his knees. His eyes moved slowly over Desney. She seemed so innocent under the circumstances, and he'd noticed how distressed she was when she spoke to the police. "I think you should rest," he said softly, rubbing her shoulders gently. He knew he needed to sleep, too, not having slept properly since hearing Teadra's confession. But somehow he felt he needed to watch over Desney. "Later we'll have something to eat and decide what to do," he added.

Desney nodded, stupidly drifting into the guise of the damsel being rescued by her buccaneer. Though surprised that her head wasn't hurting her in the slightest, she decided to take his advice and curled herself up on his sofa, drifting into a peaceful slumber.

Nine

"How you feeling?"

Wade's voice was calm. Desney looked across at him from the sofa where she was lying, having slept for half the day to recover from her ordeal. He was standing over her, a cup of hot tea in his hand, wearing a brooding expression.

"I'm feeling a little better," she managed, swallowing on a dry throat. She sat up, encountering a lethargic buzz inside her head. It was a reminder of what had happened earlier that day, and it alerted her quickly to where she was presently.

Wade's house was expansive. It stood in the quiet village of Farnborough, just outside Surrey, near London on a quiet, tree-lined road. With little sign of habitation, the rural area boasted historic cottages and mansion-sized houses of Victorian design. Wade's was one of the latter. She had recalled seeing the large garden on their arrival, the sweeping hallway leading to rooms on both sides, and the small outer buildings which she assumed were the old stables that had at one time been used for ponies who worked the nearby fields.

The room she was in felt comfortable and homely, painted in shades of fuscia and water lily with nicely fashioned Italian statues, lilac-colored leather sofas—one of which she was now lying on—and large windows that overlooked a private flower garden, where she could see the steeple of a local church in the distance.

As her stockinged feet touched ground, soft carpeting warmed her toes and she stretched her limbs before taking the cup Wade held out toward her.

"There's no sugar," he said, depositing himself in the seat next to her. "I can get some if you like."

"I don't take any in my tea," Desney smiled, gratefully taking a sip and closing her eyes briefly to enjoy the full effect.

"I was thinking," Wade began, glancing briefly at his watch, "that after you drink your tea, we should go back to the studio."

Desney gasped. "Is that wise?"

Wade rubbed his knees with both hands. "The police might want to question you again," he began, "and we need to know what is going on before any public announcements are made."

Desney looked down at the floor for her shoes. She'd taken them off when Wade had insisted that she lie down for a while and try and get some sleep. He had then disappeared upstairs, presumably to telephone his office. She was surprised she had slept at all, but Frederick's pre-dawn call had obviously deprived her of the full quota.

Her black court shoes were within reach and she slipped into them, dangling the teacup precariously in her hand. "Should we leave now?" Desney felt unsure. Leaving as they had done after being questioned by the police and before the body had been moved, and then returning some few hours later was beginning to fray her nerves.

"It's two-thirty," Wade acknowledged. "We may as well."

Desney downed the rest of her tea and placed the cup on the end table. She stood up and was instantly surprised at how weak she felt. The room swayed around her as she made an attempt to steady herself.

She felt Wade's hands instantly around her waist and almost fell back against him as the delicious, warm wave ran through her body. Desney was alert to his firm fingers, gripping hard to keep her upright. She was aware of how much she had missed his touch, missed the sweet sensation of simply being in this man's arms again.

"Careful," his voice came from behind. The breath of him brushed against the back of her neck and tickled along her nape, sending tingles down her spine.

"Sorry," she mustered softly. "I seem to have lost my step."

He let her go and Desney felt suddenly bereft. "You got your balance now?"

She wanted to lie. "I think so."

She turned and Wade looked down into her face. Something inside told him that Desney had been affected by his touch. In truth, he had felt it, too—that quickening of his emotions as his inner being yearned for that certain poignancy it seemed only she could give. It reached into the core of him there, more deeply than he had ever felt it before.

Although Wade wasn't sure what it all meant, it was enough right now for him to store the information to return to later. "Let's go," he said, surprised at the husky sound of his voice.

Desney was attentive to the soft burr of it. "Wade?" Her velvety brown eyes widened.

His, too.

"You're scared," he said, reading her thoughts. His hands rose to rest on her shoulders.

Desney welcomed the familiar feel of his fingers rubbing into her shoulder muscles through the wool of her cardigan and the flowered silk blouse. The brief massage seemed to enliven her. "Can we wait a while?" she asked. "Just until I feel ready."

Wade nodded. He wasn't sure he was ready, either. But he was a man who preferred to deal with things quickly, and he would rather that they did leave now. The plea in Desney's eyes swayed his better judgment. "If you're sure," he said, absently running his fingers from her shoulders down her arms until they rested in her hands.

Desney squeezed them, grateful that he wasn't going to rush her. "Thank you." She was about to retake her seat, when she felt the subconscious pull of her body toward Wade's tall frame.

Their eyes locked, and suddenly they were aware of how much they wanted each other. Desney did not know whether it was the strain of the morning's ordeal, the shock of finding Frederick Fitzgerald's body, or the scary-exciting feeling of knowing that Wade was so close to her again that caused the tension to build. All she knew was that she needed to release it.

When Wade placed one hand beneath her chin and silently brought her face within inches of his own, she did not ask why. The rapid beating of her heart was all the answer he required. And when their lips met, nothing more needed to be said.

The kiss was burdened with stress, but it excited Desney. Wade seemed to capture her in large bitefuls and she was instantly swept away with every movement. Their tongues licked, and their mouths nibbled at each other's soft lips, deepening the wondrously arousing taste of passion.

They moved to the soft leather sofa, where their fingers began to take part in the process of strife and tumult. Nestled against each other, Desney kicked off her shoes and allowed Wade to probe further into her mouth. Her eyes closed, the world fell at either side of her, and her only consciousness was of love-pecked kisses that worked their way from her mouth to her earlobe with frenzied appetite.

He shifted so that he was on top of her, moving his hands up and down her silky legs while he settled in between her parted legs. Desney's own feverish fingers were quick to work, removing the tie from around Wade's neck. He, in turn, loosened the buttons of her cardigan and then her blouse, plucking at each one like they were strings on a violin sending an echoing noise around the room, until her bosom was revealed to his stare. His gasp was one of delight and apprehension.

There was a jittery panic about the way they were taking each other. Amplified by the trauma of the day, their senses were sharpened. Desney was wild with the inflamed passion that had magnified between them. It affected Wade in much the same way, making him tear at the zipper on her skirt and her panty hose, like he'd turned into a hungry barbaric animal.

His predatory instincts prickled Desney's nerve endings, making her equally as savage. She attacked the belt buckle of Wade's jeans while rubbing her palms frantically against his loins. She unzipped the zipper to feel her way to his hardened shaft beneath his shorts. He stiffened and she was immediately thrilled at the beastly gaze that met her watery eyes.

"Is this an act?" Wade whispered, suddenly pausing on the brink of feral glorification to proceed with caution and searching her face for clarity. His smoldering gaze was filled with smoky desire, causing his green-brown eyes to look as dark as a coal pit.

Desney was ennobled by his hesitation. "No," she whispered, raising her mouth to his, the heated word raw on her breath. "This is—"

"You claiming me," Wade acknowledged, seconds before accepting her lips again.

Desney reached into his hair and removed the band that kept his locks in place. The kiss at its most potent touched the pit of her sexual desire where heated sensations were fighting to burst free. Desney felt the fragile silk of her bra and panties rip from her, never to be worn again. Still in her blouse, the kisses traveled downward, over her peaked nipples, past her navel to the core of her being that begged to be blessed by his sensual tongue.

When she felt the wetness on her bud, his saliva drip down her inner flesh, Desney's mind was driven mad. His tongue swirled fully inside, a sweet invasion, slipping back and forth in a devastatingly thorough exploration. He was in ardent worship. Her scream could be heard as far as that village church she'd spied through Wade's large windows. No bell could have chimed louder. The ecstasy was quick and unexpected. Her panting was loud and appeared almost dramatized, but Wade knew that it was not.

Before Desney could descend from her high, his finger was inside her, probing her carefully, keeping the fire alive while he began to slip out of his jeans. Desney moved her buttocks in time to his hand movement, her eyes wide as Wade's naked body became evident to her wondrous gaze.

Still in his unbuttoned shirt, she could see the hair on the honey-brown skin of his chest, his torso hard and firm like a black emperor. He was on his knees between her legs, his finger still working its magic. She lay waiting for him to give her the final release, the breaking of the sexual tension between them.

And Wade was obliging, removing his finger to break open the condom he'd extracted from his jean pocket, placing it over his large manhood with dexterity. The lapse was no less thrilling than their earlier recess, only now it was filled with an electric friction that sizzled in the air. Desney wanted ownership.

Mounting her attentively, Wade gently commanded by raising her buttocks to maximize the pleasure. Fully buried, the thinness of the condom couldn't veil his senses, which began wheeling instantly. His gentle movements fed the tumult, devoured the strife, ate into the tension which had tormented them both, and finally the last aggressive flux of Desney's pelvis caused them both to gasp aloud.

After several minutes, Wade raised his head, tossing back his mane of locks before he leaned on one elbow, his weight slightly displaced to one side of Desney. She was dressed only in her blouse; her walnut brown body serene and beautiful. Attired only in his shirt and smelling of languid satisfaction, with his fingers he traced a trail down the line between Desney's breasts, stopping at her navel.

"I don't think we should have done that," he whispered, his mouth inches away from her lips in impish male after-play. "Do you?"

Brushing her palm against the sleek black hair of his chest, Desney felt her breath begin to ease, fascinated by the slow softening of his manhood inside her. "Yes," she felt compelled to reply, "I do."

Something had shifted inside Wade. If he analyzed it, he knew it was the drifting from panic into oblivion. He felt as if a flash of lightning had seared through him when they came together, and after that, only this peaceful radiance. "Why?" he managed to say.

A languid warmth spread through Desney. "Because it was what we both wanted. What we both needed."

Wade nuzzled a kiss against her neck, still having not moved from deep inside her. Yes, they had both needed this to blow away the stress that had built to such a maddening pitch.

Teadra had been the last person he expected to call him. It had been just over three years since he saw her last—three long, agonizing years of wondering why she refused to meet him at the altar. That abandonment had been the inciting event that brought him to England; he had wanted to get as far away as possible from the memories.

At first, he told himself that Teadra had been too ambitious for him, that her dreams of becoming a famous actress, her sights set on Hollywood, had fogged her mind to what was truly important. Then he convinced himself that they were just too different. She was not as intellectual as he. A woman with a thick Afro-Spanish accent, with parents from Antigua, didn't understand that he was a lover of words and loved communicating. Her main assets were her face and her body. The reasoning seemed simple enough. They were incompatible.

But her revelation last night, that she had aborted their child, threw him completely. He did not expect her to tell him that. In his mind, she was passing through town and wanted to reacquaint herself with an old face. He did not understand her motives for telling him the truth after so much time had passed. Was she intending on hurting him? He didn't ask. He simply made his farewell at Maxim's where she had told him, and left.

Suddenly he realized that the last three years had been a traumatic episode in his life and that he had given himself time to repair and heal. There hadn't been anyone else until Desney, even though women were readily accessible to him and were not shy about telling him so. But he had to get things straight in his mind.

He wondered whether this was why he had developed the habit of prying into other people's lives. Was it so that he could form an understanding of his own? Understand why he should question his manhood even after having made love to Desney, a woman so unlike Teadra in so many ways? If he had been able to maintain some form of control, he would not have chosen this way as an answer.

"Does this compromise my article about you?" It was the first thing that sprang into his head as he thought of how they were going to relate to each other from here on.

How to relate after their torrid romp was an area that worried him, but Desney seemed more than accepting of the situation. "You can describe the color of my torn lingerie," she chuckled devilishly. It was her way of banishing the awkwardness of the situation, for Desney had not expected them to end up this way, either.

Wade picked up the thread, visibly relieved. "I thought you said you never wore them," he reminded, now shifting his weight.

He moved to her side and Desney buried her face into his long, fragrant locks, breathing deeply of his masculine scent as she snuggled into him. "I was trying to take the upper hand," she admitted, recalling her outrageous statement on her first confrontation with him in his office. "I sort of hoped you would take it seriously."

"I did," Wade acknowledged, nipping her chin in fun. "I lost many a night's sleep dreaming about discovering the truth firsthand."

"Now you have."

His arm went around her and drew her closer. "Guess I can say my interview on you is now officially concluded."

Desney turned sideways and looked at him strangely. His statement sounded too ominous for comfort. "Are you suggesting what I think you are?" she gasped.

Wade returned an odd look. "What's that?"

"That this, what we just did, was the big conclusion of your shadowing me?"

Wade laughed deeply. "You do have a low opinion of me."

"It's no worse than what you thought of me," Desney recalled. "I told you that before."

"No." Wade's tone hardened, signaling his wish to cut the conversation right there. "I did not plan that as an encore to my interviewing you. I thought that was more your speciality."

Desney flinched. "This wasn't one of my brazen performances, if that's what you're implying."

Wade took a deep breath. "Why are we arguing?"

Desney was confused. Guilt. That's what it was. Penitence at realizing that no sooner had she poured out her troubles to Cheryl, resolving she would never again fall into playing the poker game of love with Wade, than here she was tapping the deck in approval, allowing him to take charge once again.

Hadn't Cheryl made it abundantly clear, reminding her that she hardly knew the man? That what she did know amounted to nothing more than what Matt Doran had disclosed, added to her own measly limited facts? And then of course there was his old relationship with Teadra Lopez. He had withheld that information, so was he truly hiding something? Cheryl's words played in her ears until she felt compelled to say, "I'm just feeling silly doing this after seeing you with someone else last night."

"I tried to explain to you about her," Wade defended.

"I know," Desney sighed. "It's just that . . . either I'm with you or I'm not. I don't do in between."

"Nor instead of," Wade corrected her, planting a kiss on her forehead. His mouth lifted at the corners. "So what do you want this to be? Me dating you? You want me to be your boyfriend?"

Desney glanced at him with a bewildered expression. Was this what she was asking? "Sounds good," she smiled. "But I would like to know about last night—"

"Teadra," Wade groaned.

Desney noted that he moved his weight uncomfortably against her and seemed unsure. "If you don't want to talk about it, I understand," she wavered.

"You deserve an answer," Wade sighed. "I got a call from her earlier in the week telling me she was in town and could we meet, talk. I thought, why not?"

"So you met last night," she ventured.

"First time in three years," he said softly. "She hasn't changed much. A little older around the eyes."

"And?"

"I realized she was not concerned at all about my life," he concluded flatly. "All she cared about was herself. How her parents had footed the bill for our canceled wedding, how she'd aborted our baby because she was afraid she'd lose her career. How she was scared to tell me because I might force her to do something she didn't want to do. She was . . . selfish."

"I'm sorry," Desney sympathized, wondering why he was skipping over the news so flippantly. "I can't believe she would want to tell you all that after three years unless . . . unless she wanted a second chance."

"I'm over her," Wade said emphatically, pulling Desney closer to his chest. "I wouldn't even attach the word 'relationship' to what we had."

"Are you really over her?" Somehow Desney felt unsure. "I mean, how much of this first, second, and third love stuff do you believe?"

Wade sighed in annoyance. "Matt Doran. What was he? Your first, second, what?"

"First," Desney flinched, peeved.

"Would you go back to him if he begged you?"

She didn't need to think. "Not on a bet."

"Then why would you think I would with Teadra?"

"Because," she paused. "Because you've analyzed in your head what you want and you told me that a man makes a choice. I don't know. I need to feel—"

"That your heart is in safe hands," Wade confirmed. "Don't worry baby, you're in good hands."

He took her lips again and Desney sank into him, amazed at how easy she was in accepting him and everything he had told her. Her mind drifted as she remembered the urgency with which they had made love, recalling the touch of his fingers on her body, making her senses flare with desire.

She went over the ecstatic moment of penetration, his infinite care as he eased into her, filling her perfectly. The sense of completeness as he moved inside her, not like an invading force, but a joint force of merging, internal sweetness, making her heart tremble as his renewed kiss promised a repetition.

His head lifted and his eyes locked into hers. "This." His finger drew a lazy circle around the mud-colored birthmark below her left ear. "Were you born with it?"

Desney's hand unconsciously reached for the same spot, touching it briefly. "Yes. You can say in your rewrite that I consider it a good-luck charm because it gets me noticed every time." Her intimate gaze intensified. "Tell me about you. Do you have any distinguishing features?"

"No," Wade declared. "But my grandfather has an old war wound."

"Your grandfather is still alive?" Desney gasped.

"Yeah," Wade laughed. "He's 106 years old and was in the Sixth Battalion of the British West Indies Regiment at the base command on Taranto in Italy. During the First World War, the black soldiers held a three-day mutiny in Chirlino to protest the way they were treated; he suffered a gunshot to his leg."

Desney was alarmed. "Did he lose the leg?"

"No," he reassured her. "But he has a scar on his calf where the slug went through."

"Is that how your family came to live in Italy?" Desney asked, showing real interest.

"I guess so. After the war, my grandfather, Joshua Beresford, and most of the four thousand soldiers who served with him were returned to the Caribbean, but were displaced in Cuba instead of their homelands because the government feared more unrest." He propped himself up on one elbow and continued. "But as soon as my grandfather could afford it, he returned to Italy then came back home at the start of the Second World War. When that was over, he and some of the other soldiers finally resettled there."

"That's quite a history," Desney said in awe.

Wade nodded in agreement. "He was seventy-two years old when I was born, and my father, Seth Beresford, was fifty-two. He had me late in life. He was twenty-two years older than my mother, Ruth."

"Wow," Desney sounded out. "What was he like?"

"Very firm, disciplined. He learned all that in the army during the Second World War. He used to tell me when I was a kid that it made him a man, and that I shouldn't be afraid to fight for what I believed in."

"And what do you believe in?" Desney prompted.

"I believe in God, free speech, free will, and the right to be free," Wade remarked protectively.

"No danger of you being bound down by anything," Desney joked.

Wade chucked her chin with his finger and thumb. "And what about you?"

"I believe in being true to oneself," she confessed.

"Hmm. Any reason for that?"

"I like playing roles, as you know," she explained. "But at the end of the day, I always remind myself who I am and what I stand for. You see, in the final analysis, it's between me and God and nobody else."

"Ouch," Wade adopted a purposeful frown. "That's why you hate prying reporters like me?"

"Nothing's off the record with you guys," Desney hurtled right in. "It really is an imposition I take issue with. I think the things that I stand for are much more important than the color of my lingerie or whether I sugar my cornflakes or not. I hope someday you'll be able to see that and start chasing stories that will really matter to people."

Something in Desney's tone made Wade's body harden. He pulled away from her and sat up, his fingers buttoning his shirt. His wounded expression made Desney suddenly realize she had hit the same nerve she had touched when challenging him about his vocation at *Bribe* magazine.

"Don't presume to tell me what's best for me," he said in a tone that had a bit of an edge.

"I didn't mean it to sound like that," she relented.

"I'm thirty-four years old," Wade spat out. "I know what I'm doing. Those of us born in the sixties are the ones reshaping the world today. This is my turn."

Desney was thrown. "I . . . I was only saying you could do better than delving into people's private lives."

"*Bribe* sells two million copies a month," Wade continued, jumping from the sofa and reaching to the floor for his shorts and jeans. "Our work is good. I can stake my journalistic reputation on that."

Desney watched him as he pulled his shorts over his lean hips. "Careful," she said, sitting up on the leather sofa. "You don't want to say something you might regret."

"About my work?" Wade paused to shuck off the condom he was still wearing. "Never. At least I don't do drugs!"

Desney stared at him in disbelief. "I've told your assistant editor and now I'll tell you, I'm not a crack slinger," she railed. Remembering their mission to return to Elstree and face the situation regarding Frederick Fitzgerald, she added, "Look, life is too important to be taken this seriously. Let's just get dressed and—"

"I followed you," Wade interrupted, pulling his shorts over his buttocks. "Every Saturday around lunch time you go down to the Black Drug Workers Forum and stay, on average, two hours, before returning home. Am I right?"

"Nothing is sacred with you, is it?" Desney was shocked. She said he would be right behind her, ready to put a knife in her back, and here he was, doing precisely that. "Yes, I do visit there," she admitted painfully, quickly re-fastening the buttons on her own blouse and reaching for her skirt. "I'm on a mentor's program to help young teenage substance abusers. My job is to help give them a goal to aim for, which is why I do it. The center wanted my help and I gave it to them."

Wade's own shock at hearing Desney's vindication eclipsed his sight of the condom in his hand. He hadn't checked it before—didn't think he needed to, having used his regular brand successfully in the past. But his eyes widened when he saw the burst latex. He turned and faced Desney, the blood drained from his face.

She was almost dressed, delving her arms into her cardigan, her own expression a flurry of upset and discomfort. He didn't know what to say, or whether he should in fact say anything at all. Less than an hour ago, they had both released the stress of hearing about Frederick Fitzgerald, and now he had added to it by accusing her wrongly. Could he risk battering her emotions any further by disclosing that he had probably used protection which had passed its sell-by date?

"Sorry. I'm always saying stupid things," he backed down, quickly wrapping the condom in a tissue. A new train of thought convinced him to say nothing. She was his girlfriend now and besides, if there were any consequences—if he was lucky—this could be his final chance. A baby would be just the thing to bind him with the woman who would enrich his life. The one who would be his third, last, and only true love. "How long have you been on the mentor's program?" he asked, forcing a grin.

"Nearly a year," Desney said, a little shakily. "It was something I didn't want you to find out about. That part of my life is personal, and I can't believe you followed me."

"I'm sorry." He placed the tissue on the table and walked over to her, pulling her gently into his arms. "If you don't want it in the rewrite, then I won't put it in." He kissed her forehead before tipping her chin to look into her face.

I hope it has your eyes, he thought, *and your wonderful smile.* He kissed her lips *And all the features that make you special.* He'd never thought it was possible to get everything from one person, but now Wade believed differently. "Your life means everything to me," he said with renewed hope. "Let's keep it that way."

Ten

"Where have you been?"

Those were Shawnee Van Osten's first words as she watched Desney enter the green room with Wade Beresford by her side. Everyone was there, perched on chairs or standing around the room, sipping coffee, and deeply engaged in conversation. "You've missed all the excitement," she said with a huge smile on her face.

"What's going on?" Desney asked, unsure what to think.

She was not oblivious to the gaze Matt Doran threw her way as he caught sight of her escort. It was obvious he felt something was going on, but Matt's bewilderment was not what concerned Desney right now. She was more interested in why there were no police officers outside Elstree Studios, why the area where Frederick had been lying had not been cordoned off. Why, indeed, was everyone in the green room not looking as solemn as she thought they should?

"Frederick Fitzgerald is strapped up in a bed at North Middlesex Hospital," Pete Hinchliffe volunteered, his back against a nearby wall, a Styrofoam teacup in his hand. "He's not dead."

"What?!" Desney's mouth fell open.

"No one thought to take a pulse," Shawnee said dryly, even though it was she who played the soap's resident nurse. Crossing her legs in the chair so as to show off their shapely curves, she said, "You should've seen the paramedics when they came in and tried to move the body. They were all over Frederick, attaching a cannula into his vein, an ESG monitor, cervical collar, oxygen mask, pulse-oximeter, the works. They even gave him chest compressions at one point."

Matt was perched on the edge of the counter next to the coffee percolator, his hands resting on his knees, and looking calmer than when Desney had last seen him. "His breath was on the brink of failing," he added.

"So he's alive?" Desney questioned, relieved.

"He's in a coma," Shawnee concluded flatly, shaking her shoulders as though she'd just walked in out of the cold. "It's so chilling. It's just like that storyline we did last year when Frederick was—"

"This has nothing to do with Frederick's role as Dr. Khumalo," James snapped as he entered the green room with a clipboard in his hand. "He got shot in 'It's a Wide World,' not bludgeoned on the back of the head." He caught Desney and Wade in attendance and changed his manner bluntly. "Decided to come back and snoop around?" he barked at Desney.

She was lost. Desney had not been a cast member in the soap last year, so she was unaware of there having been a plot line with parallels to what was happening now. "I came to see what was happening about Fred," she swallowed. "It's reassuring to know that he's all right, after all. Has anyone told his wife?"

"She's at the hospital now," James confirmed, transferring his gaze to Wade. "I thought I made it clear I didn't want you on my set."

"He's here with me," Desney instantly cut in.

"Well, we're going into an emergency story conference right now," James replied. "So ask him to leave.

I don't want any media personnel within a mile of this studio until we're ready to make a statement. He can get the news like everybody else."

Desney knew when to concede. As the senior writer, James was within his rights to protect the soap and the plot line that went with it.

"Can I see you later?" Wade whispered, deciding not to take James's objections personally.

Desney nodded, squeezing his fingers. "Why don't you come by my place around seven o'clock?"

"That's fine," he agreed. Shooting a dark look James's way, he left the room.

"Okay, everyone," James announced, his gaze homing in specifically on Desney. "Until we find out what really happened to Frederick, security has been stepped up. And this is not official, but I'm revising the storyline for the show. I'm going to pitch to the producers that we shoot a double murder."

Desney was exhausted when she finally arrived home. Her watch said 5:43. Wade would be arriving in a little over an hour. She frowned, recalling her day. James hadn't said two words to her the entire time she was on set. She knew it was his way of holding her responsible for inviting Wade Beresford there. In her mind, he also made her feel small, ineffectual, and naïve.

James was a man suspicious of everybody. Even gardeners, janitors, and cleaning ladies constituted a threat to him. Desney had often felt that he was a victim of his own success, that the characters he invented for "It's a Wide World," were as real to him as the humans that surrounded him in daily life. So in his mind, it was quite feasible that a common street person would be an assassin in disguise, a woman with a baby a Secret Service agent holding a wired-for-sound doll, and a car mechanic with a monkey wrench a terrorist with an Uzi.

Scriptwriters were imaginative people, but this was no reason for him to treat Wade Beresford with such distrust. She wondered whether it was his affair with her agent that made him so cagey. She had grown to trust Wade. So far, he'd been true to his word.

He had also explained to her some of the sorry things that had happened in his life. They were not excuses, but the knocks in life that were common to most people. And losing his child the way he had done, never knowing that he had fathered one to a woman who had jilted him on his wedding day, must have been like a knife turning in the wound—an impossible thing for most people to get over.

He could have been bitter. Maybe he had been at one time. Teadra Lopez was an actress and so was Desney. Perhaps this was why he initially held such a dim view of her profession. Teadra had done a very selfish thing, and it had left its mark. But *she* loved him now, and she wondered how he felt about that.

Desney kicked off her shoes and walked into the kitchen. Flicking on a light, she switched on the kettle for some tea. She knew how she felt about Wade; she was in love with him. Despite the arrogance she had first come up against, she now sensed a deeply soft and gentle nature. It touched her heart in ways she couldn't explain. He was no longer the enemy. Suddenly, she felt like he was everything she had been looking for. Everything she wanted.

She decided she would have just time enough for a bath before he arrived, and headed straight for the bathroom and turned on the taps. The hot steaming water gave her an idea, and she applied scented bath salts, then impulsively decided to light some candles.

The soft light created just the mood she wanted to help her relax and meditate.

Returning to the kitchen, she made herself of cup of chamomile tea. Sipping it slowly, she walked over to her bedroom and picked out some underwear. A slight chuckle left her lips when she remembered telling Wade that she didn't wear them. If only she could be so bold! Still, she had been thrilled by the look he threw her way on hearing it. Her heart warmed with the knowledge of his desire for her as she undressed and slipped into a bath robe.

She was about to return to the bathroom when the intercom buzzer made her jump. She wasn't expecting anyone so soon after arriving home. Frowning, she padded barefoot into her sitting room and pressed the speech button. "Yes?"

"It's Wade." That sexy hint of an Italian accent.

Desney panicked. He was early. He wasn't due until seven o'clock. She paused to think, looking down at herself, knowing there was no time to dress.

"Desney?" His voice sounded impatient.

"Come on up," she invited, pressing the release button.

Desney ran immediately to the bathroom and turned off the taps. The hot water had steamed the entire room, making it a clouded haven where one could retreat from all thoughts of the world. She was sorely tempted to sink into the scented abyss and forget all her woes and tribulations, but she had to let Wade into her apartment first—she could hardly leave him outside while she bathed.

The sudden knock on her front door reminded her that he was indeed here. *He must have run up the stairs,* she thought. Clasping the belt around her bathrobe, she went to the front door, placing her cup of chamomile on a coffee table en route.

Wade was stood at the door looking dapper, a bottle of white wine in his hand. Dressed in fresh clothing: a clean pair of black jeans, black sweater, and a red jacket, and with a wide grin on his face, he looked completely adorable. But Desney could also see that he was drained, probably having spent the remainder of his day catching up with an endless barrage of work at his office for a forthcoming edition of *Bribe* magazine.

"You look pooped," she said, opening the door.

Wade's eyes roamed over her from head to toes, knowing she lay naked beneath her robe. "And you look like a temptress," he smiled weakly, closing the door behind him.

Desney chuckled as he planted a wet kiss on her lips before following her into the sitting room. "I was on my way to a bath," she told him gingerly. "James worked me so hard today, I don't know if I'm coming or going."

"What's his problem, anyway?" Wade asked, walking over to the kitchen to place the bottle of wine on a nearby counter.

Desney leaned against the kitchen door and folded her arms beneath her breasts. "He's now talking about changing the storyline," she divulged. "We're all going to be given new scripts on Friday and just one week to memorize our lines."

"Any news on Frederick?" he inquired.

"Still in a coma," Desney answered sadly. "I just hope he comes around soon and is okay. Maybe he can even tell us all who did it."

"Hmm," Wade mused. "Any glasses?"

Desney eyed the wine bottle. "Italian Asti," she smiled knowingly. "A favorite of mine. What's the occasion?"

The smile faded from Wade's face. "That vocation

thing you were telling me about," he began, as Desney indicated with an index finger a glass cabinet above his head where he reached for two glasses. "I've decided that you were right."

"That's good," Desney nodded.

"When you told me about your mentoring program, I felt guilty," he explained, placing the two wineglasses on the bench. "You've done so much with your life, and there was I belittling it all in my magazine."

"Well, you said you're going to make amends," she reminded him.

"That's not the point," he persisted. "I didn't know you and yet I accused you of so many things. That's why I've decided to do something I would never have thought to do had it not been for you."

Desney was intrigued. "What's that?"

Wade turned the corkscrew as he spoke. "I have a friend who owns a news channel network on digital TV," he began, popping the cork. "He's wangled it so that I can join one of his crew on a mission to Sierra Leone. I'll be working as an investigative reporter."

Desney was no longer fascinated. She grew alarmed. "You're leaving?"

"Only for three weeks," Wade explained, pouring the wine. "It was what you said about my work, about the fact that I could do better, write something that's worth reading. That got me thinking. I thought about it at my desk, after I left you. Tony was being a real pain and suddenly I realized more than ever that you were right."

She may well have been right, Desney thought, but she had never thought it would come to this. "What about—"

"Your rewrite," Wade interrupted, handing her a glass. "The draft's written up; I'll let you see it tomorrow. I think it's probably best that I don't add

Frederick, but I did have the idea of putting in a section about your first marriage to Matt Doran."

Desney's mind was elsewhere. She was more interested in their relationship than the rewrite, but Wade seemed oblivious. Something was different. He was charged, ambitious. He had an air about him that told her he was looking forward to a future. *That's what was missing,* she realized when she thought back to her first analysis of him. He did not strike her then as a man who looked ahead, but he seemed very much like that sort of man now.

"What about the danger?" she asked, referring to the peril of traveling around a country at war.

Wade took a large sip of wine and leaned his back against the kitchen counter. "I thought you explaining about your past life with Matt Doran could be a sensational part of the feature," he explained. "There'll be no danger if you take the heat off being blackmailed by Frederick by releasing the story yourself."

Desney's heart sank. They were on two different subjects. Could he not see that she didn't want him to go? "Do what you feel is best," she said softly, replacing her wine glass on the counter. "I'm going for a bath."

"Wait a minute," Wade restrained her. "I'm doing this for us."

Desney's mind went blank. "What?"

"If you're going to be with me, then I want to start thinking about our future," he assayed. "You said you didn't want me to do *Bribe* magazine, so I'm widening my horizons. I want to prove to you that I can do this."

Desney gazed into Wade's eyes. The challenge was there. It was written all over his face, too, in the tilt of his dark brows, embedded in the lines of his forehead, chiseled into the cleft in his chin. He seemed filled with new hopes and dreams. Desney felt moved by his sincerity. How could she deny him the chance when she had harped for so long that he do something worthwhile with his talent?

"You're serious about going, aren't you?" she asked, searching his expression. Her voice trembled at asking the question, but Desney knew that was because she couldn't bear the loss of him when she had just claimed him as her own.

"It won't be for long," Wade promised, setting his glass down on the counter. He pulled her into his arms and inhaled the tangy smell of her. "Major Abu, the former Defense Minister, is said to have escaped Sierra Leone and is now in Abidjan. It's rumored that he has a security vault where he has deposited twenty five million dollars in gold bullion. The crew and I want to get hold of the story before this new guy, General Kabuda, gets hold of Major Abu."

"You don't need to do this," Desney implored tearfully, running a hand down his narrow locks of hair, which were pulled back into his usual style.

"Yes I do," Wade insisted. "If it all goes well, then it's a résumé marker to get me into TV news; then I can sell the magazine."

"Sell *Bribe?*" Desney was truly taken aback.

"You don't like what I do and—"

"I didn't expect you to make all these changes for me," she gasped, leaning back against his arms. "I know I don't like what you do, but you're going too far with this. You're going abroad for three weeks, and we're just getting to know each other!"

Wade pulled her back into his arms again. "Three weeks go really quickly," he insisted. "Before you know it, I'll be back and we can really get things going."

Somehow, Desney didn't feel convinced. "I don't know," she said. "Will you come back to me?"

"I'll come back to you," Wade promised, pressing a kiss against her lips. He had meant it to be a brief one, but the moment he felt her body against him, his instincts took over.

His lips grazed hers again, sweetly and sincerely. She was soothed by the gentle, moist pressure of them on her mouth. Her eyes closed and Desney drifted into oblivion. All she could feel was the fast thudding of her heart and Wade's tongue teasing her, tasting her, melting and devouring her like ice cream.

Her arms ran over his neck, her fingers finding their way into the tousled length of his hair that spilled over his shoulders as he pulled her closer. She could sense his arousal for her, feel the hardness in his loins against her soft bathrobe.

"I need a bath first," she mouthed against his lips.

He answered her with succulent little kisses between his words. "I'll . . . join you and . . . wash . . . your back."

Her oblong bath tub was big enough for two, and Desney smiled, aware that she would more than welcome the company. "I hope you're good at giving back rubs."

"The best in all the world," Wade assured her, kissing her again.

Making love in the steamy haven of her bathroom was more than Desney could ever dream possible. Nothing in life had ever prepared her for such uninhibited sensual indulgence. There was something so childlike and pure about Wade's lovemaking, that there were times throughout when she had felt so perilously close to tears.

The purity was unfeigned, his passion so unabashed, his every movement so gently erotic, that she had been thrust into ecstasy time and time again until the water beneath them had grown cold. The jacuzzi spa had added to their delight, causing them to giggle as they rubbed and caressed bubbles into one another. In the afterglow they talked and touched, reacquainting themselves and committing to memory the tiniest sun spot, chickenpox mark, or dimple each discovered about the other throughout their bodily explorations.

And each time Wade was ready to take her, Desney was struck by his hesitation in using a condom, thinking that perhaps he saw it as an impediment to consummating the sincerity that now existed between them. Finally spent and lying in her bed by his side, among the tousled sheets, she watched him now, tracing with her fingers along his heavy eyebrows, seeing the fatigue in his eyes.

"When do you leave?" she asked, her voice sounding husky, as though she might break into tears.

"This weekend," Wade whispered, landing a kiss on the tip of her nose.

"I don't think I can bear this," she murmured weakly, feeling vulnerable as she snuggled into his chest, inhaling the clean smell of his flesh. "So much is going on right now."

"You'll be all right," Wade assured her, when a fleeting thought crossed his mind. He could well be returning to discover her pregnant. Perhaps he should say something now. But how? He didn't want to lose her. Not like this. Guilt rankled his mind. "Desney?" He brushed a finger against her cheeks. "If . . . if at any time you feel you need to tell me something, you will tell me."

She clung to him even harder. "I've told you everything I need you to know," she paused. "There is one thing."

Wade's body stiffened. "What is it?"

Desney sighed. "I don't want this in your feature about me," she warned.

Wade turned and faced her, unsure what to expect. "Whatever you say."

"It's about me, about my family," Desney began. "It's the reason why I'm on the mentoring program at the Black Drug Workers Forum."

"Go on," Wade encouraged, seeing her nervousness.

"Remember I said I had two sisters?" she continued. "Well my older sister, Rhea, was a drug addict. She overdosed once and the hospital managed to save her. She's the owner and organizer of the Forum I do the program for."

Wade's eyes widened in newfound admiration. "You're supporting her?"

"We keep it quiet," Desney went on. "If people knew I was affiliated, it would take the focus off the real work that needs to be done there. I help out but stay incognito. I like it that way. It's what my sister and I both want, and that's why I didn't want you to know. I don't want her project compromised because of who I am."

Wade pulled her close and hugged her tightly, kissing the top of her head. "You're truly nothing like what I expected to find in an actress," he told her truthfully. "And your sister . . . she's the one who wanted to be a—"

"Singer," Desney supplied. "Her addiction was like the plague," she attempted to explain. "Like the one of the firstborn in Egypt during Moses's time. It afflicted the eldest child in the family. Our parents were devastated. When I came back from America and saw her, it felt like looking at a ghost."

"What was the drug of choice?"

"Heroin."

"But she survived."

"Only just," Desney breathed. "You wouldn't know it to look at her now. It was a long haul, but she pulled through."

"That's why you knew so much," he acknowledged.

"Yes," Desney admitted. "At the Forum, she's trying to advocate an ethnic monitoring program as part of the government's index of registered addicts. Rhea tells me that data on drug use is difficult to collect because of the illicit nature of the activity, but she's persevering to break down the stereotypical view of addicts being criminals rather than people in need of help."

"How does she get funding?" Wade asked, riveted by this knowledge pouring forth from such an alluringly attractive woman.

"It's easier to get money for a donkey sanctuary than it is for a black project," Desney said sadly. "But I've donated a good amount over the past year, and Rhea was lucky to get some lottery funding a few months ago."

Wade shook his head, scarcely able to believe the remarkable achievements he had found in Desney Westbourne. It made him feel even more guilty about what little he had achieved in his own life. "What's the plan?"

Desney sighed. "She wants to lobby the government's Research and Statistics Office to develop an ethnic-based self-reporting survey in which people are asked to declare their drug use. Only then can the Forum, and others like it, begin to look at factors such as racism, unemployment, and poverty in the effort to help users kick their habits."

"And the mentoring program?"

"That's for users who have already gone through some form of rehabilitation and need role models to help them see their goals." A brief smile spread across Desney's face. "My work is mostly in that area. I enjoy it. It's what youngsters need today."

Wade felt ashamed. "I have a confession to make,"

he hesitated, on the brink of telling her the truth, that he may have, in fact, given her a baby. But fear propelled him in another direction. "When I saw you go into the Black Drug Workers Forum, I thought *you* were on drugs."

"Me?" Desney laughed.

"My mistake," he quickly amended. "Deep down in my heart, I knew that you couldn't have been. Otherwise I wouldn't have . . ." His voice trailed. He wouldn't have done what he had done. Risked everything to be with her. Risked falling in love with her.

"You do think the worst of me," Desney reiterated. "I don't even know how to inhale a cigarette."

Wade smiled. No risk to his unborn child there. Desney noted the sparkle in his face. Her velvety brown eyes widened expectantly. "What?" She chuckled.

"Nothing."

She knuckled him tenderly in the chest. "Are you holding something back from me?"

Something inside Wade jumped. She knew. He stared at her, but all he could see was her deep desire to know everything about him. It felt as though time had slowed down, just for him. Slowed so he could savor every minute sensation, every devouring kiss, every quivering touch. Loving her had made him feel truly blessed.

"I'd like to know who this is." He held up Desney's soft toy and they both chuckled at its big wide eyes.

"That's Poxy, my pet rabbit," Desney giggled. "He sleeps with me every night."

"Well, I'm throwing him out," Wade declared huskily, tossing the white fluffy toy to one side. "You've got a new bed mate now."

Desney snuggled into him, then thought to ask him something. "This isn't about you running away, is it?"

Wade inclined his head slightly. "From what?"

"Having to face up to what Teadra did."

"No." Wade pulled her into him. His voice caught on her name. "I promise I'll come back and be everything you want me to be." He covered her mouth with his, sealing his oath with their lips in a vow that he knew would never be forgotten.

Eleven

She went into the private room crammed with flowers. Desney stared at Frederick, propped up against four pillows, his head bandaged, and his body hooked up to an EKG monitor. His eyes were closed to the world. As she looked at him, she realized she had never been in a real hospital ward before, though she knew all there was to know about the experience.

She had played the part of a student nurse. Her father had excelled in his profession to become a surgeon before his retirement, and though she had never been an actual patient before either, she was one under Dr. Khumalo's care on "It's a Wide World." *By the time Frederick wakes up, the story on Cinnamon Walker's marriage to Matt Duran will have broken,* she thought. There would be no avenue for him to blackmail her then.

Still unaccustomed to carrying a handbag, she placed her keys on the edge of his bed and added her pot of fresh flowers to the hoard that filled the room. *You have friends, Fred,* she mused, glancing around the otherwise empty room. No doubt other visitors would arrive later, and despite the fact that Frederick had behaved like a craven little weasel, Desney was still his friend, too.

Returning her gaze to the bed, she grimaced and then tightened her cashmere coat around herself as though she felt a sudden chill. She realized that a small window was open, admitting the cool November air. Wade had been gone twelve days now. She had checked his rewrite before he left. The parting had been tearful. Tony Barbieri was with her when they had seen him off at Heathrow Airport. He didn't look too pleased, either; Wade had left him with much of the responsibility for *Bribe* magazine.

And in Wade's car returning to London, Tony drove in silence hardly throwing two words her way. She couldn't figure what was wrong with the man. All her attempts at conversation had fallen on deaf ears. She had finally retreated into silence and decided to dream instead about her dashing buccaneer at the helm of a strong ship.

The door behind her opened suddenly and Matt Doran breezed in. Desney was surprised to see him. He didn't appear surprised to see her.

"Hello," he gestured, shifting his gaze toward the bed. Matt's hair was freshly shaven close to his scalp, and he was dressed casually enough for the weekend— just a pair of black trousers and a warm grey jersey sweater beneath a black leather jacket.

"Decided to use your Saturday to see him, too?" Desney asked as he placed a signed get-well card by the jug of water on the bedside table.

"I don't really know him," Matt admitted, licking the thin line of mustache above his pink lips, "but I thought I'd come anyway. Respects from one cast member to another."

She had never told him what Frederick had planned to do, about his revealing that they had once been married, and Desney decided it was probably best that she didn't. She couldn't see what purpose it would serve, anyway. When the police had finally questioned them all on the studio floor that day, no one knew a motive for why Frederick had been clubbed on the back of the head.

The investigation was still an open one. As she stared down at him again, seeing that Frederick's face had aged, his skin color faded to an ashen gray, his expression innocent to the world, she wondered whether they would discover anything at all. Would he ever come back?

"Did you know about the storyline they ran last year?" she asked Matt, suddenly curious, deciding she would be cordial and polite. "Frederick was in a coma once before in 'It's a Wide World.' "

"I heard Shawnee talking about that," Matt nodded indifferently. "Why? Do you think they're connected?"

"I don't know," Desney said, looking out the window. "Just wondering, that's all."

"It was before we were put on the cast, so I suppose that puts us in the clear," Matt breathed with relief. "Anyway," he paused. "Haven't seen you with Wade Beresford lately. Lost the hots for you, has he?"

"You wish," Desney said peevishly, retrieving her keys from the bed. "He's in Sierra Leone."

"What's he doing there?" Matt was surprised. It was the first mark of emotion Desney saw on his face since his arrival.

"News assignment," she answered. "There's more to him than just his magazine."

"New edition out yet?"

"Friday, next week." Desney wavered. "There's a good rewrite about my life that I think you'd find interesting."

Matt stood rooted to his spot for a few brief seconds before it finally dawned on him. "You haven't!"

"I have," she said in satisfaction. "The truth would one day come out anyway, so I decided why not explain what I did on my own terms. Don't worry," she added, seeing Matt's mouth widen with consternated disbelief. "It'll add to the ratings and you'll be even more famous, which is what you've always wanted, isn't it?"

She dug her hands into her coat pockets and was about to leave when Matt lunged forward and caught her arm. "What I want is you," he responded with a sincerity that put Desney instantly on guard.

"Matt!" His grip tightened around her arm. "You're hurting me."

"I've never meant to hurt you," he mewled, his grip loosening slightly. "I know I did a very wrong thing when we were younger. I was just desperate, that's all. Mindless and foolish. I didn't mean to piss away your money on cocaine."

"You spent my inheritance on drugs?" Desney gasped, astonished. "You're an addict?"

"No. It was more recreational than dependency," Matt said desperately. "The rum, the vodka, they didn't help to—"

"Matt," Desney tried to break free, smelling the liquor on him now. "I'm in love with someone else."

"Not Wade Beresford," Matt spat the words. "That man—"

"Would never have touched what my grandfather left me in his trust fund," Desney finished. "I can never forget what you did, especially now that I know where the money went. I was thoughtless, too, but not anymore. Just leave me alone."

He hung on, bruising her beneath her coat. He had a surprisingly strong grip. "A man can't make a mistake, can he?"

"Depends on what kind of mistake," she said, glaring at him.

Matt studied Desney's hardened gaze. Their relationship on set was tolerable enough. His part had developed to the point where the viewers now knew they were heading for a love liaison. How he wished it were true off set! "Will it be a mistake when I kiss you on set next Friday?"

"It'll be an act," Desney reminded him sternly, looking directly into his face. "Nothing more. Nor will it ever be."

"Then maybe we should rehearse the scene now."

"Get off me," she snarled, fighting him like a wild thing as he pulled her into his arms.

She was so caught up in getting away from him that when the sudden, aphasic sound of someone coughing reverberated in the room, interrupting Matt's determined protestations of love, it went ignored until a second pronounced cough plummeted them both into utter silence.

The machines that were hooked up to Frederick began to bleep all manner of cacophonies, and Desney turned to find his anxious face alert and staring in bewildered shock. Frederick was attempting to sit up, but was too encumbered by the drip tube, respirator, and other medical attachments, that all he could move were his eyes, which seemed to make an earnest plea.

Matt released Desney as though he had just witnessed the miracle of resurrection. He backed away two steps, and neither of them spoke. Desney's alarm melted with the knowledge that Frederick was wide awake.

"I'd better get the medics in here," Matt stammered in disbelief, edging backward toward the door.

No sooner had he turned the knob than the door burst open and an entire medical team rushed in. "We saw the monitor," a doctor explained as he rushed over to Frederick's bed and signaled others to restrain the patient. "How long has he been awake?" He turned to Desney.

"I . . . just now," she blurted, disoriented by the way

everyone was jumping into action. A technician was tampering with one machine, his assistant with another; one doctor flickered a torch into Frederick's eyes, and the leader spoke briskly to his patient.

"Can you hear me?" he asked, his voice professionally pitched. "You're at North Middlesex Hospital. I am Doctor Wesley, attending physician."

Frederick's mouth formulated into a weak smile, acknowledging the question. "I am Doctor Khumalo," he replied weakly. "From Kenya."

Dr. Wesley turned to Desney, confused. "I thought his name was Frederick Fitzgerald!"

"It is," Matt confirmed. "Dr. Khumalo is the role he plays on the TV soap we work on."

"I see," the physician nodded. "I wonder . . ." His voice trailed as he returned his attention to his patient. Desney moved closer in order to hear what was going on, stopping when she reached the foot of the bed.

"Doctor Khumalo," the registrar began. "Do you know who Frederick Fitzgerald is?"

Frederick's eyes widened, his voice weak. "No. Should I?"

"Do you know who these people are?" He indicated Desney and Matt, who leaned forward so that they were within his view.

"No," Frederick answered, his expression blank.

Dr. Wesley turned toward Desney and Matt. "I think you two had better leave," he advised tersely. "We're going to need to run some tests to ascertain whether he's suffering from temporary or acute amnesia."

"Amnesia . . ." The word hung in the air when Desney repeated it.

"We'll call his wife," the doctor concluded.

Desney faced Matt, annoyed. Their arguing had obviously woken Frederick, but it was a hollow awakening. She felt only sympathy for the doctor who would have to deliver the news, and for the family who would receive it. Frederick had been married eighteen years, and now he probably would never even recognize them, or indeed anyone he had ever associated with, ever again.

Outside the door, she heaved a labored breath. She felt sick. Her head had become light, her insides nauseated, and she suddenly felt hot. Desney panicked as she felt the urge to vomit.

"What's the matter?" Matt asked.

"You stay away from me!" she struggled to tell him. "I . . . have to . . . go."

She put her hand over her mouth and ran down the corridor to the nearest restroom, and in an instant her head hung over the bowl. Nothing came; only spit and her fretful breath fell from her lips. A while later, she was at a basin, sprinkling cold water over her face as the tide of heat that had swept over her began to subside.

What was that? she asked herself, confused. Desney was realistic enough not to put it down to Frederick recovering from his comatose state, or Matt Doran trying to manhandle her. He was harmless in his own way—nothing like the dangerous man she had met just two months ago who had stolen her heart. But Wade was far away from her now, in another city, another land. Was he in danger or was he safe? There was no way of her knowing.

No postcard had arrived. He hadn't telephoned, and she had no email address for him to reach her, either. The latter was something she needed to resolve. Most of the cast members now had web sites; she was far behind the times.

She wiped her face with a tissue and looked at herself in the mirror above the basin. The reflection of a troubled woman looked back at her. *Who are you, really?*

she thought. She patted her cheeks as though she might force color into the flawless walnut brown of her complexion. She certainly wasn't Cinnamon Walker, the role that was putting her in more demand with every new episode of "It's a Wide World." And she wasn't convinced that she was Desney Westbourne, actress.

She wasn't dreaming anymore. Since Wade's departure, her buccaneer had failed to materialize. The ship was gone, too. There were no sunsets, no deep kisses at the helm, and she was no longer a damsel in need of rescuing. He was gone. Perhaps this was her way of coping, she thought. Of dealing with Wade's leaving so suddenly just as their love was blossoming.

But now she was sick. Inside, she still didn't feel quite right, though her reflection made her seem normal enough. It was a feeling like something was there, when she knew she had skipped breakfast and hadn't yet eaten lunch. *That's it,* she concluded logically. *I'm hungry.* She would go home and eat something, then chill out in front of the TV. And above all else, try and remember the words of Wade's promise to her.

Six days later, Desney applied the finishing touches to her face, brushing more mascara onto her eyelashes than what had gone on earlier in makeup. Then her mouth pursed into a tight O of concentration as she reddened her lips.

With a sigh, she recapped the lipstick and screwed the mascara brush back into its bottle. Surveying herself in the mirror above her dresser, the artificial face of a stranger stared back at her. She wore great swathes of blue eyeshadow, which did not compliment her velvety-brown eyes, but was more in harmony with the costume she was wearing for this take.

Suddenly, she was consumed by nerves. She felt sick at the pit of her stomach. The entire week had gone by with her body filled with turmoil. She could only imagine two things that might be causing it: the release of *Bribe* magazine that morning and her screen kiss with Matt Doran, which she had yet to perform in less than ten minutes.

She had refused to be intimidated by him in the rehearsal hall at dawn, the new call time James had set so that the new storyline could be filmed as early as possible. The fact of Frederick's amnesia had filled much of the conversations that morning and had been an excellent buffer to divert her mind from the awful, looming kiss. As far as she was concerned, she could do the job in one take. And besides, she felt so committed to Wade, she couldn't bear even the thought of acting out a screen kiss.

The jitters were still in her stomach when she walked onto the studio floor. The same level of chaos that had gone on all week still pervaded the area. Everyone seemed agitated and nervous. James had circulated revised pages of the script all week, making changes almost every day and taping complete episodes within twenty-four hours.

The last-minute ideas came on colored paper, either as an abridged memo or story outline. Sometimes the cast would only be given the night before to memorize complete scenes. It was all beginning to feel too disruptive.

Matt Doran spotted her arrival. He noticed her painted face and her hair swept up from the nape of her neck, with soft tendrils falling about her ears. Then his gaze moved away from her frightened eyes to the black fishnet stockings and stiletto heels beneath her dressing gown.

Embarrassed, Desney blurted harshly, "What are you gaping at?"

"Nothing," he replied, a smile lurking on his lips. "I was just thinking how much I'm looking forward to this scene."

"I'll try and make it as unpleasant as possible," she assured him, unknotting the belt of her gown and handing it to a stage hand.

A wolf whistle escaped Matt Doran's lips when he saw the black basque edged with green lace, which hooked at her waist and forced her breasts enticingly upwards. Beneath the basque, her navel was visible and at the thighs he saw her silk lingerie. Wardrobe had done an excellent job. He felt the fire in his blood instantly. "I don't think this is going to be unpleasant for me," he joked, though his eyes rested on her with undisguised yearning.

Desney suddenly felt giddy. *I want Wade.* Her heart sank as she gazed blankly into Matt Doran's determined expression. Her whole body was racked with a sickly tension akin to the claustrophobic feeling of being stuck in a high-rise elevator. Everything was closing in: the air, her breath, the studio floor around her. Even Matt seemed to be swaying unusually as he advanced closer.

She had no awareness that she'd even hit the floor until she found herself there a few seconds later. "Are you all right?" The voice was Pete's.

"I . . . I," she was weakened, looking into all the faces around her. "What happened?"

Pete had her on her feet and back in her dressing gown within minutes. "I think you should sit down," he said, motioning her back toward her dressing room. "You fainted."

"Maybe that hit you got on the back of the head

when Frederick got conked has affected you," Shawnee mustered with surface concern.

"It's all this pressure and overtime," someone else protested.

Desney glanced behind her to find Matt Doran staring, intrigued. He was probably thinking the same thing she was, Desney thought as she allowed Pete to help her into the chair that she had left only minutes earlier. Another glance at herself in the mirror, and she couldn't see it; it did not show in her face. But the one word was on her mind. *Pregnancy.* Slowly the truth dawned.

Following the nausea attack at the hospital when she had visited Frederick, the rest of the weekend had been filled with similar bouts, most of which manifested as a revulsion for food when she woke up. Nothing relieved it, either. Tea, light biscuits, chips. It all had wanted to come right back up the moment she swallowed.

A depth of anxiety struck as she thought of how her pregnancy could have happened. She had used protection with Wade. They had been careful. Her mind spun with the sudden realization that the condom they had used must have failed. It terrified her. Her breath caught in her throat as she felt again that nightmarish, loathsome loss of control. "I need to visit the drug store," she told Pete, almost absently. "I need to take something."

"I can go get you whatever you need," Pete enthused eagerly. "Headache tablets, tampons, birth control, pregnancy test kit . . ."

Desney looked up at him. He was such a kind, sweet boy. Tall, spectacled, looking like the sort who had never had a girlfriend. But at twenty-two, he was much smarter than she had given him credit for.

"I didn't fool you," she said quite cynically. "I seem

to have been fooling myself." Her period was due four days ago but hadn't arrived. It was still early. Very early. There was still a wide margin for error. "I could be making a mistake."

"How late?" Pete inquired.

"Four days."

He nodded. "Too early."

She smiled weakly at him. "Aren't you too young for all this?" She tried to add a chuckle to her voice, but failed as tears welled up into her eyes. "What am I going to do?"

Pete grabbed a chair and sat down beside her, affectionately rubbing a warm hand across her shoulders as the shocking knowledge worked its way in slowly. The reassurance was timely and was what Desney needed. She wanted to be told that she was talented and beautiful, that she was a woman entitled to fears such as this, but in her heart she had to accept the fact that she might be carrying Wade Beresford's baby.

"Wait a couple of weeks," Pete smiled. "It could be stress. My mother used to get that when she was overworked at the school. She used to be a principal and they get more stressed than anyone."

Desney chuckled, wiping one side of her cheek with the back of her hand as she listened to the wise voice of late adolescence. Somehow, it felt like the voice of reason. "You're right," she nodded, feeling decisive about his solution. "This new storyline has got us all on edge. James won't even let us see the entire script until one week before filming. And there's been so many revisions, I think I'm feeling the strain."

"He's paranoid," Pete agreed. "I haven't seen him like this before."

"What about last year?" Desney asked, diverting her mind onto this new subject in the hope that she could momentarily forget her situation. "Did he behave like this when the storyline of Frederick's coma went down?"

"No," Pete admitted, "though that was big. The ratings shot up like never before."

Desney paused for thought, then patted Pete on the knee. "I think I'm ready to go back on set now before James starts sending out a search party."

Pete was most obliging and agreed to walk her there. Everyone was on the studio floor waiting for their cues when she returned. All the studio lights were adjusted and the sets and props were in place, though the camera operators were still setting up. Desney searched the floor for James. He was the only person missing.

She wanted to know how soon she could leave the studio and go home to telephone Tony Barbieri. Maybe he had heard from Wade, she thought. He was due back in three days. And besides, she needed time to ponder all the changes that having a baby would bring to her life.

When she finally caught sight of James, he looked explosive. There was nothing calm about him. Desney assumed that the producers upstairs hadn't approved his newest script changes. Then she experienced a pervading sense of doom when he marched directly toward her with a copy of *Bribe* magazine in his hand.

It was the latest edition. His body leaned forward as he displayed it to Desney. "How did your lover get this?" he demanded, spreading the copy wide open in front of her, then turning to display it to the entire studio floor.

It was a double-spread feature. Desney hadn't yet seen it, but of course she had approved the content. "I gave Wade Beresford an interview," she declared calmly. "I did tell you he was doing a rewrite."

"How much did he pay you?" James demanded savagely. "Ten thousand? Twenty?"

"I . . ." Desney was stumped. They had never discussed a fee. "It wasn't about money," she explained.

"Then pray, do tell. What *was* it about?" James shot back at the top of his voice. "Revenge? More fame? Or was it a lame, girlish crush to try and please him?"

Desney gasped. "My former marriage to Matt Doran is my own personal disclosure," she said angrily. "I wanted it out in the open."

"What?" The studio floor fell silent, all ears peaked as James glared at her. "You were married to Matt Doran?"

Desney shrugged her shoulders. "A long time ago," she said casually. "That is what we're talking about, isn't it?"

"Hell, no!" James railed, flapping his hands around like a butterfly, as though she were dim for not seeing the point. He thrust the magazine at her. "I'm shitting kittens because of this!"

Desney's eyes widened as she caught the headline: "COMA VICTIM IN DOUBLE MURDER PLOT."

"You leaked the story, didn't you?" James accused hotly. "After everything I said about Wade Beresford."

"This . . . this isn't the story I gave the magazine," Desney protested. "I . . ."

"Save it," James dismissed. "Your contract has just expired. You're fired."

"James," Desney implored, innocence marked across every feature of her face. "I'm not responsible for this." She flicked through the pages, alarmed at the old footage of Frederick in a coma on "It's a Wide World" and recent pictures of him in hospital. "This isn't the story I gave Wade. I don't know where *Bribe* got this."

"It cites you as the source," James pointed out in disgust. "Right there on page seventy-five."

Desney found her anxiety spiraling as she looked

around the studio floor. The accusing glances from each cast member were filled with shock. Even Pete, not daring to look at her, turned away to avoid her seeing the doubt in his eyes.

Flipping rapidly through the magazine, she found the commentary about an entirely new storyline: How Dr. Khumalo was going to get stabbed when he discovered her illicit love affair with Nick Palmer, and the key suspect would be none other than herself as Cinnamon Walker, with Nick also winding up dead.

James had only given them the restructured plot two weeks ago. It didn't take amazing powers of deduction to work out that there had been a story leak; that the magazine had known about the revised plot line all along. They knew that Matt was going to be axed, although only she and a few others may have been aware that he was on a three-month guest contract.

"I've been framed," she offered in defense, aware that she had just thrown out a classic soap line. "Why would I want to do this?"

"Name recognition," James said contemptuously. "You were a nobody before you joined this show. A few minor successes, a stint on Broadway, and the Hackney Empire. Nothing major until I gave you a part right here. I don't even want to look at you."

"James!" Desney was tearful. The nausea was attacking again, but she made a supreme effort to ignore it. "Don't embarrass me like this."

"The moment you began fraternizing with media scum, I knew we were heading for trouble," he warned, pointing a finger firmly at her. "You're in violation of clause 17B in your contract, which states clearly what can and cannot be disclosed to the media."

"I didn't tell him anything," Desney cried, searching the entire studio floor for even one friendly face.

But the looks of accusation did not soften. Shawnee faced her as though she had heard the worst news in the world; Matt simply hung his shoulders and turned his face away. The other supporting cast began to quietly disperse, as though wanting to forget that she existed. And James didn't want to hear any more excuses.

He glanced at his watch, then ignored her completely as he turned to Pete Hinchcliffe, his decision made. "Get the other writers down here now," he ordered. "And regroup the cast in the rehearsal hall in ten minutes. So help me God, we're going to do an emergency plot change." His gaze returned to Desney. "Feel free to take your dismissal upstairs to the producers, but somehow I think they'll side with me on this one."

"You're making a mistake," she objected proudly.

"Somehow, I don't think so," James returned, glowering at her as he stalked off the studio floor.

Desney turned toward Pete, but he was already going about his business. A few moments later, she stood rooted to the spot, utterly alone. The studio floor was completely dead. Desney looked around, disbelieving that Wade could do this to her. As far as she knew, the three-page feature she had approved was solely about her and nobody else. The only other party mentioned was Matt Doran, and even then she had been kind, never mentioning his indiscretion on how he had bilked her out of what little money she had inherited.

But somewhere between her approving the feature and its publication, she had been hoodwinked. A terrible thought crossed her mind. Wade suddenly disappearing abroad as he had done—was this all part of it, too? Had he really intended on betraying her like this, all for the sake of revealing a sensational story to boost sales?

It still didn't answer exactly where he had gotten

the story leak. Maybe another cast member had stolen the new script. It didn't detract from the truth though. Wade had stabbed her in the back, just as she knew he would. From where she was standing, the knife wound felt pretty deep. She felt like her career had just gone up in smoke.

When Desney returned to her dressing room to change, she was surprised to find Pete there, looking distraught. "I couldn't just walk away," he said tearfully, handing her the small card in his limp hands. "I wanted to give you this before you leave us all for good."

It was an old, worn card that she recognized instantly, the kind that often came attached to flowers. The inscription, "MR. ANONYMOUS" was clearly visible. Desney shook her head, distressed. "What is—"

"I was the one sending you the roses," he admitted bleakly. "You deserved them. I liked to see you smile. It used to make my day just to see you smile."

"Pete," Desney voiced weakly.

"I have to go now," he pressed, his voice filled with distress. "I don't think I can like you anymore."

He left, swinging the door hard behind him. Desney sank into her chair and wept. The tears came more out of disillusionment than anything else. That everyone could turn so easily against her without allowing her to explain. And the wrenching pain was hampered further by the knowledge that she could be pregnant by the one man responsible for it all.

In her mind, Wade Beresford had a lot to answer for. Why would he approve a completely new slant on her story without checking it with her first? And why would he disappear on a job abroad so hurriedly, had it not been because he knew about the volcanic eruption that was about to hit the newsstand?

And James. She sobbed even harder as she recalled

his face and the awful things he had said. If he had set out to humiliate her, he had certainly succeeded. She couldn't go back onto the studio floor now, even though she was expected to perform a screen kiss with Matt Doran. Obviously, James had canceled that now. If he was regrouping everyone in the rehearsal hall, that had to mean a last-minute plot change, and new lines probably, for fresh takes in the morning. If so, and if indeed her contract had been revoked, then that could only mean one thing. James was planning to kill Cinnamon Walker.

She wiped her eyes with the back of her hand, thinking that she may as well get dressed and go home, when there was a firm knock at her door. It was Matt Doran.

Desney saw red. "If you're here to gloat—"

"Love is rotten when it happens like this, the hard way," Matt interrupted, boldly admitting himself into the room. "You're going to need friends like me now that you're 'in between roles,' as they say."

"Out of work," Desney rebuffed.

"I just wanted to see that you're all right, that's all," he said smoothly, closing the door and leaning against it. He rubbed his jaw absently. "I have a theory," he began.

"Shouldn't you be in the rehearsal hall?" Desney said sharply, getting to her feet and leaning her weight on the high back of the chair to face him head-on. "Someone's playing silly games, and I just want to find out who it is."

"This has all the hallmarks of a Wade Beresford stunt," Matt said wryly. "You don't need to look any further."

He was probably right, she conceded. Wade had arranged the rewrite; only he had told her when the feature was due. And all the tangible evidence was printed among the pages of his magazine.

"I'm going home," Desney breathed, too sick to deal with it all. She reached for her clothes on an adjacent chair.

"You can't just walk out between takes," Matt said, blocking the door. "What about our debut—"

"Didn't you hear James say he's going to do a rewrite?" Desney reminded him. "That means I'm going to be cut from the cast, and you'll probably get a one-year contract."

Matt fell silent. "What are you going to do?"

Desney felt renewed strength suddenly fire up within her veins. "I'd like to tear down the House of Beresford," she countered angrily. "But I think a little visit to his office to find out who was paid for that feature will do instead."

Twelve

The British Broadcasting Corporation was the first breakfast network to call Cheryl on Monday morning. By the time she was on the phone to Desney, they had upped their financial offering for an exclusive TV interview in a bid against the rival early-morning program, "Loose Women."

Desney was in the same withdrawn state in which she had left the studio. Neither James nor any cast member had called. Instinctively they seemed to respect the barrier she had erected around herself, and left her well alone.

For three days she had hidden herself from the scrutiny of the world. Since the scene with James, a sense of affront and humiliation had festered deep inside her like a contagion. Even now she could still hear him deriding her, as the tears had scalded her eyes, his cruel words echoing in her head, emphatically blaming, growing in volume until her brain was full of it.

But somehow she did not lose control of herself. Each morning, she washed and dressed casually, mostly in jeans and a sweater, forgoing jogging in favor of television until she had seen a doctor. The doctor's appointment was not yet on her agenda, anyway. There was still a part of her that hadn't yet come to full terms with herself.

She ate moderately, not really preparing food, but stealing small snacks to ward off the bouts of nausea. And all the time, she had replayed James's sense of wrong, hating his paranoia and his eagerness to incriminate. As she saw it, she was being carried away by an evil Grand Inquisitor, but there was no one to hear or heed her protests of innocence; and so, fighting alone, she somehow had to free herself from capture.

She was startled by a continual jangling that suddenly invaded her silence, irritating her to the point that she had to pick up the telephone. She was convinced that it was her sister Rhea, calling from the Black Drug Workers Forum to say she had just read or heard about the coverage in *Bribe*. Or perhaps it was her parents from Grenada. She hadn't heard from them in a while. Shelagh, her younger sister, rarely called. She was too busy exploring the frontiers of law enforcement.

She knew that eventually somebody within her social and professional circle would call, so Cheryl's bubbly voice was not unexpected, though it did nothing to assuage the sullen atmosphere that had gradually filled her apartment over the past few days.

When Cheryl spoke, Desney was curled up in bed, the curtains drawn to shut out the world, the phone cradled to her ear. "I got the news from James. Why didn't you tell me?"

She heard the awkwardness in Cheryl's voice and absorbed it within herself. "I didn't think you would believe me," Desney explained. Her voice was husky, her throat dry from all the crying she had done.

"You could have given me the benefit of the doubt."

Desney's mouth twisted into a bitter smile. "Would it have made any difference?"

"Depends," Cheryl taunted, "on whether you want to do something about it."

Desney sat up slightly, her head propped up against two pillows. Poxy, her soft toy, was nestled against her stomach, where she held on to it for comfort, much as a child would. "What did James tell you?" she asked.

"Well, he was nettled," Cheryl began. "Said you sold the new story line to Wade Beresford for a handsome fee. I did try to tell him that I didn't think you'd do anything like that."

"And?"

"He said to let you know he'll want you back on set to do a final take on the show. Then Cinnamon Walker is going to disappear."

"I see."

"I did convince him not to kill the character," Cheryl added with encouragement. "It'll be you walking out on the family."

"What about the romance storyline he was setting up between Cinnamon Walker and Nick Palmer?" Desney inquired. Though she didn't welcome any liaison with Matt Doran, she needed to know all the same.

"That's been scrapped," Cheryl confirmed. "I did my best, Desney, but as your agent, even I'm not supposed to know this much. I cannot dictate what the scriptwriters do."

"You did your best," Desney agreed, cradling the phone tighter to her ear before adding quite cynically, "I suppose he was pleased that the ratings shot through the roof?"

She was, of course, referring to what she had read in the newspapers that morning. It had arrived with the mail, and there had been a postcard from Wade, too. She could hardly allow herself to read it, knowing that he was expected back in England that very day. He had betrayed her, yet something else was gnawing away at her, something she was fighting against and that added still more fuel to the fire.

The pregnancy test she had purchased on leaving the studio had proved positive. She was expecting Wade Beresford's baby, and every time she thought about it, she was overwhelmed with shame and embarrassment. How could she have been so stupid?

There was also the matter of her reputation. It was her consideration of this that had prompted her to take the test early, purchasing the most sensitive detector the pharmacy had. She was an actress who wanted to pursue her career further, and she had never been suspected of a cowardly or dishonest act before.

But now, it had been fatally compromised. The news of a baby by one of Britain's most controversial journalists would only pour more poison into the ears of many of her friends and acquaintances in the profession. Her love child could maliciously be used to break her heart.

In truth, and within the confines of her soul, she had already accepted that her heart very much belonged to Wade. She couldn't explain why she felt so calm, knowing he was still keeping his distance. But how could she face seeing him to tell him how much she had missed him, longed to be in his arms and to feel him deep inside her taking her into ecstatic oblivion, when it would be a betrayal of everything she believed in?

And yet she kept returning to the inescapable truth. Without Wade's love, she would simply cease to exist. As he had said, without love there is only existence. Wasn't that the most damning treachery of all?

For three long days and nights, these contradictory thoughts had paralyzed her brain. Combining that with what she realized was morning sickness, she was incapable of performing even the simplest chores. Her time and every passing thought were subordinated to the battle raging in her head. Should she see Wade? Shouldn't she see Wade? Should she tell him about the baby? Should she lie?

She had no clear idea what to do because she was dealing with a resourceful, ruthless man. He could either desert her or take command. Did he love her or had he played her for a fool to get his story? The thoughts were still whirling in her head without conclusion, when Cheryl burst into a paroxysm of laughter.

"Yeah, he was pleased with the ratings," she admitted.

"What happens now?" Desney asked, sounding downbeat. She hardly cared under the circumstances; her mind seemed to occupy a different dimension.

"First, James will be sending over a final script to you by courier, which he wants to shoot early on Sunday," Cheryl explained. "Then I suggest you do a talk show while the heat on this scandal is hot and vindicate yourself, if only for your reputation's sake."

Desney was silenced.

"As your agent," Cheryl reminded again, "I suggest you go with BBC. Conrad Waldorf is good, and they're paying the most and have the widest audience."

"When do they want—"

"Tomorrow morning," Cheryl cut in. "It'll just take a phone call and they'll have their standard contract 'round to me by lunchtime."

"What about Wade Beresford?" Desney's voice was cracking with emotion.

"People like Wade don't do anybody any favors," Cheryl rebutted harshly. "You're going to have to climb out of your ivory tower, stop dreaming about pretty bows and flowers, and recognize the real world, honeychile."

Desney's face felt tight with suppressed emotion. She reasoned in her head and quickly deduced that she was having a baby and was effectively now out of work. She would need the money. Wade may decide not to support her, and she had already decided she wasn't going to abort her child. She couldn't do to him what Teadra Lopez had done. An introspective look stole across her face as she adjusted to the situation, balancing the possible advantages of a BBC interview over the disadvantage of doing nothing at all.

Her courage had buckled when she had decided against visiting *Bribe*'s offices on leaving the studio three days ago, only to find herself vomiting at the curb instead. It was just as well she had gone straight home to deal with the suspicions that her body confirmed. She saw no reason trading salvos with Tony Barbieri, the monkey, when it was the organ grinder she had the beef with. At least this way, on live breakfast TV, she could offer her point of view and take the cash all the way to the bank.

"Set up the deal," she ordered Cheryl, after a half-minute's deliberation. "I'll do the Waldorf interview with BBC."

"Good," Cheryl applauded. "I'll see if I can trick James into sending over the latest clip of the soap."

"Are you still sleeping with him?" Desney blurted out as they concluded their conversation.

"He's still on the menu," Cheryl admitted cheerily. "And no," she added, as though sensing the calculations going on in Desney's brain. "I did not sell any pillow talk between James and me to *Bribe*, okay?"

"Okay," Desney replied.

The phone clicked dead and she clung to the handset for a few seconds. Then Desney tossed back the sheets. She was resolved; she would go down to Wade's office after all. If she were going to go on live TV in the morning, the least she could do was fish for information first. Wade had not told her exactly what time he was due back, or even whether he would be arriving during the morning, afternoon, or evening.

She hated such ambiguity in people. His only indicator was his postcard. It was eleven days old. Ironically, it should arrive on the day he was expected home. He had said he was well, that the weather was extremely hot, and that he had witnessed much of the fighting from news camps set up within close proximity. Her heart trembled when it occurred to her that he could have been killed. Perhaps he had been. Or, perhaps he had been wounded or injured. A lot could happen in eleven days.

She hurried to her wardrobe and pulled the louvered doors open. A striped gray skirt and white shirt with black Donna Karan jacket seemed suitable for the occasion. As Desney quickly dressed, mentally planning how she would style her hair, she had no thought of how she would react if she were to find him there.

The thought didn't really weigh on her mind until, having driven half-way across London, she found herself walking out of the elevator car onto the floor housing the suite of offices for *Bribe* magazine. The reception desk was unmanned, as it had been on the day she had first barged in there, so she breezed past it toward Wade Beresford's office

There was his name, still inscribed on the door where she stood, peering in to see who might be there. Wade would have to step up on security, she thought, considering all the people he must have upset during the short, illustrious life of the magazine.

She had just placed her fingers on the doorknob when a firm hand came down hard on her shoulders. "Looking for someone?" a harsh voice asked.

She turned to find herself facing Tony Barbieri. He hadn't changed much since the last time she saw him. His attire was very much the same, street-styled and menacing, his gold tooth still in place, his persona appearing as though he had just been sprung from jail. She had never thought to ask Wade where he recruited him.

"I was wondering whether Wade is back," she answered lightly. "He—"

"No, he isn't," Tony interrupted.

"When is he—"

"That's none of your concern," Tony snapped, with a conclusive tone. "Perhaps you'd like—"

"I won't be making an appointment," Desney cut him off. She was sorely tempted to add some innuendo about being the expectant mother of Wade's child, but better sense prevailed. "Just tell Wade I'd like him to call me about the matter in the current edition." She thought it was perhaps best to put over her concern politely, considering how Tony had been and still was so very much against her.

She was entirely unprepared for his outrageous attack. "You're nothing to Wade, do you know that?" he lashed out. "He doesn't really go for girls like you— air-brained bimbos with a habit."

"What?" She retreated back on her heels.

"I've got you pegged," he snorted in derision. "You're going to use him, just like the others. Whore!"

"How dare you!" Desney said, outraged, thinking that Tony could only be likening her to Teadra Lopez and perhaps the other women Wade had admitted into his life. "I don't know where you're going with this, but you can take it out of my face."

"Your face," Tony laughed. "That's all you girls have. A face. A man like Wade needs more than that, sugar. Do us both a favor, and leave him well alone."

Desney's scrutiny sharpened suddenly. Exactly what was Tony saying here? Was he implying that there was someone else vying for Wade's affections? She eyed him carefully, then bit her lip, rolling her car key nervously between her fingers. "Why would I want to leave him alone?" she asked. "We're lovers."

The last two words, she noted, fell hard on Tony's ears. He seemed to shrink back into himself at this revelation. "You're kidding me." His voice went weak. "You're a liar," he added, as though denying it would make it untrue.

Desney felt unsure of what she had just been pulled into. Instinct warned her that maybe she should be making plans for a getaway. "I have to go," she stammered, looking at her watch.

Tony seemed unable to accept that. "You're going nowhere," he said, holding firmly onto her arm. "I want to talk to you."

"No." She looked around, seeing no one around who could help, though Tony's raised voice seemed to suggest to the workforce that he was perhaps escorting her off the premises. They were probably used to it, she thought, seeing actors, actresses, and other celebrities burst through the doors of *Bribe,* enraged over some sordid feature or other. It probably explained Tony's appearance, why he needed to look so predatory and harmful. "We don't have anything to talk about," she answered firmly.

"I think we do," Tony mustered, ushering her forcefully into Wade's office.

It looked the same as when she had last been there, every piece of wall space filled with *Bribe* covers, with two more additions. The imposing steel desk in the center of the room and the mesh chairs were also as before. Even Wade's popcorn bowl was evident, though it was empty.

The doors were glass, Desney reminded herself with relief, so Tony could hardly expect to murder her or cause her any injury without at least someone being aware of what was going on. "What do you want?" she demanded.

Tony walked the length of the room toward Wade's desk and leaned his bulky frame against the corner of the steel desk. He folded his arms and contemplated Desney warily as she stood facing him in the middle of the room close to the door. At least she had an escape route, she thought, looking directly into his watchful expression.

"Wade needs me," he said. "I look after him and pay attention to his every requirement."

Desney shrugged her shoulders. "Is this going somewhere?"

"I want you to leave him alone," Tony blurted out.

Desney paused, pondering the statement. Shock suddenly registered on her face as the enormity of the news began to sink in. "You're gay?" she asked.

"Queer as a football bat," Tony bragged. "And Wade is mine."

"Wade isn't like that," Desney gasped weakly. *He can't be,* she prayed. Not this wonderfully intimate man who would soon be the father of her child.

"You don't know him like I do," Tony went on. "Just leave him to me."

Desney stood staring at him for several long seconds. She couldn't possibly be hearing what she was hearing. It seemed ludicrous. Unreal. She was certain she had just been thrust into the Twilight Zone, to an alternate universe where such things could be. "I don't believe you." Her voice bore out in the shattering of her illusions. "You're lying."

The tears had just begun to well up in her eyes when she heard the door behind her open. She did not turn. Her face was still fixed on Tony, disbelieving everything he had said. But on doing so, she saw that his eyes had moved upward above her head, and then sideways as the newcomer advanced into the room.

"Desney!" The voice was familiar.

She turned instantly and gasped as if she had seen a ghost. She felt a sense of *déjà vu* on finding Wade standing there before her like a miraculous aberration, handsomely dressed in a gray suit, white shirt, and maroon tie, his face cleanshaven, and holding a briefcase in his hand. His hair was pulled back and tied at the back like he always had it, and a wide smile was planted firmly on his face as he tossed his briefcase to the floor and rushed head-on toward her like a footballer about to score a goal.

Desney felt herself crushed to him instantly. The hug was familiar, too—intimate, warm, and genuine. Everything within her reciprocated, and she flung her arms around his neck and inhaled the full, clean scent of him. She could hardly believe he had been away. The weeks seemed to fall away the moment he rubbed his cheek against hers. And when he pulled her from him slightly to look down into her tear-streaked face, she recognized all the features of her dashing buccaneer: the green-brown eyes, dark brows, square jaw line and the cleft at his chin, all set off beautifully by his honey brown skin.

Even the monkey grin, wide and wonderfully inviting, made her promptly forget the godawful things Tony Barbieri had just said to her. "Hello, stranger," she smiled, her heart pumping so fast she could hardly contain it. "I . . . I . . ."

The tears fell unexpectedly. They were tears of relief, but compounded with everything that had gone on while he was away, everything that she had yet to deal with, and the more pressing matter of Tony being in the room. But Wade was oblivious to all this.

He simply took Desney into his arms and pulled her mouth into his.

The kiss fired his soul immediately. He had waited three weeks to taste Desney again. He couldn't wait to tell her of his amazing adventures, of the people he had met, the suffering he had seen, the terrible circumstances of a country torn by war. The experience was a life-changing one. For the first time in his life, Wade had seen a side of life that made him realize there were many other ventures to strive for other than just those within the purview of his magazine.

But all those matters were pushed to the back of his mind as their kiss deepened to fill every vacant crevice within his body that had longed to be touched again by the feelings only Desney could give him. Three weeks without holding her, twenty-one days deprived of her voice, her scent, the sound of her laughter. The time seemed eternal.

This is the one, he had told himself time and time again. She was the one who would enrich his life, bear his children, become his companion and lifelong friend. And he couldn't wait to tell her. He was eager to let her know. But again, all thoughts were washed away as his mouth moved seductively against hers.

Then the thought bore in on him—the possibility that she was pregnant. Nothing about the way she was kissing him suggested anything. He sensed some reserve, but that was to be expected. And her lips were trembling, but then again, so were his. Her body felt the same, too, as his hands moved along her curves and contours. She looked gorgeous, as usual, so there were no signs there either.

He liked her hair like this, pulled back from her face. And the striped gray skirt and white shirt were fetching against her walnut brown complexion, complimented by her black jacket. She appeared more businesswoman than TV icon, and the sense of this new dimension revved his pulse rate as his tongue caressed hers.

Desney's taut thread of tension snapped again. Only Wade's kisses had the ability to do this. He was truly a man who knew how to push all her buttons. But as much as she needed his kisses, as much as she wanted this moment of loving him never to end, she was painfully aware of Tony's presence in the room. She tried to still her lips as a sign that she wanted to pull away.

Wade sensed the finality and lifted his head. He was surprised, as Desney, when they found Tony Barbieri standing next to them. His face was enraged, his arms akimbo at his hips.

"Get your hands off my man," he demanded, pushing Desney forcefully away. She stumbled two steps back but was able to catch her balance.

"Man, what's wrong with you?" Wade derided. "What's going on."

"He says he's—"

"Wade you know I love you," Tony interrupted suddenly. "I always have. I—"

"Wait a minute." Wade put more distance between himself and Tony by walking over to where Desney was standing. "I'm not that way," he said sternly. "You know that."

Tony was devastated. "Is it because of her?" He pointed directly at Desney.

"I like women. *Just* women," Wade countered, his face still showing his shock. "She's special. This one I want to be—"

"You can't do this to me," Tony persisted. "After everything I've done for you; the way I've kept this magazine afloat while you were gone."

"That's your job as assistant editor," Wade declared

firmly. "I'm straight. I don't know what else you want me to say."

Tony's anger grew. Desney could see it in the changing features of his face. "I made you!" he screamed at Wade, his voice now bordering on hysteria. "Even now I've got your magazine selling double, triple the copies it normally does."

"That'd be the coverage on Desney which has contributed to that," Wade reminded him, turning toward her and holding her wrist, which only served to rile Tony further. "We agreed on the Matt Doran feature."

"Haven't you heard?" Tony spat out. He looked at Desney. "Tell him, honey."

Desney was surprised. She had thought that Wade had been behind the latest coverage, but it appeared he knew nothing at all about it. "There's a coverage in *Bribe* about Frederick's coma, and an entire story leak from 'It's a Wide World.' "

"What?" Wade's eyes widened with the news. His eyes roamed across Desney's innocent features and strayed toward Tony. "You two concocted this?" he asked.

"No," Desney cut in. "I only found out three days ago, and James fired me on the spot."

"You're fired?" His gaze moved accusingly at Tony. "How did we get the story?"

"I did it for you," Tony yelled.

"How did we get the story?" Wade insisted.

"Tip off," Tony declared. "I thought you'd be pleased. I did it to get her out of your life."

He was being amazingly honest, Desney thought as she contemplated Tony's bare-faced audacity in explaining everything so forthrightly. The turmoil of it all made her want to sit down. She pulled her wrist from Wade and inclined her head toward a chair. He quickly obliged by pulling one of the steel mesh chairs forward and watched as Desney slumped her body into it.

She felt nauseated again, another reminder that she was suffering from morning sickness. But at that moment, it seemed nothing compared to the rapid-fire revelations coming of Tony.

"Are you telling me you planned all this?" Wade seethed, resting his hands firmly against the back of Desney's chair.

"Whatever," Tony relented without concern.

Wade shook his head. He was totally unprepared for what he had returned to find. "Who gave the tip off?" he demanded. "I want his guts for garters."

"He's cool, he's cool," Tony said lightly.

Wade took a menacing step forward, stopping between where Tony stood and where Desney was seated. "If you're going to override one of my decisions on a feature that I approved," he said in a deadly tone, his mild accent a little more pronounced than usual, "the least I expect is to know who gave the tip-off and how much we bloody coughed up to pay him from the coffers, considering I didn't offer any money to Miss Westbourne."

"I got the tip-off from Frederick Fitzgerald," Tony admitted at last, his voice slightly frightened.

"Frederick!" Desney gasped in unison with Wade.

"It was before I heard he got rushed into the hospital with a coma," Tony concluded.

Wade's eyes narrowed. "When was the last time you saw him?"

Tony became fidgety, beginning to move nervously around the room. "Man, it was early in the morning, at the studio where he works."

"At Elstree?" Wade asked, astonished.

"Yeah," Tony nodded. "He wanted us to meet early,

real early. Said he had a copy of the latest script for me."

"Was that on the morning he got rushed into hospital?" Desney asked suspiciously, looking up at Tony.

"What's it to you?" Tony lashed out. "I ain't the one who did it. Of course, when I heard about it, I embellished the feature a little. I remembered an old plot 'It's a Wide World' did, and sort of merged the whole thing together."

Wade was silent, disbelieving. "You did all this for me?"

"I thought you'd be pleased," Tony trembled. "I love you. We always said we were going to do great things together. Break huge stories. Big, career-making stuff that would break a celebrity right out of the water."

"It's done that, all right," Wade groaned. "Miss Westbourne's been fired because of it."

"I don't need this kind of rejection," Tony bristled, feeling sorry for himself. He looked so weak and insecure, Desney quite rightly felt sorry for him, too. "You left me under so much pressure," he wailed.

"Do you know how this looks?" Wade raged. "We could be in the middle of a murder."

"Frederick's out of his coma," Desney interjected. "I haven't heard anything since I last saw him, though he's still suffering from amnesia."

"Amnesia!" Tony mouthed, halting his pacing.

Wade's eyes narrowed even further. "Did you two fight before you left the studio?" he inquired in a stern voice. "Did you hit Frederick Fitzgerald with anything?"

"I never touched him, I swear," Tony whined. "He was walking around when I left him. He took the whole five thousand in cash, too."

"You paid him five thousand quid?" Wade blazed, suddenly seeing red.

"It was an exclusive rewrite of the script," Tony chimed. He didn't seem to have any qualms at all about what he'd done. "It was worth the fee."

"Get out," Wade said, his face full of rage. "Just . . . get . . . out."

Tony's face pleaded. "Wade, Honey, don't do this to us."

"Tony." Wade's voice lowered to an even deadlier tone. Desney felt the chill of it from where she sat. "If I find you on these premises in five seconds, my hands will be around your neck. I said get out." He reeled out a long litany in Italian, and Desney lost the meaning, if not the intent.

"You're putting *her* over *me?*" he shrilled. There was no shame in the man.

"I'm doing more than that," Wade declared harshly. "I'm going to marry her. Now just leave us alone."

"It's your loss, man," Tony whimpered. "You keep her. It's all good. I can find somebody else. I don't need you. I don't . . ." He was muttering all manner of maledictions as he left the room.

But Desney wasn't listening. What she had heard was the word *marry*. It seemed to hang in the air like an angel's halo. Something sparkled about that one word as she turned her face up and looked at Wade.

But his eyes had grown angry. There was no vestige in his face of what he had just said. Wade's mind had dropped into overdrive. "I don't believe what I've come back to," he railed. "This . . . Tony . . . the article. What's going on?"

"And welcome home, too," Desney said with the hint of a smile.

Wade glanced at her. "Darling, I'm sorry." He walked over to her and pulled her out of the chair.

Facing her, he snuggled her against his chest, inhaling the scent of her hair. "I didn't plan to see you like this," he muttered weakly. "The plan was to pop in here, see Tony, and then rush over and take you into my arms." He planted a kiss on the top of her head. "But this!"

"You didn't know about Tony?" Desney asked, concerned, her cheek pressed hard against his chest where she could feel the thudding of his heart.

"Hell, no!" Wade railed. "I don't suffer fools lightly, but . . ." He was obviously still digesting the twists and turns of it all. "I'm going to have to talk to him. He should've gone to the police about Frederick. How is he?"

"As I said, he's out of his coma, but he can't remember anything," Desney verified, content that she could now put everything Tony had told her entirely from her mind.

Wade hugged her closer. "God, it's so good to feel you again," he gasped, rubbing his hands over her arms and shoulders. "Having you near me arouses my flesh, speaks to my spirit, and rocks my soul. I don't know what I would do without you."

Desney shook with pent-up emotion. "I kept telling myself you couldn't have been behind that story," she told him quietly.

"You thought I would do something like that to you?" Wade asked in wonder.

"I don't know what I was thinking," she admitted shakily. "My mind was on a roller coaster of denials and blame. And James, he's been horrendous."

"He was the one who fired you?"

"Yes," Desney went on. "At the time, I felt that you were responsible."

"But we agreed on the feature before I left for Africa," Wade objected, his voice quaking as though pained. "Why couldn't you trust me?"

"I don't know," she replied, her own voice weak. "The last three days were heartbreaking, but I did, in my heart, trust you in the end. I kept believing in the promise that you made me, and somehow that got me through."

"That I'd come back to you?"

"Yes."

Wade rubbed a reassuring hand up and down her back. "Now do you believe me?" he breathed hoarsely. "I could never hurt you."

"More than anything," Desney admitted, recalling his mention of marriage, but feeling unsure of whether to remind him of it. It still felt almost surreal having heard him mention it in the first place. "How was Sierra Leone?" she asked.

"It was hot," he drawled. "And you should see the conditions these people live in. So filthy. They have nothing, Desney. Just their dignity."

She picked up on the sorrowful tone in his voice. "You worried for them, didn't you?" she swallowed, placing her arms around his waist and hugging him closer in a comforting way.

"It made me think," Wade exclaimed, his thoughts now in a different gear. "What function do we serve? Why am I here? You were right, sweetheart. I'm not breaking news. *Bribe* is trivia. It's fashionably sleazy gossip and intrusion. And look at the trouble it's gotten me in. Tony was on a one-man crusade to impress me. I don't mind what he is. I just wish he would've told me. I've known him since I was twenty years old."

Desney felt his fists clench behind her in white rage. "He didn't tell you and you didn't suspect," she assayed calmly. "He'd brought me in here to tell me to leave you alone."

"What?" Wade thrust her from him gently. "He didn't hurt you did he?"

"No," Desney assured him, recalling that members of his staff could just vaguely see through the glass doors from their work spaces.

"I'm sorry," Wade gasped, working both hands across Desney's shoulders. "I don't know what's happening anymore. Sometimes, I feel like I'm a barge drifting down the river, going nowhere. I finally decide to do something constructive with my life, and people . . . Tony . . . there's always someone trying to mess it up."

"Don't let them," Desney said, gazing into his green-brown eyes. The desire for her was still there; she could see it. It warmed her inside, knowing that they still wanted each other, knowing that three weeks had only made their hearts grow stronger.

Wade looked at her thoughtfully. "I've bought you a present," he said lightly. "But it's at home. Why don't you come back with me. We can catch up on . . . everything."

The innuendo felt so sweet and delicious to Desney, she couldn't say no. "I'd like that," she said. It would also give them the opportunity to talk. Being in his home might also give her the opportunity to tell him about her present condition.

Thirteen

The advent of December made the village look different. It was 3:00 when Desney's car arrived in the driveway just behind Wade's car. The trees were now bare, the countryside around was discolored, and the church in the distance appeared much closer than it had before.

Desney followed Wade into the house and kicked off her shoes. Taking refuge on his sofa while he took her jacket, she watched as he switched on the TV and inquired whether she wanted a cup of tea.

"I'll take some warm milk," she told him with a smile. Lately, it had been the only thing that calmed the nausea of morning sickness.

Wade's brows rose at her suggestion, but he did not question it, just hung up her jacket and disappeared into the kitchen. The silence around her made Desney turn on the TV. Ironically, an episode of "It's a Wide World" was airing. Her heart stirred as Shawnee's face, dressed smartly in her nurse's uniform, zoomed up in front of her.

She missed being on set. Although the three days since her last visit there had passed almost timelessly, her heart still fell when she thought of all the energy she was missing. Of course, there was the chance for her to remedy all that with her BBC interview in the morning. It would perhaps be her only chance of vindicating herself.

That was no guarantee that James would give her her job back once she revealed who had really sold *Bribe* the story leak.

Frederick Fitzgerald, she reminded herself again, appalled that he could've stooped to such a level. She could only imagine that the motive was one of vengeance. His impotent rage at James's plans to remove him. And the £5,000 fee would certainly go far alleviating his sense of wrong.

Wade arrived back in the room with the hot milk and handed it to her on a saucer. Desney looked up at him and took it carefully, the smile still on her face as he glanced over at the TV.

"Watching your favorite soap," he said with a grin. He removed his jacket and threw it behind the sofa.

Desney chuckled as she tasted the sweet warmth. "It's the best there is," she returned.

He sat down beside her and rubbed the back of his hand against her cheek. She seemed to look a little pale suddenly. "You okay?"

Desney smiled. The feel of his strong fingers against her soft cheek was soothing as it was comforting. "Just a little tired," she answered. "Nothing to worry about."

He nodded. "I think I'm still a little jet lagged. I got into London just after five-thirty this morning."

"You haven't slept yet?" Desney asked, surprised.

"I took a nap on the plane. I just wanted to check out the office and see you." His smile widened. "It feels so good to have you here."

Desney took a large gulp of the warm milk before answering. "It's a wonderful home. Very traditional, and so rural."

"I love the country," he said calmly, bending down

to unbuckle his shoes. Kicking them off, he relaxed more comfortably against the sofa and breathed a long sigh of relief. "It's calming." He closed his eyes and Desney glanced over at him. The light made him look a little more gray around his hairline, but it wasn't evident unless you looked closely. Still, it made her realize that he was more worried about things than she had surmised.

"Did you visit Abidjan?" she asked.

"We went there," Wade confirmed, his eyes still closed. "The circumstances of the people were the same as they were in Sierra Leone. All they have is their faith. But we got the Major Abu story."

"The former defense minister," Desney recalled. "That's great. What was it?"

"He didn't escape. He had instructed his wife to move out of Sierra Leone and into Abidjan before the West Africa peacekeeping force, ECOMOG, intervened and started the war," he explained. "So she did. She escaped to Cote d'Ivoire with the sum of twelve million U.S. dollars hidden in a trunk."

"What?" Desney laughed. "So it wasn't twenty-five million in gold bullion?"

"No." Wade opened his eyes briefly and looked at her. "She placed it all in a security vault in Cote d'Ivoire, but now she doesn't know how to get the money out without security vault officials becoming suspicious."

"What is she going to do?"

"Well, the money belongs to the state of Sierra Leone," Wade explained, closing his eyes again and leaning back deeper into the sofa. "But she believes that the money belongs to her husband."

"And where's he?"

"They shot him two months ago," Wade concluded.

Desney shrieked. "I see." She sipped her milk. "So why are you interested in the story now?"

"There's a rumor that this General Kabuda has mandated some of his loyalists to search for her and Major Abu's son. They want to retrieve what she calls the family treasures.' "

"Did they find her and her son?"

"No."

Desney sighed in relief. "I'd hate to think that they'd kill a woman and her child."

"They would," Wade confirmed.

"Then I hope they never find her," she said, sipping the last of her milk.

"We did," Wade declared mildly, opening his eyes again. "In a refugee camp in Cote d'Ivoire."

Desney smiled. "And you got your story?"

He nodded and watched Desney place the milk cup and saucer on the floor. It was the break he was waiting for. Wade leaned forward and pulled her closer. "I want to take you to bed," he whispered.

His green-brown eyes ensnared her and she was instantly captured. "Mmm," she moaned and leaned into him, accepting the mouth that met hers. The kiss was deep and sweet and filled her mouth with the promise of eternal fulfillment, love, and sincerity. And then Wade was on his feet, picking her up like a babe in arms.

She laughed as he carried her through the sitting room door and into the hallway, before taking the stairs two at a time. He bore her weight effortlessly, pausing twice to savor her lips before venturing on again. At last she was in a room with a king-sized bed and windows so large they overlooked the entire meadow at the back of the house.

The view was breathtaking, Desney noted, as he placed her on the bed among lemon-colored sheets with little lime green speckles. She could see the threat of rain on the horizon coming in among the overcast clouds, casting varying dark shades across the room, but in no way spoiling the bright yellow design of the walls, carpeting, and bedroom fabric, set against the beautifully carved pieces of black Italian furniture.

"Nice room," she approved with a giggle.

Wade loosened his tie and lay down beside her, propping himself up on one elbow. With deliberation he traced a finger down the center of her chest, resting it on the top button of her white blouse. "I'm going to undress you slowly," he declared in a hoarse whisper. "Starting with this button right here."

Desney trembled as he unbuttoned it without effort. First one and then another. And another, until he was spreading the blouse at either side of her waist. Her lacy bra was revealed to his hungry gaze. "You want this, don't you?" He suddenly seemed unsure.

Desney nodded and reached out to loosen his tie a little more. It was all the consent Wade needed. He pulled her into him and took her mouth in a hot, wet, bruising kiss. His eyes were filled with desire as he gently pushed her into the mattress, the kiss deepening as he felt her ignite beneath him.

His fingers worked their way around the flesh of her waist, into the blouse and behind her back to loosen the clasp of her bra. Desney let out a moan as she felt the bra release her breasts and Wade's hands cup them from the sides. His warm touch against her hard nipples had her gasping for breath, her body straining upward and toward him as he rolled one brown bud between his finger and thumb.

Then, as his lips left her mouth to reach for that same nipple, her mind drifted dreamily as he took it into his mouth and slowly licked and sucked on it, as if it were something sweet. Desney inhaled deeply, hazily, surfacing and submerging back into oblivion.

Her arousal grew, and she panted as Wade transferred his attentions to the other nipple and performed the same, exciting process of tasting it, rolling it, and darting his tongue around the peaked, hardened area until she wanted to scream for mercy.

His mouth claimed hers again, smothering that very plea as his caressing arms enfolded her against the sculpted hardness of his chest, molding her into each sinewy curve until the desire and wanting took her over completely. Wade's body instinctively responded to the feel of Desney's hands down his spine, shivers of delight coursing through him as his mouth opened to the intimacy of her kiss, a feeling of hard possession sweeping over him as her tongue invaded and told him that he was wanted. Needed. Truly missed.

It spoke to him as never before. He had to make this woman his. He wanted her to be pleasured. His every impulse demanded that he make love to her, and he responded to the urge so primal, so innately a part of him, he neither challenged nor questioned why.

His eyes glittered deep green as he knelt and undressed. She missed none of it, remaining still and watchful, waiting until he was fully unclothed before he began the agreeable task of removing every item from her body.

Desney's skin was a flawless walnut brown, unmarked by any blemish but the small birthmark by her ear. Wade began to kiss her thighs in earnest, loving their taste and silken texture.

And then he was licking her, kissing her, playing a wonderful teasing game with his tongue around her most sensitive areas. That forced her head back onto his pillows and to quietly beg to become one with him. Wade always seemed to heighten the sexual tension, even when he reached for his condom and applied it in the artful, disciplined way that made Desney's heart warm in awe of just how careful he had consistently been.

When he finally joined her to him, the possession was a new kind. Deep inside her, all portals invaded, she felt rekindled anew with the fire that took them both to a new plateau completely. Totally spent, their emotions ragged, Wade withdrew and buried his head into Desney's chest.

He felt at peace against the softness of her flesh and inhaled the salty scent of her sweat, having decided that he was going to make Desney his. Perhaps this would be the best time to ask her, he thought, raising his head slightly.

"I want us to get married," he blurted out suddenly, then closed his eyes, wishing he had worded it differently. "I mean," he offered Desney a wide monkey grin, "will you do me the honor of being my wife?"

Desney chuckled, finding the whole line of questioning funny. "You weren't expecting to do that?" she said knowingly.

Wade chuckled beneath his breath. "Let's just say I should've rehearsed it." He paused to search her face for an answer. "And?"

Desney smoothed a stray, tangled lock of hair over his shoulder, quivering with excitement as she searched his face. The love was there. She saw it in all its glory. He didn't need to say it. She knew. As she was sure he knew of her love, too. It had crept up on them like a fog in the night, with neither of them asking for it or even aware of it until Wade's journey to Sierra Leone had parted them, proving their dire need of each other.

"How long shall I give it?" she teased.

"How long should you give what?" Wade asked, curious.

"To think about it," Desney answered, her tone intriguing. "Half an hour, ten minutes?"

"What time is it now?"

"Three fifty-seven."

"Give it until three fifty-eight."

Desney giggled until a full minute had passed. Then, propping herself on one elbow, she turned to face Wade and she said, "Yes. I will marry you."

He crushed her into his arms and she smiled. Under the present circumstances, she didn't want to tell him about the baby. The moment, she felt, belonged to them, to their commitment to one another. And it was such a beautiful moment. Perfect.

As she lay against Wade's arms and he pulled the sheets over them to keep warm, she could see through the large windows that it had begun to rain. The clouds had opened and were pouring down onto the world all their burden. And she heard the wind, too, shifting with the rain. Seeing the wide meadow in front of her, where Wade's house hid among the spreading oaks and lofty poplars, she felt sated and happy, though she knew it would be short-lived.

Tomorrow was the BBC interview. She had yet to tell Wade about it. She would do that later, maybe after they'd eaten and before she returned home. There was still the call to Cheryl for details about when and where she should be, her timetable, and what to wear.

But she thrust those things from her mind and thought only of Wade as he drifted contentedly into sleep and she pressed her body closer to him.

It was 7:30 that evening when Desney returned angrily to her apartment. She and Wade had argued. It was a case of "Why didn't you tell me this earlier?" against "I didn't think it would be anything to do with you."

Of course they were debating her upcoming breakfast TV interview on the Conrad Waldorf show. Wade had been totally against it. They had awoken at 5:00 and spent two hours debating before she decidedly left and came home. Her stomach was now complaining because she had refused to let him make her something to eat.

"But you haven't been talked through it by anyone," he had argued, his face beginning to show the signs of his jet lag. "You might end up incriminating rather than vindicating yourself."

"I have no choice," she replied. "I'll take my chances."

Her answering machine was flickering, and when she pressed the button, she heard Cheryl leaving all the details she required. Cheryl had said it would be fine, but Wade evidently did not trust the agent because he knew about her affair with James Wallace, and he told Desney so. She couldn't say she was surprised. It was his job to know such things.

"You could be walking into a trap," he added as food for thought. "There's no knowing what questions they're going to ask you."

"I'll pre-check it all with Cheryl," she assured him.

She was still thinking about this when the intercom buzzer leapt into action.

"Who is it?" Desney inquired.

"Courier Express."

That'd be the revised script, she thought as she pressed the release button. It was. She tipped the courier and ripped open the envelope as he departed. Yellow pages met her gaze. James always had his final amendments printed on this color paper as an alert to all the cast members and the executive producers upstairs, that there would be no further changes.

She flicked through the pages, noting the new storylines, deletions, and additions for episode 108. As she did so, she placed the script on her kitchen counter while she made soup to settle her stomach, reading as she went. Ten minutes later, the soup tasted just fine, but her lines did not.

While slowly sipping the broth at the kitchen counter, reading edit #11C, Desney quickly recognized that Cinnamon Walker was not going to have a walk-off part after all. She was expected to OD on crack cocaine on a grotty urban sidewalk. The shoot was scheduled for Thursday.

Desney's senses screamed at the revelation. James was being harder than she could ever have expected. The soup suddenly tasted sour in her mouth. Her sister Rhea had nearly OD'd once upon a time. Desney didn't feel she would have a problem reenacting her memories to play the role. That was not what was bothering her.

What she found upsetting was James's ability to do this knowing that she had done nothing and that there were at least six months outstanding on her current contract. The fact that he had even been given the go-ahead confirmed the backing of the producers upstairs. She wanted to scream at the sense of betrayal.

The need to absolve herself felt stronger than ever. Wade couldn't possibly understand how she was feeling. He had just gone through an adventure of his own in Sierra Leone. In her mind, he had not yet shifted gears to absorb her present circumstances.

She pondered that thought as she lay alone in bed that night. *What a home coming,* she mused, her anger abating only when the image of Wade appeared in her head. Her heart went out to him. The fact that they had quarreled on his first day back home upset her, but she had just wanted him to understand. He hadn't called, so he was probably still angry at her, was probably thinking to himself that he couldn't believe what kind of day it had been.

Desney decided against picking up the phone herself, thinking it best to give him time and space to assimilate all the information. She made a firm decision instead. Tomorrow morning she would go on breakfast TV and tell the truth.

Her name was Kelly and she was enthused.

She smiled. Even when Desney did not reciprocate, she continued to smile. A solid block of enthusiasm; that's what the girl was.

"I can't believe it's really you," she trilled, smiling even wider as she led Desney down the corridor to a small, empty room backstage. Kelly flickered through a pad in her hand before adding, "Conrad Waldorf will be interviewing you at . . . eight thirty-five. Would you like something to drink?"

Desney gazed into flashing blue eyes. There was nothing about this girl that was not vivacious. "Water will be fine," she accepted.

Another smile and the girl disappeared. Desney looked around her. The room was small and drafty. She shivered slightly as her gaze caught sight of white-painted brick walls, an open window, and the lingering scent of smoke. A steel ashtray filled to the brim with cigarette butts lay on a wall bench facing her, next to which was a wooden chair—the only chair.

Hardly the Ritz, Desney thought as she took a seat, glaring with distaste at the bare wooden floor. She had heard that the BBC was not renowned for its room decor. Dressed formally in a beige Dries Van Noten trouser suit, white blouse, and brown ankle boots, she looked the picture of confidence, though inside she was a bag of nerves. Cheryl was expected at any minute, and she knew if anyone could calm her nerves, it would be Cheryl. But she would rather it be Wade.

He still hadn't called, even though he knew of her plans that morning. She had gotten up, dressed, applied heavy makeup to her ragged profile for the sake of the cameras, styled her hair elaborately in intricate African twists, and left her apartment after picking up the phone just once—Cheryl checking that she was on her way out the door.

She couldn't resist telling her agent about her engagement to Wade, though the retelling was brief.

There was a knock at the door and Cheryl breezed in. She was a picture of misery. "Oh you're there," she muttered in annoyance. "We've been looking all over for you."

"We?" Desney asked. "I just got here."

Wade Beresford walked in behind her. Desney's heart raced the moment she saw him. He was the last person she expected to see that morning. "What are you doing here?" she gasped in surprise as he walked over to within inches of her, and towering like an Egyptian statue, took hold of her hand.

He was smitten by her appearance. His heartbeats went from a trot to a gallop on seeing how beautiful Desney looked. "I was thinking about your sense of justice and decided that you needed my support," he said, his gaze at once penetrating and apologetic.

Desney took in his presence: the dark blue suit that made him appear so majestic, the gleaming black shoes, the pristine white shirt and blue patterned tie, and the hair that hung in loose locks around his shoulders, making him look even sexier than ever before.

Her eyes glittered in response, telling him so. "I'm so happy you're here."

Cheryl's sarcastic voice intruded. "When you two lovebirds have finished," she gibed, "I'd like to go through the procedure with Desney."

Desney reared back in her chair, slightly embarrassed. "Okay," she smiled, switching her gaze from Wade to Cheryl, encouraged. "Take me through it."

Her water arrived, and Conrad Waldorf himself popped his head around the door twice before she was finally asked to leave the backstage room and have a seat among the suite of comfortable sofas in front of the cameras.

The lights were much brighter than what she was accustomed, and the set was smaller. Budget was obviously a consideration. But of course the BBC accepted no commercial advertising and was funded entirely by the viewing public via a TV license, often dodged by many who hated coughing up the fee.

"Am I all right here?" she asked one of the stage hands.

"You're fine," he nodded.

Kelly was on hand again, this time in her capacity as floor assistant. "Do you feel comfortable?" she enthused. "The cushions are not swallowing you?"

"I'm just fine," Desney replied softly.

The smile grew wider. "I still can't believe it's you," she insisted, wide-eyed. "You make my heart bleed for Cinnamon Walker. But she's going to win through, isn't she? I just know she is."

Desney nodded and strained to catch a glimpse of Wade and Cheryl, who were standing off-stage, but within her view. He waved and she inclined her head. Conrad Waldorf, all silvery hair, glasses, and a modest suit, now joined her, seating himself within knee-touching distance.

"The cameras roll in two minutes," he said, with a friendly smile, offering a well-manicured handshake. "Don't worry, we'll take it as it goes."

Desney smiled courteously as Kelly made her exit. Another set of lights seemed to dim suddenly, and Desney realized that the cameras had jumped into action. There was an autocue for Conrad's introduction. Desney swallowed.

They were on.

"Hi. I'm Conrad Waldorf. Welcome to another morning with 'Waldorf Breakfast TV.' I'm here with 'It's a Wide World' star actress Desney Westbourne. We'll be talking about her controversial role as Cinnamon Walker and her latest revelation that she was once married to guest star Matt Doran, as well as discussing fresh rumors about Frederick Fitzgerald, who plays Dr. Khumalo. All that, coming up right after the news."

And cue. The cameras switched and the news desk kicked in. Conrad turned toward Desney and patted her knee. "You okay?"

She smiled a little nervously. "I think so." She nodded her head to assure herself. A fresh glass of water was placed on the small teak-colored table in front of her, which was strewn with all the morning's newspapers. She reached down and took a sip from the glass.

"We're back on in two minutes," Conrad prompted, quite friendly. "Anything you want to ask me?"

Desney shook her head and smiled. She had already prepared herself to "take it as it goes." She glanced quickly across at Wade, standing backstage next to Cheryl, and smiled as he threw her a reassuring wink. Knowing he was close was all the consolation she needed.

She relaxed a bit more with Conrad's genial banter, hardly noticing the moment the cameras switched. Desney blossomed, easing into her public mode and presenting herself smoothly for an immaculate performance. She told Conrad about her childhood ambitions, about growing up in London, the Italia Conti Stage School, and Matt Doran. She told him about the annulment, her years in New York, and her first acting job, and about how joyful she had felt to know that she was making her mark in the world.

And, of course, she talked about "It's a Wide World," about her role as Cinnamon Walker, and the reasons why she had accepted the part—emphasizing the growing tide of drug abuse problems in England.

It was all reminiscent of the stuff she had told Wade. It seemed eons ago that they had agreed that he shadow her so he could learn everything about her life. Now he was part of her life, but that was something she would not reveal to Conrad or her viewers. Some things were private.

Conrad was easygoing and understood the normal, human side of her life. He nodded in acceptance and dismissed trivial lines of questioning as he moved along. Then there was the subject of *Bribe* magazine.

"COMA VICTIM IN DOUBLE MURDER PLOT," Conrad repeated, a copy of the latest edition now resting in his hands. "Frederick Fitzgerald was struck on the back of the head. Rumor has it that a cast member did it to boost ratings. It's startling in its similarity to an earlier storyline . . ."

"I wasn't a member of the cast at that time," Desney interrupted.

"But you were with Frederick when he got the blow to the head, which corresponds with the double murder plot outlined here in *Bribe* magazine."

"I . . ."

"And you were, of course, the cast member who *Bribe* earlier reported had knocked him out cold,"

Conrad finished. "Do you have a vendetta against Mr. Fitzgerald?"

Desney tried to smile sweetly. "No, I do not," she affirmed sternly. "I respect him and his talent very much. I visited him at the hospital only recently. He's recovering."

"He was in a coma," Conrad interrupted. "I believe you and Matt Doran were in his room arguing at the time Mr. Fitzgerald awoke?"

Desney realized that the situation did not look good. "We were simply talking," she amended.

"About your annulment?" Conrad asked. Desney noted his tack and attitude toward her had changed suddenly. "Isn't it true that Mr. Fitzgerald was attempting to blackmail you by disclosing news about your marriage to Mr. Doran?"

Desney gasped. How did he come by this information? "I don't know—"

"It's speculated that you were the cast member who tried to harm Mr. Fitzgerald."

"Me!" Desney was appalled. Her voice shook with it. "I didn't—"

Her attempt to explain was brutally interrupted when Wade Beresford walked onto the stage. Conrad looked amazed to see him towering above them, but he remained calm and directed his face toward the cameras. "We are joined by Mr. Wade Beresford, publisher of *Bribe* magazine."

"Hello." Wade smiled and took a seat. "I'd like to clarify something if I may."

"Go ahead," Conrad smiled evasively.

"We were working on an independent feature with Miss Westbourne before my assistant editor overrode her feature and replaced it with the current commentary," he began. "My assistant editor made that decision in my absence because he had received a story leak about the plot for 'It's a Wide World.' "

"And . . . Miss Westbourne provided that story?" Conrad let the implication hang.

"No," Wade confirmed. "Frederick Fitzgerald did."

Conrad's face grew startled. "Are you saying—?"

"He leaked the story of the revised plot line for 'It's a Wide World' before he got knocked on the head," Wade finished. "And at this point we cannot speculate who wanted him harmed, because he's suffering from amnesia."

Conrad paused. "It was suggested to me that this is all an elaborate publicity stunt to increase the show's ratings." He took the issue sideways, not knowing where else he could go with the main subject.

"I would like to affirm to you and all the viewers," Wade continued, "that my magazine does not endorse 'It's a Wide World', nor are we linked with any publicity efforts to raise its ratings. When information of the nature we received is provided to us, we either pass on it or buy it."

"As an advocate for free press," Conrad approved.

"Certainly," Wade concluded.

"And your relationship with Miss Westbourne," Conrad broached, turning toward Desney. "Your agent tells me wedding bells are in the air."

Desney gasped, hardly daring to turn her head and glare at Cheryl. "I . . . I . . ."

"Yes, we do plan to get married," Wade returned steadfast, lacing Desney's hand into his.

Desney peered into his green-brown eyes, resentment growing within her that he should announce something so private on national TV. She hadn't yet told her parents, her sisters, close friends even. This was the worst way for any of her family members to learn of it, without having heard it from her first.

"Are we hearing the patter of tiny feet?" Conrad leered, prying in the hope of discovering any further revelations.

"You'll just have to wait and see," Desney chided, a dangerously sweet smile still planted on her face, though her eyes were putting Conrad on notice.

"I'll take that as a confirmation," Conrad reaffirmed, turning to face the cameras. "We were with Desney Westbourne from 'It's a Wide World' and Wade Beresford from *Bribe* magazine. Tomorrow, my guests will be Tyra Banks, supermodel, and heavyweight champion of the world Lennox Lewis. From me, Conrad Waldorf, good morning."

When the camera switched, Wade glared at Conrad. "How dare you try and implicate Miss Westbourne in the attempted murder of Frederick Fitzgerald?" he raged.

"I thought you were a nice person," Desney added angrily. "But you're nothing but a slimy little toad."

She rose out of her seat, finding that Wade had joined her, and marched off the stage. Cheryl remained rooted backstage and looked most apologetic, realizing she had inadvertently let a little piece of news slip. But of course, everything was likely to be repeated if heard within Cheryl's earshot, Desney thought. She made no comment. Instead she tried to find her way out of the building.

"Desney!" Wade rushed after her.

"I suppose you're going to tell me I told you so?" she bellowed.

"I'm sorry." He restrained her at a set of double swinging doors. "I couldn't help barging right in there to sort that man out. I could see where he was going with it and—"

"So you decided to announce to the world that we're getting married," Desney interrupted. "Didn't it occur to you that my family would've liked to know that piece of news first? Or yours for that matter?"

Wade rocked back on his heels. Suddenly, he realized he hadn't been thinking. "I didn't think—"

"No, you never do," Desney fired off. "How would you have liked if I revealed to all and sundry that I'm carrying your baby?"

Desney gasped when she suddenly realized what she had said. She tried to think how to take the words back, but she couldn't. The truth had slipped out. Wade stared at her as though the world had suddenly lost its bottom.

"Pregnant!" The single word hung in the air, sending an eerie echo down the corridor.

Desney's only recourse was to seek a way to explain. "I hadn't planned to tell you until I'd seen a doctor and was certain for sure," she appended calmly. "It's—"

"Not a surprise," Wade said absently. He shook his head,. "I was thinking . . . maybe . . ."

"Maybe what?" Desney asked, feeling a tightness in her chest.

Wade closed his eyes, sighing heavily. "Our first time, the condom . . ."

Desney felt hot. "Don't tell me it was past its 'sell-by' date, please!" she implored him suddenly, tears now welling into her eyes. "Please don't tell me you were that stupid." She leaned against the wall, feeling suddenly weakened and sapped of all energy.

"No . . . no." Wade pulled her against him. "Desney, listen to me. It wasn't like that."

"What was it like?" she shrilled, waiting for the truth. A chance that it was a miracle, *that* she was prepared to believe, but not because of some banal human failing.

"I wanted to sort it out in—"

"Sort it out," Desney gushed. "You can't just sort things like this out."

"If you'd let me explain," Wade demanded. He paused and saw how distraught she appeared. His heart reached out to her. "I thought I'd been stupid, but I hadn't been. I checked the wrapper. The condom failed. Baby, it was an accident."

Desney paused to compose herself. "You knew about it, but didn't tell me?" she remonstrated, shocked by the disclosure. The tears were building. "Don't you see?" She tried to think. "Now I don't know if it's me you want, or the baby."

Wade was struck. "What?"

"You had an inkling that something had happened, and it warped your judgment."

"Desney," he broke in.

"You'll have to prove to me that you really want me," she said, lowering her voice. "If you're not sure, then don't."

"What . . . ?" Wade glanced sideways in annoyance as a few members of the BBC staff walked by through the swinging doors. Only when they were out of sight did he speak. "What kind of ultimatum is that?"

"What does your heart want?" Desney asked stubbornly.

"You, for my wife," Wade raged.

"My heart wants that, too," she admitted. "But what does your head say?"

Wade looked directly into her velvety-brown eyes. "My head says it's the right decision."

Desney nodded, tearfully. "My head agrees with you."

"Then what's the problem?" he demanded. "The Bible says a man's heart will plot its way and God will set his feet aright. Well, I know where my feet are going."

"Was this before or after?" Desney insisted. "I need to know."

"Before."

A part of Desney reluctantly believed. She couldn't understand why she was clutching at straws. Insecurity probably. "Am I going to be your third and only love?"

Wade cast his eyes heavenward. "I can't go back Desney," he told her in earnest. "I could never love the women in my past the same way again, because my love wasn't strong enough the first time round. We are allowed to change our minds, even our fragile hearts."

"Wade—"

"Life is too important to be taken this seriously," he said. "And about not telling you any sooner, you can't make me feel any smaller about that. I'm already shrunk."

He was right, Desney conceded. The heart was a fragile thing, not to be trifled with. At least that was how she'd always seen hers. All her life, she had hoped to find a man who would at least keep it safe. Wade had done that. He had kept her in his heart, too. In all honesty, he could have pretended ignorance about the birth control failure. But he had stayed, accepting responsibility. That had to mean that he respected her. Respected her right to know.

"Just tell me why you did it?" She had to ask.

Wade took her hands and kissed the back of them like a man desperate to hang onto everything he had ever longed for. "I wanted you to have my baby," he admitted selfishly. "I wanted to look into his velvety brown eyes and know where they came from, see the thin, small nose that you have, the same slender neck, your wonderful smile. It had to be you."

Desney was weakened by the admission. Wade had described a love child in every sense, and her love for him grew stronger in that very moment. "I was scared about having this baby," she told him truthfully. "But not anymore."

Wade smiled and pulled Desney into his arms. "I just want you to do me one favor," he chuckled, nestling her against his firm chest. "If it's a boy, don't call him Otto."

Desney giggled as she closed her eyes and let the pure bliss wash over her, deciding that as soon as 'It's a Wide World' was put well and firmly behind her, she would prepare for her best role yet—that of being a mother.

Fourteen

It was a story that had legs and it was running. By the time Desney arrived at Elstree on Thursday morning to do her last take for "It's a Wide World," the whole studio was talking about the Waldorf interview she'd given at BBC.

There was her marriage engagement to Wade, of course, and the speculation that she was pregnant, but above all that, there was a pervading sense of apology in the atmosphere—much of which was due to the fact that she had disclosed the true identity of the culprit responsible for the story leak.

Shawnee was the first person to confront Desney on her arrival on set. "I would never have guessed it," she enthused, her eyes sparkling. "You and Wade Beresford!"

Desney simply offered a mischievous smile. "I'm glad it's my last day," she said, "but I'm going to miss all this."

"Well I think it stinks, James letting you go like this," Shawnee continued, her own sense of guilt showing beneath the flawless art of her makeup. "For the record, I never did believe it was you."

Like hell you didn't, Desney thought, feeling truly vindicated. She was already dressed and ready for the take, the clothes unironed and torn, her makeup applied to give the appearance of an addict afraid of going cold turkey, her wig teased to look like it had been dragged through the streets before being placed on her head. The thread of the storyline was that she had reached the last vestiges of coping with her life and would overdose on crack cocaine. It wasn't the way she had wanted to leave the soap, but with the way things had played out thus far, Desney had no alternative but to accept the final script changes.

"You're so kind," she lied, offering Shawnee a manufactured expression in acceptance of the closest thing to an apology that she was ever likely to get. "When—"

Her further speech pattern was broken when Matt Doran emerged on set. "Desney!" he exclaimed. He rushed over like a man in a hurry. "I saw your interview Tuesday morning. Boy, have you got guts."

As usual, Desney was aware that he had been drinking. Nothing had changed about Matt in that way, except that he looked a smidgen more sober than usual. His charismatic manner was much the same, too, as were his impeccable good looks. But those, as always, remained ill spent on her. "I had to do something," she admitted, accepting his hug.

"You did it in style," he agreed, finally pulling back to contemplate her. "James has been looking pretty nervous ever since."

"That's right," Shawnee butted in. "I think he might be the one in violation of your contract now if he lets you go. To think," Shawnee added, her thoughts in full swing. "You could sue. That's what I'd do if I were you."

Desney digested this new information carefully. Of course it was very likely that the producers upstairs, in light of the fresh piece of evidence Wade had supplied on national TV, would be hopping about wondering exactly how they were to keep one of their star actresses after falsely accusing her of leaking plot lines. She could effectively sue for wrongful dismissal. In a court of law, the resulting judgment could earn her a bundle. It was a thought that had never crossed her mind before, but it did now in all its Technicolor glory.

"You're probably right," she admitted to Shawnee, thinking it was a matter that she should best discuss with Wade. "I think I'd better talk to my lawyer."

"I don't think there's any need to be hasty," a voice behind her interjected. Desney turned to find James standing directly behind them.

He looked much the same as when Desney had last seen him, though just a little more tired around the eyes. Even so, his tall, bulky frame seemed slightly menacing—a reminder to all that he was indeed the man in charge and not to be trifled with. "James!" Desney smiled with pretended sweetness. "I got the script, read my lines, and I'm waiting, ready to go."

"Can I see you in my office?" he said, his tone much more formal, even concerned.

Desney was neither surprised nor worried. She had suggested as much to Wade only that morning when she had left his bed and dressed herself for work, saying that she expected James to corner her about her contract. At the time, Wade had advised her to demand some more big bucks as an incentive to bring her back into the soap.

"You're worth more to them now," his voice repeated in her head. She stopped off at her dressing room to pick up her bag before following James toward his office. "Don't have them pay you the money that's on your contract. You've got them by the balls. Milk it for all you've got, in fact," he had said, pausing to pick up his dictaphone. It was the one he had used to interview her at Floriana's. "Take this." She accepted the small tape recorder. "I want to hear what the man has to say for himself. No harm in protecting yourself in case things get rough with your contract."

It sounded cutthroat, but it had strengthened her nonetheless. To find herself suddenly in a powerful position over James Wallace felt about as good as it was going to get. And so, after Wade had kissed her and given her the supportive hug that she needed, she had placed the tape recorder in her bag and driven to Elstree Studios, prepared for the confrontation.

It seemed unusual to Desney to see James this way. He was never a man so easily anxious or apprehensive. In fact, she would never have attached such a word as uncomfortable to the fabric of his character. But James seemed unsettled. By the time she had reached his office and taken a seat in one of the deep leather chairs, "It's a Wide World's" senior writer and director seemed about as restless as a young man about to ask for his first date.

"Miss Westbourne," he began, the formality of his address to her taking Desney by complete surprise. "About your contract . . ."

"Yes," she said, resting her bag on her knee and sliding to her hand discreetly inside to switch on the tape recorder.

"I think we . . . I . . . have judged you very hastily." James took a chair at his desk and placed his elbows up against the wooden table, resting his chin against his clenched fingers to contemplate Desney steadily. "You see, I'm very protective when it comes to my work. To me, everyone poses some kind of danger, and . . . my work is everything I have."

Desney nodded, understanding this. "I know," she agreed. " 'It's a Wide World' is you, and you are 'It's a Wide World'."

"You understand," he said slowly, a slight crease

leaving his forehead. "I've always been straight with people and I expect them to be straight with me."

Desney nodded, waiting for it.

"When I reacted the way I did, to the *Bribe* feature," he continued, "it was out of feeling a sense of betrayal. I hope you can see your way to overlooking my . . . let's say, dastardly behavior."

That's putting a fine point to it, Desney thought, keeping her velvety brown eyes firmly fixed on James's face. It felt nice to see him squirming like this, as befuddled and self-deluded as he really was. Only someone with such hidden traits could develop such a myriad of dysfunctional characters and share them with a TV audience, who in turn supplied him with all the adoration he needed, spurring him on to invent ever more twisted plot lines.

Maybe that was what James was—truly twisted. For surely he couldn't be expecting her to sit there now and accept such an abstract apology. When was the word *sorry* going to materialize? It didn't.

Desney gave him time to reflect on it, but still the one solitary word failed to pass his lips. Instead James asked, "So, how do you feel about still running the take on the overdose scene, but in episode 109 you wake up in hospital?"

It was a tempting prospect, Desney thought. Her contract would still be valid, she had already added considerably to the ratings on the show, and a comeback in the most promising role of her career as Cinnamon Walker would be a slot worth keeping. But something held her back. It wasn't so much the money, Desney realized.

Her eyes strayed sideways, wondering why she was hesitating. Wade had recommended that she demand a twenty percent wage increase or threaten them that she would walk. And now Shawnee had suggested that she could actually sue. That wasn't an option she had discussed with Wade that morning.

She was pondering the best answer to give, when Desney suddenly noted something in one of the leather chairs in the far corner of James's office. She recognized it immediately. It was the brown hat she had worn on the day Frederick had been bludgeoned. What on earth was it doing in James's office?

"Desney?" James prompted.

Her eyes shifted quickly back. "What's the pay structure?" she temporized, her eyes straying back toward her hat.

"Pardon?" James was obviously taken aback.

"Surely you cannot expect to pay me the same salary per episode after all the publicity I've brought in for the show," she answered carefully, re-shifting her gaze. "I'm told I could sue for unfair dismissal."

"Now Desney," James cautioned, dropping his elbows suddenly and clasping both hands in front of himself on the desk. "We're getting into an area here that's straying from—"

"You owing me," Desney finished. As she eyed James more closely, she suddenly remembered when and where she had last left her hat. She had it in her hand when Frederick had suffered the slug at the back of his head, moments before she herself had slumped to the ground.

She had never seen who hit her or Frederick, but whoever it was had . . . taken her hat. She could only imagine that forensics would find blood stains on it, or something else that could point the finger at the perpetrator. Or maybe her hat had been used to wipe away fingerprints and then taken absently. Her mind wandered in all directions, not sure whether she was arriving at correct conclusions to anything. But her instincts told her to take the matter of her hat being in James's office seriously.

It could mean nothing, but maybe whoever had taken her hat was trying to hide evidence. Suspicion suddenly flooded Desney's mind. She felt certain James knew something, and while her tape recorder was rolling, she wanted to know what.

A new line of questioning instantly sprang to mind. "I was thinking," she began craftily, "about the five thousand pounds *Bribe* paid Frederick for the story leak. Tony Barbieri at the magazine told Wade and I that he handed the money over to Frederick in cash, only I've come to realize it wasn't found on his body when paramedics got to him." She looked across at her hat once more, and quite gingerly rose from her chair, marching toward it. "My head nearly went on the block for this entire mess James. The least you can do is split the money with me."

Desney noticed the shock emerge on James's face, which he tried to mask with a loud, hearty chuckle. "You're kidding me, right?"

"No," she answered, keeping her voice cool and equable, diligently reaching for her hat. James watched her with alarm as Desney took a firm hold of it. "Frederick doesn't remember anything because he's suffering from amnesia, but my hunch is that you knew he wanted to get back at you for planning to axe him from the show."

"He deserved what he got," James lashed out. He then blinked as he realized that Desney had opened her hat. He saw the muscles move in her cheeks when she discovered what was hidden in there. "Of course you can't prove anything," he added.

"I'm not planning to," Desney admitted, keeping her voice as calm as she could while her startled gaze fell upon five thousand pounds wrapped tightly together with three elastic bands. "I just want a share of the pie."

"And what if I'm not willing to give you a slice," James threatened, leaning back into his leather chair as though he had just reminded himself that he had the upper hand. So what if he had taken the money from Fred and hidden it in Desney's hat; who could prove anything other than that he was rightly dispensing justice by making sure Frederick didn't profit from the story leak?

"Then I'll have no choice but to disclose to *Bribe* magazine details of your secret torrid affair with my agent, Cheryl Carlton."

James was enraged. "You—"

"Temper, temper," Desney cautioned, returning her hat to the leather chair with the money still inside.

"You're bluffing," James blustered, his eyes ablaze as he watched Desney reseat herself. "You can't prove that I did anything to Frederick."

"But you did," Desney replied, determined to force him into an outright admission. "Frederick was—"

"A trumped-up idiot," James finished. "Weeks of work," he ranted on. "I wasn't going to let him hand over weeks of my well-kept storylines to the media. 'It's a Wide World' belongs to me."

"So that's why you tried to kill him?" she ventured.

"I didn't want to kill him," James relented, a deep sparkle springing into his eyes. "Just maybe lame him a little."

"Why?"

"Because he stole from me," he snapped. "I was in my office when I discovered that my file holding the new storylines was missing." He sighed. "The only person who had been in my office that morning was Frederick Fitzgerald. He had come in early to plead that I renew his contract. So I followed him. Caught him red-handed passing my file over to some guy in the parking lot."

Tony, Desney surmised. "So you waited until he returned to the building?" she asked, amazed at how calm she was keeping herself.

"Yeah," James confirmed, secure in the knowledge that as long as Desney thought she was in for a share of the money, she'd not take his admission further. "The studio was empty. I confronted him, we argued, and then I hit him with this." He picked up a solid paperweight from his desk. "You can call it premeditated if you want. I call it teaching the guy a lesson."

"But you could've killed him," Desney insisted, her eyes widening. "Me, too."

"I didn't hit you with this," James confirmed, a little more softly. "I used the back of my hand on you. You weren't supposed to be there so early anyhow."

"I wanted to try and find Matt," Desney told him, deciding to disguise her efforts to prompt further revelations from him. "Frederick wanted to blackmail me."

James's little smirk suddenly broke into an all-out grin. "Let me guess, your marriage to Matt Doran."

She nodded.

"Then he deserved everything he got," James repeated, approving of his actions. "And you can't prove shit."

"I'd still like a cut of the five grand," Desney ventured, "or I'm taking this conversation to Wade Beresford."

"The lover," James spat out. "Or should I say husband-in-waiting?"

"Whatever."

James pondered for a long moment, as though calculating an equation in his head. When he finally spoke, his voice had softened slightly, as though having conceded to the inevitable. "Okay." He leaned forward in his chair. "So I'm sleeping with Cheryl, and I put Frederick Fitzgerald in a coma. How much is it going to cost me to keep you quiet and get you back on the payroll?"

Desney smiled. This was all the information she needed for the police. "Give me twenty-four hours to think about it," she said. "In the meantime, I'd just like to do the take."

It seemed a business decision that James could readily accept. He stood up signaling that their meeting was at a close. "Get back to me tomorrow," he suggested, happily acknowledging that they had reached a meeting of minds. "I must say, you surprise me Desney," he added. "You've got real potential, and now that we understand each other, there's going to be some big changes with your character on screen. I've got plans for you."

How Desney kept herself so composed throughout the morning was another matter entirely. She'd returned to her dressing room, switched off the tape recorder, pressed rewind to make sure she'd gotten everything, and then returned to the studio floor to act out her role on set.

It was three o'clock in the afternoon when Desney reached Wade's home in Surrey. He wasn't home, but she had a key. She decided to utilize the time waiting for Wade by taking a long, hot bath, immersing herself and the speeding train of her thoughts regarding James Wallace into the depths of warm water.

When Wade finally arrived home a little after 6:00, Desney was refreshed, but she had become panicky when she realized exactly what she had endured throughout the day. Wade detected her fretful composure the moment he walked into the sitting room and caught her seated against the sofa, feet up, twisting her fingers in apprehension.

"Your day was that bad?" he asked, concerned and at the same time annoyed that he had been too busy himself to afford time to be with her.

"I think you should listen to that dictaphone you gave me," she stuttered, hardly able to tell him.

Wade's brows rose as he looked into Desney's face. "That bad?"

"Worse." Desney pointed at the tape recorder she had extracted from her bag and left on the coffee table.

Recognizing the deep level of concern on Desney's face, he took off his jacket, sat down, and played it back. Ten minutes later, Wade was on the phone. Desney didn't need to ask; he was calling the police.

By the next morning, the news was hitting the TV screen. Desney and Wade were huddled together in bed at his home while the newscaster relayed brief coverage about James Wallace being brought in for questioning.

The reporter did not specify charges, but only stated that James had offered to help them with their inquiries. It was all tantamount to gaining his full confession, Desney thought, now that the police were in possession of her tape.

"He'll probably get off scot-free," she told Wade sadly, curling up beside him as he rested against two pillows, eyes closed to the world. He was awake and listening, but his thoughts were also elsewhere. "Men like James Wallace always do," Desney added.

She eyed Wade curiously, seeing the acknowledging smile on his face. He looked adorable at this early hour of the morning, when the dawn had just broken and the wind was rustling among the trees outside, and after they had just shared a night of passionate love. They were naked beneath the sheets, his loose-hanging hair against a night's growth of stubble giving him a wild look.

She recalled the scene of their love play throughout the night: his kisses and gentle advances, his caressing of her every niche and womanly curves. He had worshiped her very human body and soul. Making love to her with all the care and attention that only a man in love could give. And when he had taken her to the brink time and time again, she had welcomed falling and drifting gently down in blissful contentment. She brushed a light kiss against his unshaven cheek, a reminder to him that the morning had dawned.

"No faith in the justice system, then?" Wade murmured softly, opening his eyes to absorb the tangled mess of Desney's hair. He had made it like that, running his fingers through it during the night, making her lips sore with so many kisses that he noted their chapped appearance even now. He pulled Desney to his chest and marveled at the way she lay against him, content and relaxed.

"I'm just thinking about Frederick," she sighed, nestling against Wade's ribs. The central heating in the room had made it warm and cozy, making her remember that the weather outside was hovering just above freezing. "Not that he deserves my sympathy, but he hasn't recovered from his amnesia, and he could've gotten himself killed."

"So, you think James will get off with the charge of grievous bodily harm?" Wade asked, taking the remote control from Desney's hand and flicking through the channels. He noted a cartoon while the channels jumped by, and left it there.

"He'll walk," Desney said flatly, aware that James could no doubt afford the best lawyers money could buy. "Mind you, that five thousand pounds that was paid to Frederick will probably show up in his bank account sooner or later."

"Not if he's disbursed the cash," Wade noted shrewdly.

"But I saw the money," Desney breathed. "He hid it in my hat."

"It could be your word against his," he replied. "And that recording you made might not hold up in court. It could be ruled as inadmissable evidence, because you made it without his prior knowledge or consent. And we can't prove anything at the magazine, because it's the nature of our business to pay for stories in cash. It goes with the territory."

Desney absorbed the information. "Then it's Frederick I feel sorry for," she went on. "He should never have stolen from James in the first place and tried to sell it to the media."

Wade flinched and Desney sensed the movement in him. She inclined her head slightly, fretful that she had destroyed the euphoria that had enveloped them the entire night. But his face remained calm and brooding.

"I've found a buyer for *Brihe*," Wade told her matter-of-factly.

Desney looked into his eyes. "Really?" She had wondered what was on his mind that morning.

"He wants to pay me two million for it."

"What!" Desney sat up and leaned one elbow against Wade's pillow to find a wide monkey grin spreading across his face. "That's brilliant," she gasped in surprise, a smile breaking across her own features. "Why didn't you tell me?"

"I'm telling you now," he said, brushing the back of his hand against her cheek. "And I sold the Major Abu story, too."

"Yeah?" Desney's smile widened.

"Yesterday," he murmured, burying his face against her neck, where his hot mouth tickled the side of her throat. "I'm thinking it might be an idea for a documentary."

"Hmm," Desney moaned, closing her eyes to savor the sweet sensation of being close to Wade. "You are full of surprises today. What else have I missed?"

"Your present," Wade whispered, resuming his meanderings about her neck. "I wanted to tell you last night, but after sorting out the James Wallace thing, and submitting to the shameless way you seduced me . . ."

"The way *I* seduced *you*," she exclaimed in mock outrage, knuckling him in the chest. "Weren't you the guy who, after that police officer left, picked me up off my feet and carried me to this very bed?"

"My intention was to tuck you in and allow you and my baby to get some sleep," he laughed.

"Your intention was to remind me what a good lover you are," Desney returned, enjoying the feel of his fingers rubbing softly against her bare stomach. He would not be able to feel the baby for some months yet, but she instinctively welcomed the way he felt her as though he were able to sense their love child.

She turned her head upward and offered her lips to him. Wade accepted the kiss, pulling her lips into his and drugging himself with the sweetly seductive pleasure that filled his body. His hand moved up and down her spine, the other explored her breasts, down her navel, and stopped at the sensual core of her, increasing her yearning for him. He needed her again. And she needed him. He felt it with his every stroke against her tenderest flesh.

"Wade . . ." Her gasp was weak and filled with longing. Desney descended into a world of her own where everything seemed more real than ever. Only a few months ago, she had only known of Wade Beresford's existence through the media; now here she was, in his bed, his future bride and the mother of his unborn child.

Wade's restraint broke. He pulled Desney into him and kissed her with heightened passion. "You have the loveliest breasts," he told her, "the softest skin." He nibbled her lips. "You're mine." He felt her, supple and responsive beneath him, and his mind closed to everything but the feel of her warm flesh against his own.

Pushing aside the sheets, he bent his head and took her nipple gently between his teeth. He lapped at it like a cat lapping milk, his lips pulling against the solid peak until Desney could barely stand the upwelling inside her.

"You're making me . . . need you," she muttered into the air.

"I know," Wade whispered, silencing her again with his mouth. He lavished his full adoration on her, melding his tongue with hers, running it along her teeth, tasting and smelling the delicacy of her arousal, knowing what she wanted.

Desney melted from his attentions. And drifted. Her arms rose without conscious volition to slide about his neck, her fingers twisting themselves into his black, heavy locks. Desney was lost, overpowered by everything that Wade had to offer. The potent weight of his arousal unleashed the desire within her as she savored his lips and bit gently against them.

The blood was drumming in her ears, too as her whole body, charged like a battery, ready to take him on. The rush of emotion was so intense, Desney hardly knew how to contain it. Her eyes closed as Wade's hands moved around her possessively.

She threw her head back against his pillows, reveling in the way he followed her head there, his lips never leaving hers once as Wade tasted her mouth. The tip of his tongue lightly caressed the inner moisture that spoke of Desney's desire, his heart pounding, his skin feeling soft and silky beneath her fingertips.

Desney relaxed against the pillows, sensing her feminine delicacy against Wade's hardness, the dark hair on his chest tickling the sensitive tips of her breasts. And then his lips were on those tips once more and Desney groaned low in her throat as she felt the moist warmth of his tongue flicking over her nipples.

His hands roamed her body, in intimate familiarity with all of the zones that spurred her to yield to him. Her own supple hands reached the most intimate parts of his body, across the back of his shoulders, down the center of his spine and to his buttocks.

And Desney touched him there, where he lived, rubbing gently against the turgid crown and hardened rod that throbbed between her fingers. Wade's pining moan told her he was ready. His own fingers stole between her legs, slipping into the moist depths of her; she was ready for him as well. Her thighs instinctively parted to accept him, wrapping around his body as Wade penetrated the molten portals of Desney's core and filled her entirely.

She felt the stir of him, the hardened manhood gently invading. Every fibre of her body accepted him, pulled him in. His tender thrusts propelled her into another dimension of ecstasy, where nothing existed but the feeling of this man inside her, touching her very soul. She clung to his wet skin and dug her nails in as the brink drew ever closer, closed her eyes tighter to force back the sweet tears that wanted to escape, kept her mouth locked to Wade's for fear that he would escape her. And when she fell over the edge, her body convulsed in shudders joining with the tremors that shook Wade's.

After a while, when the world had returned and her breathing had steadied, Desney placed her hand against her belly. Their love child was safe. She was reminded of the deep sense of lovemaking that she shared with Wade, which had given her such a wonderful gift. What other memento could he possible give her, when she had already received the greatest prize?

"Wade?" A satisfied smile bloomed on her lips as she turned into his arms and faced him. The pure lines of fulfillment were etched in his face as he lay on his back and glanced across at her. Desney felt warmed that he looked so at peace with himself. "What is it?"

"What?" Wade asked, his voice husky and parched.

"The present," she reminded him. "You said—"

"Oh, that!" A spark of humor lit the green-brown gaze. "It's a yacht."

"A yacht?" Desney pulled back slightly. "What kind of yacht?"

"The best in Italian tradition," Wade declared. "The *apreamare Emerald*, built in the shipyards of Sorrento. Teak decks, solid GRP construction, twin diesel shaft power—"

"Wade, what are you talking about?" she interrupted, confused.

"I've chartered a yacht for us," he smiled, bending his head to plant a satisfied kiss to her temple, where her hair still hung disheveled and damp. "How does two weeks in the Caribbean sound?"

Desney squealed. "Wade!" She threw her arms around his neck and hugged him for dear life. "This is a wonderful surprise. What made you decide?"

"Hmm," he drawled mysteriously, his eyes twinkling

with a spark of exaltation mingled with rising passion. A roguish monkey smile spread across his handsome face, curving his cheek and making Desney distinctly apprehensive.

"What?" she queried suddenly.

"I was hoping we could get married while we're out there," Wade admitted finally. "Now that you're pregnant and you're no longer working on 'It's a Wide World,' I was thinking—"

"Wade," Desney interrupted, nervous. She sat up now and leaned on one elbow, facing him. "I'm still an actress. At some point, after the baby is born, I'd like to go back into TV. I mean," she sighed, "when did you make this decision? Is it because I'm pregnant you want us to rush and get married?"

"No." he said firmly, his mild Italian accent suddenly sounding more pronounced. He paused for reflection, realizing that Desney needed to be clear on a few things. "This isn't about me standing in the way of what you want," he began. "I'll always support you with your career, whatever you decide." He reached for her shoulder. "I'd already decided I wanted to marry you before I went to Sierra Leone," he confessed, gently stroking along the top of her arm. "Before I left to go there, I thought about you often. And how you made me feel. How you made me see my life, the things that were missing, the things I needed in it." Wade looked steadfastly into Desney's eyes. "Before you, Desney, I was lost. I've been lost most of my life."

Something inside her shook. "Wade . . ."

"Listen," he whispered softly, putting a finger against her trembling lips. "Until I met you, I always felt this searching need. I was searching . . . searching, but I didn't know what for. I got knocked back twice and thought, what the hell? So I gave up. And then . . ."

"What?" Desney murmured.

"I met you."

Tears welled in her eyes.

He sat up to join her, propping himself up on one elbow, his expression serious and intent. "I remembered you saying something about a buccaneer coming to your rescue," he continued softly.

Desney chuckled weakly. "Yes," she nodded. She remembered it well. It was on the first day he had agreed to shadow her for the *Bribe* feature and they had gone jogging together in Hyde Park. "I told you I preferred a gallant buccaneer with whom my heart will be safe," she remembered.

Wade nodded at the reminder. "It made me start to think about the sea and sunsets and being at the helm of a ship, sailing you away into the horizon," he revealed.

Desney laughed against happy tears. This was her dream. Just as she had imagined it time and time again.

"When I asked you to marry me," Wade went on, "it wasn't supposed to be the way I did it. I wanted to be on one knee, not making love to you."

Desney laughed out loud. She couldn't help herself. In her mind, making love was preferable. "It was beautiful the way you did ask," she whispered against his lips, kissing him there to assert the truth of her words.

Wade accepted the kiss and squeezed her shoulder, feeling aroused again. Only this woman had the power to do this to him. "Desney," he said softly, needing her to understand him. "I want us to get married on the yacht and take a honeymoon cruise." He saw that she had given him her complete concentration, and he appreciated her even more for it—that he was faced with something quite genuine and not a lie. "I want to be that buccaneer you dreamed about that comes to your rescue, busted toenails and all, and whisk you off into the sunset."

Desney threw her arms around his shoulders again and accepted everything Wade had to say. He wanted her. Not just because she was carrying his baby, but because she was everything he needed in his life. And she wanted him, too. He was the man of her dreams, the man who wanted to keep her heart safe.

"But the magazine," she said, suddenly aware that reality had a way of forcing its way in.

"I sign on the dotted line next week," Wade explained, "then hand it over to Cowie Publishing Company."

"Then the answer is yes," Desney proclaimed, as only a woman in love could. "After we get married—"

"We can either buy a new home or live here," Wade announced, realizing that they needed to make plans.

"Buy a new home," Desney readily insisted. "I'll sell my apartment. I want something that will be ours. All ours."

"Okay," Wade nodded, with a deep, husky laugh. "And I'll be taking a new job at the Reuters News Agency," he added.

Desney stared at him, thoroughly amazed. "You didn't tell me this."

"I thought I'd surprise you," he countered. "I start in January and I'll be working on those real human stories you convinced me I had the talent to do." He bestowed another kiss on her lips. "And a year from now, maybe two, I'll go independent and set up a small news agency of my own, specializing in hardcore ethnic minority issues. Probably float it on the Internet."

"Wow, you are ambitious," Desney crooned.

"Got a family to support now," Wade drawled in mock seriousness.

"Oh Wade." She started to cry. She couldn't help the tears from falling. She had never set out to change him, had never believed it possible that he could change. But somewhere between meeting him in all his arrogance and falling in love with him, he had learned to acknowledge himself; he had changed. She had enriched his life. "I don't know if I deserve to be this happy," she cried, as he pulled her into him and hugged her, pulling her slowly down with him back onto the bed and between the sheets where he warmed her with his body heat. "I'm having my first baby, I'm in love with its father and—"

"Its father loves you, too," Wade confessed. He kissed the tears of joy away. "You deserve to be this happy, Desney." He patted her tummy, a gentle reminder that they now had a future together to work toward. "And we both deserve this baby."

That remark earned Wade Beresford another heartfelt kiss.

ABOUT THE AUTHOR

Sonia Icilyn was born in Sheffield, England where she still lives with her daughter, in a small village which she describes as "typically British, quiet and where the old money is." She graduated with a distinction level Private Secretary's Certificate in Business and Commerce and also holds a Post Graduate Diploma in Writing. She is currently CEO of her own corporation, The Peacock Company, which manufactures the "Afroderma" skin care line for people of color. *Roses Are Red* was her first title for Arabesque, followed by *Island Romance* and *Viloets Are Blue,* the sequel.

She would love to hear from her readers:

P.O. Box 438
Sheffield S1 4YX
ENGLAND

E-mail: peacockcompany@cs.com